Her Place In Time

Part 2

Old Bill's family suffers more tragedy and Cindy Lou learns harsh realities about the choice she's made between her two suitors. The decision made, she moves into a new life head-long and head-strong, but without some of the most important people in her life by her side.

The man she's chosen is changing - and not for the better - while the one she rejected makes her regret her decision more and more each day.

As others try to help Old Bill's family cope with many terrible changes, the townspeople and those they've long rejected must come to terms with one another. Will the choices Cindy Lou and her sisters made stand, or will time and the revelations of long-held secrets cause their new lives to crumble?

Copyright ©2008, Amy K. Jones & Jason M. Jones
All rights reserved.

No portion of this book may be reproduced in any manner, form or medium without prior written permission from the author.

discditcher@gmail.com

Made in the U. S. A.

Dedicated to my wonderful husband and precious family members.

Her Place In Time

Part 2

Chapter 1

Thunder rumbled the floor under Esther's feet and lightning cut scars across the dark sky, eerily lighting the room, as she rocked in her chair, knitting furiously. For days, there hadn't been any sign of the rain's end and she was weary from her tears and the ever present sensation of unrest in her belly.

To pass the many hours, and stay clear of her older sister's critically watchful eyes, she'd stayed up in her small new room, knitting a blanket for the baby she couldn't imagine sharing her allotted space with in just a few months. Since she'd arrived on Sarah's doorstep with all the clothes she'd been able to grab from her closet, she'd felt entirely unwelcome.

Cory, her younger sister's new husband, had only given her the barest of notice that she was no longer welcome to live in her father's home with them. He'd woken her and Cindy Lou the day after their father's funeral and, after she'd made breakfast for the three of them, had told them their father's pre-death decision regarding her scornful condition, and her future.

She'd pleaded with Cory, but he'd ignored her entirely, refused to look at her, and told Cindy Lou to help her pack and be ready to make the long drive to their sister, Sarah's, home by the following morning. Even while the dirt mounded over her father's final resting place was still settling, she had been removed, amid many tears and angry exchanges, from her childhood home to live with her older sister, until she'd given birth to her child and found a way to become independent - if she ever could.

By the end of the hours-long ride in the pickup truck, wedged suffocatingly between her sister and Cory, Esther had been exhausted and terribly ill. Sarah had met them at her door, listened only to Cory's version of her situation and his claim to know their father's wishes, then escorted her to the smallest room in her farmhouse and curtly bade her good-night. She'd heard Sarah stomp back downstairs and fume to Cindy Lou, about her, for a few minutes, then Cory had announced that they were leaving, and they did, without Cindy Lou even coming up the stairs to tell her good-bye.

Sarah's husband, Lee, hadn't bothered to come out of his study to acknowledge her arrival, and had remained in his study long after she heard Sarah come up the stairs again and go to her room.

Esther had investigated her room and unpacked her belongings, in tears. Overwhelmed by the sudden eviction from her home, and angry beyond reason with Cory for doing this to her, she made solemn vows to herself to pay him and her sisters back, and retake what was rightfully hers - her father's home. The frightening storms had started the following night, and it didn't seem, to Esther, that they would ever stop.

As the days dragged by, Lee was rarely around and didn't seem to want a great deal to do with her. And Sarah, after giving her a stern lecture about her future, had only barely given her any attention at all. She took care of all the household chores and prepared all the meals, but refused to allow Esther even a moment more of her time than absolutely necessary, and she told Esther that Lee had only agreed to allow her to stay with them on the condition that she not disrupt their lives, and that he forbade any contact with Johnny, proclaiming the intention to shoot if he caught sight of him anywhere near his property.

Over the long miserable days, in near complete isolation, Esther's furious vows to return to her father's home, her childhood home in her own town of Farmersville, turned into carefully laid plans, worked out in her head and in mutterings under her breath, while she knitted for the baby she was loathe to carry, appearing, had anyone cared to notice, quite placid and accepting of her new living arrangements, as was her way.

A few moments of quiet passed before Esther realized that the latest storm to sweep across the landscape had abated. She'd become so miserably accustomed to the noise of rain and wind, she was startled to find everything so suddenly quiet around her. She set aside her needles and crossed the room to stare out at the dark fields from her window, fighting an urge deep inside her to run, run that very moment from her sister's home and escape the cold reality she'd been enduring for so many days.

Lightening still flashed and the ground was soggy from rain, but she gave in to her impulse and turned to find her shoes; her decision was made; she'd carry out the plans she'd made without any further delay, or die trying. What Cory had done to her wasn't right. He'd kicked her out of her own home so he could live there and enjoy all the things her father had worked so hard to give her and Cindy Lou. Cory had his own home, she fumed to herself, and she had every right to live in hers, with her baby. That, she decided, was what her father would have wanted for her, and that was what she would have.

It was very late, and her sister and brother-in-law had already gone to bed for the night, so no one would be able to stop her from leaving, she told herself. They'd only intended to keep her locked up in the house, in that tiny room, she knew, so that no one would see her and scorn their precious household. She would take only a few of the trinkets she'd brought with her and the clothes she was wearing, she decided, and sneak through the house to Lee's study where he kept his guns.

Sarah had shown her the collection, Lee's pride and joy, once when Esther had visited, after Sarah had first married Lee and moved to his farmhouse. She remembered where Sarah had found the key, and she got her hands on it easily, though it took her a few tense moments to get it to work in the old cabinet door lock.

The gun she chose was heavier than she had thought it would be and it wouldn't fit into her dress pocket like she had hoped, but she was determined not to go into the dark night alone, without any protection. There were men, she'd heard tales of, who slept out on the land waiting to rob people, and wild animals she might encounter; so she picked up the hem of her skirt and laid the gun in the loosely formed pocket, and relocked the cabinet door. Once she'd put the key back in its drawer, she slipped out the front door and escaped into the rain soaked fields, running until she reached the road that would lead her home, feeling defiant and full of hope.

For the first time in a long while, she felt really good. She was going home and no amount of mud and muck in her shoes would keep her feet from taking her there quickly.

Esther's bravery held out until, at nearly two

hours walk from Sarah's farmhouse, she saw a streak of raw electricity shoot down from the sky, miles in front of her, but seemingly dangerously close. A clap of thunder followed almost a full minute later and she shivered in fear. Not realizing that she was following the path of the storm that had only just gone over her sister's house, while she had been safely indoors, her confidence began to fail.

More lightening flashed in front of her and she turned from it to run, but after a few steps she realized what she was doing and stopped herself. To go back to Sarah's would mean being a prisoner in that tiny, airless, room. That, she decided, was worse than any storm she might have to endure to get away. She turned and forced herself to march down the road again, toward the dangerous storm.

She watched lightening continue to shoot down from the sky in front of her, fighting the urge to turn back with all her will, for a long while, before she realized that the storm was truly too far ahead of her to harm her. She did not seem to be getting any closer to it, which relieved her greatly, and brilliant light intermittently lit up everything around her, making it almost easy for her to follow the muddy road toward home.

The sky lit up all around her abruptly, alerting her to one of the shortcut paths she'd hoped to take along the way to speed her progress. It led out through a narrow stretch of heavily treed land which, though terribly dark, would give her a sheltered place to rest for a while, and maybe even allow her to continue walking until sunrise.

She stepped onto the path, and found it even more muddy and slippery than the road had been, but she felt a sense of accomplishment that she'd made it so far, so quickly, and with renewed energy she made her way toward the woods, carrying the gun in her hand now, in case she encountered anything, or anyone, dangerous along the way.

Chapter 2

Cindy Lou had spent so much time alone since Esther's departure she'd almost decided there was nothing more she could hope for than more of the same. The vagueness of her thoughts, the meaninglessness of her new daily routine, and the guilt she felt for causing her life to be in such shambles, made it harder and harder to get up each day and face her new life with her new, cruel, husband.

She hated Cory for being there and prayed he would just go away, go back to the supply store and his miserable little apartment and leave her alone. But each day she woke to the sound of his yelling and pounding on her bedroom door, which she kept not only locked, but also barred with a heavy chair Esther had favored in her many hours since her pregnancy had made her so ill, before Cory had sent her away.

She longed for her father and Esther's company and wished so much to be with them, at times, she contemplated ending her own life. With Mrs. Wilcox no longer around to offer a bit of humor or advice, the house felt utterly possessed with unhappiness, and was so quiet she was almost fearful at times.

In her mind, she talked to her father and tried to imagine what he would want her to do now that she was all alone and married to the man he'd loved and trusted so much. She felt sure he would not have approved of the way Cory was treating her, or the way he'd tormented her sister. He would have changed his mind, if sending Esther away had ever really been his plan, if he'd known he wouldn't be around to take care of things if something should go wrong. He wouldn't have wanted Cory to do things this way, especially not the day after he was buried. And he wouldn't have wanted Cory to send Mrs. Wilcox away when they needed her most.

She worried that Esther had not written to her since she'd been at Sarah's, knowing that her sister blamed her for what Cory had done. At times, her heart felt like it was going to race out of her body when she thought of Esther, in her condition, and how awful it would be for her to have, and raise, a baby in Sarah's home. She knew Sarah would overwhelm Esther with all she would have to do to earn her keep, and she didn't think Sarah would be very kind to Esther's baby at all.

If only Mrs. Wilcox could have gone with Esther to take care of her, she thought, then she could prevent Sarah from mistreating her sickly sister. If only she hadn't agreed to marry Cory so suddenly, she thought, she and Esther could be living, in great comfort, in their father's house, getting everything ready for the baby - the way they'd planned.

She wondered if there was any way to convince Cory to forget the whole marriage and go home, but she knew that would require speaking to him and she didn't want to do that. Each night she prayed for Esther to come back home and help her figure out what to do.

Cory felt like he was fighting a losing battle, trying to take charge of Old Bill's household. Only one hostile young female remained, his new wife, and he was becoming more agitated with her by the day, fed up with all of it.

He'd wake in the morning, get his own coffee, and make any food he might want to eat in a horribly silent house. If he tried to wake Cindy Lou, or get her to come out of her bedroom, his efforts were only met with the bang of one object or another hitting her side of the locked bedroom door.

When she did decide to come out of her room, if he happened to be around, he'd only catch a glimpse of her heading toward the bathroom at the end of the hall upstairs, then another closed door, locked for over an hour at a time. When she got hungry, he knew she'd sneak down to the kitchen and take food up to her room eat alone, behind that damned locked door.

He had tried to explain to her the good sense in sending her sister Esther away to Sarah's home, but Cindy Lou wouldn't understand. She'd accused him of being cruel and called him a monster, and refused to talk to him in a reasonable tone, so he'd given up and told her to just go and help her sister pack. The next thing he'd known Mrs. Wilcox was in Cindy Lou's room with her, and Esther, and he could hear the older woman filling Cindy Lou's head with nonsense about refusing to obey his orders, with her full support.

Angered by the older woman's subversive ideas, he'd banged on the door and demanded that the woman come out. When Mrs. Wilcox had appeared, he'd tried to talk to her about what he'd decided was best for Esther, but she'd argued that the girls needed to be kept together, said they'd suffered a terrible shock losing their father and that he was evil for trying to get rid of Esther simply for the sake of his standing in the community.

On hearing this, he'd lost control of his temper entirely, and ordered her out of the house.

He'd chased her down the hall, when she tried to escape to hide with the girls in their room, and he'd grabbed her arm to stop her. She'd screamed, but he hadn't let go of her; the sounds of the scuffle scared Esther and Cindy Lou so badly they couldn't make a move to help her.

Holding the woman by the arm, yelling at her still, he'd marched to the guest room and shoved her in, ordering her to get her things together. And when she had her things in hand, weeping, he'd taken her out to his truck and driven her straight home. He'd left her sputtering in a cloud of road dust, in her own front yard, a short while later, with orders to stay away from his house and his wife - or else!

When he'd returned to Old Bill's house, he'd found Cindy Lou and Esther in the kitchen, and another fight had broken out between the three of them, immediately. Cindy Lou had shrieked at him, accusing him of treating all of them abusively, and she'd vowed never to speak a word to him ever again if he followed through on his plan to take Esther away, then they had fled back up to their room.

He'd had stormed back out to his truck, furious that Cindy Lou was acting so childishly about the whole thing. He had no choice, he felt, but to insist that the right things be done for his new family, but he already deeply regretted taking on such a heavy responsibility. He hadn't really appreciated just how foolish his new young wife would be about such important matters.

He'd felt sure that if he stood firm on removing Esther, in the end, Cindy Lou would see how wise the plan was, but if he gave in and allowed the pregnant girl to stay, she would bring disgrace on all of them. She'd require attention Cindy Lou knew nothing about at her age, and her presence would disrupt all the other plans he had for Cindy Lou and himself.

He'd spent his wedding night alone, but he had no intention of spending too many more that way. And if there was to be a baby in his house it should most certainly be his own, not his sister-in-law's, he reasoned.

Though he dreaded having to do so, he'd driven over to Johnny's father's farm to confront him with the news of his son's dalliance with Esther, and the girl's pregnant condition, ready to demand that they make arrangements with him to pay for Johnny's mistake. Johnny's father had been outraged to hear such news, but he didn't try to shirk his duty.

He'd agreed that Cory should get Esther to her sister's farm, away from their community and his son, and he assured Cory that he would compensate him for his trouble, and impress on his son that he needed to take responsibility for this baby and make it legitimate, immediately. He gave Cory what money he had in his safe and Cory left him to deal with his son - when he found him.

The following morning, Cory had followed through with his promise to get Esther out of town, despite Cindy Lou's threats of "silence to last his lifetime". Neither girl had spoken to him throughout the loading of Esther's things into the back of his truck, nor the hours-long trip to Sarah's farm.

When they arrived, Cindy Lou had spoken only to Sarah, after Esther was taken up to her new room, and Lee, Sarah's husband, had summoned him into his study. He'd given Lee the money Johnny's father had given him, and explained that it was to compensate them for taking Esther in, as well as provide for the girl's needs til Johnny could be found and made to marry her.

Lee was very unhappy about the whole affair and made it plain that he would do away with Johnny if he showed up anywhere on his property, but Cory didn't care what the man did; the problem was Lee's now, as far as Cory was concerned, and he didn't care to involve himself in how Lee chose to handle things; he had his own problems to deal with.

Ultimately, Cindy Lou had broken her vow of silence almost before he could steer the truck back out onto the road for home. She told him, through clenched teeth, that she hated him. He'd hit the steering wheel angrily and tore into her at top volume for being so stupid, but she'd decided she didn't have anything more to say to him, and responded only with silence. For days, every word he spoke to her, no matter how kind or apologetic, was met with a fierce glare and, if one was convenient, a slamming door in his face.

Mrs. Wilcox, abruptly returned to her own home, had slowly gathered her senses as she'd unpacked the few things she'd brought with her from Old Bill's house, and set her house in order. Despite the harsh treatment she'd suffered at Cory's hands, she knew she was helpless to do anything about it, for herself, or for the two girls who she'd thought she might consider her own.

She knew Old Bill's daughters needed her, now more than ever, and she cried bitterly for them, and herself, but she knew that a scorned woman such as herself, so hated by the community for her past indiscretions, would have no standing against yet another woman's husband - no matter how pure her intentions this time. Cory was too highly respected in the community for anyone, let alone her, to defy him and interfere with his plans for his new wife and her sister. To make matters worse, she knew she couldn't breathe a word about the goings on in Old Bill's house, or Cory's violent treatment of her, without revealing the source of all the conflict: Esther's pregnancy. That subject required delicacy, and silence, until Johnny married her.

Maybe Cory had been right, she'd consoled herself sadly. Maybe it was best for both girls that they live apart through Esther's time, and Cindy Lou be given a fair chance at a happy life, respected by a community that would likely treat her badly because of her sister's irresponsible behavior, but it saddened her to know the heartache they were suffering.

She'd thought, so happily, that fate had given her Cindy Lou and Esther to love like the daughters she had always wanted, but it had all been ripped away from her. Now she had only herself, again, and all the loneliness that came with her solitary existence, and had for all the years since the community had shunned her and pushed her out.

Chapter 3

Doctor Miles woke early the morning after Old Bill's funeral, anxious to go down to his hospital room and see his new, unlikely, patient. He splashed water on his face, not daring to look himself in the mirror just yet, unsure whether the uneasy sensation in the pit of his stomach was from hunger, or guilt over taking the murdering Fenton boy into his home, leaving a good man like Cory to fend for himself with no warning whatsoever.

He'd half-anticipated Cory showing up at some point during the night to demand his hospital room back. He couldn't be sure how Cory or Cindy Lou had received his poorly thought out plan for them to marry, the night before, but if either had gone against it, he would know soon enough, he guessed.

For that moment, it seemed to him, everything had settled out, leaving only him, with his terrible feeling, to find a way to do what he'd felt was necessary for the Fenton boy, and get him back out of his home before the townspeople began to ask questions, and Cory started giving answers that would make every Farmersville resident determined to take care of Jimmy Fenton their own way. Once people heard that Jimmy had caused Old Bill's death, they would be banging down his door to get at him.

He made coffee quickly, after assuring himself that the young man in his hospital room was still sleeping soundly. He'd examined Jimmy's face closely the night before, but had seen no possibility of undoing any of the damage he'd done; Jimmy would only have the use of the one eye, it appeared, and his speech would forever be difficult at best, and Doctor Miles had only the barest of ideas of how to tell whether he'd suffered any brain damage. When Jimmy woke up, he decided, he'd watch him carefully to see what he could and could not do on his own, talk to him and see if he understood anything, and then worry about what to do next.

Jimmy Fenton woke in Doctor Miles' hospital room, in a full panic. His memory of all that had happened the day before forgotten, replaced with only confusion over where he was, and fear when he saw the man who'd taken him in. He looked around the room frantically, spotting Blasted, Doctor Miles' aging Saint Bernard, sleeping near his bedside, but no weapon to use to defend himself as Doctor Miles came through the doorway with a tray in his hands.

As soon as the doctor reached his bedside, Jimmy lunged, hitting the tray as hard as he could, slamming it into the doctor's chest and spilling food all over him. Before the doctor could regain his balance, or his thoughts, Jimmy jumped from the bed and shoved the older man again, grunting and contorting in pain as he did.

Doctor Miles fell to the floor, helpless, but Blasted was quick to defend him, throwing his massive body against Jimmy's weakened, painful legs, putting him into a howling heap near the door, then he sat guard beside him, unsympathetically, until the doctor was back on his feet, cursing and swiping bits of food off of him.

Doctor Miles yelled at Jimmy for attacking him, but Jimmy couldn't hear him over his own wailing. He writhed on the floor, thinking the pain he was in would surely kill him in just a moment's time, completely unaware of Doctor Miles' movements around the room, for a time.

After glaring at Jimmy for a moment, it occurred to the good doctor that if he was to help this, now bleeding, wild, young man, he'd have to sedate him. He ordered Blasted to stay with Jimmy and went to his office to get medicine.

When he returned, he gave Jimmy a shot to knock him out, holding the strong young man under his knees and by the arm to steady him. After a few more tortured minutes, Jimmy stopped struggling and Doctor Miles released his hold, and worked carefully to turn Jimmy onto his back so he could see what fresh damage had caused all the blood to flow.

He saw immediately that Jimmy's jaw was broken, snapped by the impact of hitting the floor, and was jutting out grotesquely. Blood streamed from his cheek where the bone had cut through it, and filled his mouth, threatening to drown him.

He turned Jimmy's head to the side and carefully examined his mouth, and manipulated the jagged bone with his fingers until he could no longer see it, but could feel it go flush against its other half. Then, holding Jimmy's jaw still, he grabbed the roll of gauze he'd brought from his office and carefully wrapped it around Jimmy's head, to secure his jaw with the bone in place.

It was a crude fix for such an injury, but Doctor Miles was pleased. The bone that was once again broken was one he had noted in his first examination, the night before, as having already nearly healed, but severely out of place, contorting Jimmy's jaw in in such a way that he'd not been able to close his mouth fully without effort.

He had not considered re-breaking it to correct

the deformity, but since Jimmy had done it himself, with a little help from Blasted, he had been able to reposition it, and the lower part of Jimmy's face, despite the torn flesh from the momentarily protruding bone, had resumed a completely normal appearance. He was relieved, somewhat, to see that what he'd deemed too abusive a treatment to correct some of Jimmy's deformity, was now a necessity.

It would take time for the bone to re-heal, but at least Jimmy wouldn't feel the pain from the process this time, with the medicine he could give him. Only the difficulty of getting food into him while his jaw healed remained a critical issue.

Doctor Miles drug the mattress off the hospital room bed and moved it over to where Jimmy now lay, unconscious. The young man was much larger than he, and too heavy to lift, so he carefully rolled him onto it, and put a pillow under his head. Then he left Blasted to watch his new patient while he cleaned himself, and the hospital room, up a bit.

While Jimmy slept, Doctor Miles knelt on the floor next to him, checking him over. The morphine he'd given the young man had prevented him from feeling any more of the excruciating pain from his broken jaw, but now he had to make sure he was right there with Jimmy when the medication started to wear off, so he could explain things to the crazed young man and convince him to trust him. It was a long wait and Doctor Miles nodded off a few times, but Blasted, each time he noticed his tired owner's head begin to sag, nudged him til he started and shook himself fully awake again.

Jimmy finally woke again and Doctor Miles started talking to him the moment he did. Jimmy's one working eye widened in alarm as he listened, and he felt the bandages on his head. He imagined the terrible pain must be returning, so he gave Jimmy more medicine and left him to sleep again, with Blasted staying by his side, taking full advantage of the soft mattress on the hard wood floor, pressing against Jimmy's side so he'd know the instant the young man tried to move again.

Having so recently learned to use his plastic tubes to feed through, Doctor Miles set to work cleaning one to feed Jimmy with when he woke again. He scrubbed his kitchen clean and made some stew for his dinner, setting aside some of the broth for Jimmy to sip later, wondering how the young man had kept himself alive since the night he'd left him for dead. He was amazed that there seemed to be no infections in Jimmy's quite severe wounds, but aside from his head and the weakened condition of his legs, the young man appeared to be quite healthy.

He felt sure that Jimmy must be hungry, so he hadn't given him as much morphine as he had the first time in hopes that within the hour he could give him some warm broth. He ate his dinner trying to imagine how things had gone for Cory with Cindy Lou, and what, if anything, Cory would do about Esther. If she was allowed to stay in town, he'd have to attend to her, being the town's only doctor, and he didn't want to do that. He hoped Cory'd had the good sense to send the irresponsible wildcat to her sister, Sarah, rather than allow her to stay and sully Cindy Lou's reputation by having her illegitimate baby in their father's house.

He knew Old Bill would have wanted Esther out of his house, from the fight he'd heard between the old man and his daughter the day he had confirmed Esther's pregnancy. He decided that, if Cory hadn't sent Esther away, he'd make a run to

Cindy Lou's house and advise Cory to at least send Esther home with Mrs. Wilcox to live. Mrs. Wilcox would know how to handle the young woman and keep Johnny under the gun to marry her.

Chapter 4

Esther stumbled and fell against a tree, out of breath and dripping wet from head to toe. Her nose was running and the mud in her shoes was chilling her to the bone. Another storm was atop her. Hail beat down on her through the branches of the trees above her and the wind blew chunks of bark, twigs and leaves into her face. Tears of frustration mixed with the rain running down her cheeks as she held on to the tree, desperately trying to stay on her aching feet. She'd been picking her way through the woods, on the path she'd found, for what seemed an eternity and she was beginning to worry she'd made a mistake, taken a wrong direction at a fork near the beginning of the path.

When she'd caught her breath, to calm herself a little, she cursed the icy stones that pelted and snapped against her head, and the relentless rain and lightning that were making the woods around her seem alive with evil creatures. Having vented a bit, she once again felt sure that if she stuck to the path she'd chosen, she'd be back on the road again in short order, so she pressed on, keeping a careful eye on the path before her each time lightening flashed, setting her sights on finding the end of that path before she had to rest again. She'd walked nearly all the night hours, but her speed hadn't been regular for all the slippery mud and treacherous ruts in the road, and on the path.

Finally, she spotted the clearing ahead of her and fairly ran until she reached the last of the trees.

She dropped to the waterlogged ground on her knees, panting, exhausted, and feeling nothing but weariness and pain racking her small frame. She leaned her back against a tree and waited for the next burst of lightening to show her the road from there, still struggling to catch her breath. Thunder rumbled and shook the trees and brilliant lines crisscrossed the sky, showing her not a road before her, but another puddle-filled footpath.

Grateful to see anything, but fearful of leaving the relative safety of the trees, she allowed herself to sit for a few minutes more on a fallen log and rest. Her feet and ankles began to tingle after a moment or two so she stood up and stomped her feet to set them straight again, long having given up the idea of keeping her dress free of mud splatter. She was as filthy as the many cows she'd seen, growing up, in pastures around Farmersville.

Stomping her feet didn't stop the tingling, so she gave up the idea of resting there and ran through the rain and hail for the path. Once on it, she slipped on the mud and wrenched her ankle violently, but she managed to stay on her feet and stumble forward, desperate now to find the road again, vowing not to take any more short-cut footpaths until daylight.

As daylight began to brighten the sky, the storm clouds rushed on ahead of her and she dropped her pace a little, feeling hopeful that she'd made it most of the way home already, but terribly hungry and weary. When she finally reached the water-filled ditch that stood between her and the road she'd searched for half the night, her foot slipped again, and she fell into the deep rushing water helplessly and silently and didn't get up again.

Chapter 5

Cindy Lou woke herself from a terrible nightmare, screaming. In her dream, she'd seen a vivid image of her sister, Esther's, pale, oddly swollen, face and felt certain that her sister was dead. She burst from her room sobbing, searching the house for Cory, desperate to find him and tell him to go and find Esther right away.

Cory, working on his truck in the side yard, heard Cindy Lou's screams and rushed into the house. He caught her up in his arms in the kitchen doorway and demanded an explanation. He could hardly understand what Cindy Lou was so upset about, but when he did finally hear her clearly he was horrified; his new wife had lost her mind.

Guilt and frustration overtook him, and he turned away from Cindy Lou so she wouldn't see how disturbed he was. He tried to keep his voice from shaking, as he told her to shut up and sit down, but his efforts only made his voice sound harder and colder to Cindy Lou's ears, and she grew even more hysterical.

She hurled accusations at his back and yanked out a chair from the table and tried to throw it at him, but he grabbed it, then her, and pulled her against him so she could do no more. While she screamed, punched, and kicked him, he tried to talk calmly to her and finally managed to reduce her to pitiful wails over her sister, promising he'd go to Sarah's and bring Esther home for her that minute if she would only stop crying. He couldn't find words enough to express how sorry he was that he'd ever taken Esther away.

Cindy Lou stopped crying, but didn't become any more reasonable, and she didn't stop demanding that he go and find her sister. She accused him of killing Esther and said she'd never forgive him for it, but when she told him she hated him and wished he was dead, he couldn't block out her hurtful words any longer. Angrily, he argued again that he'd only done what her father and he had thought best for Esther, but Cindy Lou only stared miserably at him until he stormed back out to his truck and started the several hours long trip to retrieve Esther from her sister's farm.

After Cory had gone, Cindy Lou sat in the chair she'd tried to throw at him just moments before, and cried. The terrible picture she'd dreamt, of Esther's face, wouldn't go away and her heart ached like it was trying to smother her.

When all her tears were spent, the heavy, sick, feeling remained and she stumbled around the house touching things of her father and her sister, trying to make some peace between herself and them. She knew in her heart that Esther was gone, that it would do no good for Cory to bring her back only to be buried, but she was anxious that he do just that.

Cory bounced along the road toward Sarah and Lee's farm, his mind reeling in confusion, the likes of which he'd never experienced. He'd been so sure he was doing the right thing in sending Esther to Sarah's right away and getting Mrs. Wilcox away from his wife and her trouble-making sister. He'd done what Old Bill would have wanted him to do, he felt sure.

He'd thought Cindy Lou would see that he was right, and that the two of them would enjoy a little time thinking only of themselves and their future, once the house was cleared. Something had gone wrong somewhere, though, because he'd never thought she would go out of her mind without her sister living with them, and it made him sick to think he'd reduced his beautiful new bride to a lunatic, convinced that he'd murdered her sister just because he'd moved her out of the house.

All he could think to do now was to go and get Esther as fast as he could and show her to Cindy Lou, convince her her sister was well and very much alive, then let them stay together in their father's house until Cindy Lou was back to normal again, if she ever would be. He would just go back to his supply store and try to get by without her.

It wasn't how he'd pictured married life would be, but the alternative didn't seem to fit his picture either, and something had to give somewhere. He couldn't go on living in Old Bill's house, fending for his insane, youngest, daughter, enduring her wicked glares and silent treatment, and add back to it the reckless pregnant daughter too. His reputation would be ruined whether he stayed or left, so he resolved to himself that he'd try to get things back to the way they had been, for Cindy Lou's sake, then get on with his life and hope she'd come back around some day.

He pulled to a stop in front of Sarah's house just before noon.

Sarah had had a bad dream in the night too, and had woken early that morning in distress. Losing her father had been a real blow, and not being able to go to his funeral and be with her younger sister's had nearly crushed her spirit.

It was hard on her to live so far away from her family and she'd known her father wouldn't live forever, but she loved Lee and felt she had to be with him despite the distance from her family. Learning by letter that her father had died in her absence, had devastated her. Having Esther, in her condition, dropped off to live with her, and for many days refusing to even speak to her, was more than she could bear.

When they'd received the notice that Old Bill was dead, Lee had offered to borrow a car and drive her down to Farmersville, but whoever he borrowed it from would have wanted something in exchange for the use of the car, something they could not spare: money. She'd assured Lee she didn't want to go, that they could not afford it, but she'd cried bitter tears, secretly, for many days on end. Then Cindy Lou and Esther had appeared on her doorstep, and just as she was about to tell them how happy she was that they'd come to be with her, since she hadn't been able to go to them, Cindy Lou's new husband Cory had interrupted her with his announcement that Esther had gotten herself into trouble and needed to stay with them.

He'd left her staring stupidly, on the spot to make room for Esther in her small home and Lee had stayed in his study with Cory and shut the door on her, so she'd had no choice but to show Esther up to the only suitably furnished room of the house without getting any explanations at all out of her. She'd gone back downstairs to ask Cindy Lou what had happened, but Cory had reappeared and whisked her little sister out the door, back to Farmersville; his duty to Esther finished.

Esther was clearly very angry to be forced to

live in her home, and hadn't seemed to want anything to do with her, so Sarah had just cooked and cleaned around her, trying to give her time to come around. She'd grown impatient after the first day and tried to press Esther for information, but after getting nothing more out of her than that the baby was Johnny's, she'd lost her temper and told Esther off, but good, for being so irresponsible. She hadn't tried to talk to her after that because she seemed determined to stay up in her room all day, knitting and feeling sorry for herself.

After a night of bad dreams about Esther dying, however, she'd decided to try again to talk to her sister, but on going up to Esther's room, she'd found the door locked and hadn't even been able to get a response to her knocking. She'd beat on the door, crying, calling to Esther, begging her to just talk to her for a few minutes, until Lee had come to find out what was wrong and had led her back to their kitchen and made her some coffee, trying to console her. He'd suggested they leave Esther alone completely until she came to them for companionship and avoid any further upsets like the one she'd had that morning.

Around noon, Cory, Cindy Lou's impossibly rude new husband, was back on their doorstep asking for Esther, telling Sarah that Cindy Lou had had a break down, and had convinced herself that Esther was dead. Now, he wanted to take Esther back home with him to prove she was indeed alive.

Lee asked Sarah to go up and get Esther while he and Cory had a word privately in his den, but once again, Sarah couldn't get any response to her knocking; this time it terrified her. What if Cindy Lou was right, she worried, what if Esther was dead, right on the other side of the door? She kicked at the door and beat on it with her fists, screaming for Lee to come help her, certain, now, that her own nightmares had come true.

Lee came running with Cory right behind him, and kicked the door open for her, but the room was as empty as Esther had left it, many hours before. Cory pushed her aside and ran to the bed, dropping to his knees to peer into the darkness under it. He found nothing but a discarded knitting needle and dust.

He jumped to his feet to confront his sister-in-law and her confused husband, demanding to know where Esther was, but neither could say. Sarah was suddenly hysterical and Lee was entirely focused on calming her, reassuring her that Esther was around somewhere, and promising they'd find her. Cory felt sick, suddenly. He ran down the stairs and out the front door, yelling for Esther.

Sarah followed him, forgetting her distaste for him, for the moment, hoping that he'd find her sister.

Lee searched the upstairs rooms, quickly, then made his way downstairs to search the rest of his house; calling out for Esther angrily, accusing her of scaring her poor sister to death, but he found no hostile female hiding anywhere in his house. He searched his study last, checked to make sure his gun cabinet was still locked, the money Cory had given him was still in his safe, and the key to his gun cabinet was still in the drawer, but nothing seemed amiss.

Cory and Sarah searched the yard, barn and out buildings, but it was soon clear that unless Lee found her hiding in the house somewhere, Esther had run away.

Cory ran into Lee as he rounded the side of the house, and punched the wall furiously when the other man admitted that Esther was not anywhere in the house. Sarah ran to her husband wailing that Esther was nowhere to be found outside either and the three of them stood, completely baffled, staring at each other for a long moment.

Finally, Sarah confessed to Cory that they hadn't seen her sister since the evening before, and that she'd tried to rouse her early that morning, but had assumed Esther was just angry with her, ignoring her, but definitely on the other side of that bedroom door.

Cory just glared at her, his mind racing, replaying Cindy Lou's outburst that morning in his head, trying to figure out what he should do next. The answer came from Sarah, at last; she told him to start searching the road back toward Farmersville and ran back into the house to get her walking shoes. She decided that she and Lee should walk the road sides, searching the ditches, while Cory searched from his truck, but when she returned to the yard, her husband flatly refused to continue to look for her sister.

Lee stormed back into the house and locked the door behind him when he got to his study. He'd had enough of his wife's family and had no intention of wasting any more of his time and energy worrying about the worst of the three of them. If Esther didn't want to stay under his roof, so be it; he had a living to make, he fumed.

Sarah didn't waste any time telling her husband what she thought of him, from the yard where he'd left her. Cory was already gone in his truck, searching the road, so she followed him on foot, searching both sides of the muddy road for any sign of her sister, wailing as she imagined the horrors Esther might, at that very moment, be suffering. A wild beast attack, a savage wanderer who had murder on his mind, a tornado or lightning strike; she was quickly as convinced as Cindy Lou had been, according to Cory, that Esther was indeed dead.

    Cory drove as fast as he dared, back down the road toward Farmersville, cursing and searching for Esther. He argued to himself that if she'd taken this road, the only one leading homeward, he'd have surely seen her earlier on his way out to Sarah's farm, but he pressed on anyway, desperate now to find her and give her back to her sisters.

    He stopped his truck and mucked through a field to ask a farmer who was checking his fields for damage from the storm, if he'd seen or heard anything of a young woman out on the road during the night, or perhaps earlier in the day, but the farmer couldn't help him. The man hadn't seen a soul, aside from Cory, for several days.

    Cory thanked him and slogged back to his truck, telling himself he was a fool for ever bringing Esther out to this remote region, and cursing the mud caked on his boots as he reached the road and got back up into his truck.

    He didn't start the motor again right away, though, noticing the deep, water-filled ditches that paralleled the road on either side of him, recalling his leap to cross over to the farmer's field and having to jump again when he'd returned, a moment before. Then it dawned on him that Esther's comparatively short legs would never give her a chance at clearing one of them. If she'd gone off the road somehow, she'd be under that murky water, invisible to him or anyone else who might happen along the road, he realized.

    Wondering how deep the ditch water might be, he retraced his steps to where he'd jumped the ditch, with a stick from the back of his truck. He sank the stick into the rushing water until it reached the ditch bottom, then took it up again to measure the water mark against his six-foot frame. The water mark reached his upper thigh.

This wasn't probably too deep for Esther to survive, he decided, trying to fight down the fear that they'd not find Cindy Lou and Sarah's sister until the ground soaked up all the rainwater. He stomped back to his truck, and glared at his filthy boots for a moment, trying to figure how far he was from Sarah's farm and how far Esther might have gotten by now, toward home, if she'd left Sarah's house before daybreak that morning.

As he stared downward, thinking hard, his eyes began to focus on something he hadn't noticed before; there were small footprints in the muddy road, just a few feet from him. He walked over to have a closer look, then followed them a few yards, then he ran back and started his truck.

They had to be Esther's footprints, he decided, and if they weren't they might at least lead him to someone who'd walked this very road since the storm had passed, someone who might have seen Esther. He followed along the trail of footprints in his truck, trying to cover the distance between himself and Esther, or whoever had left them, more quickly.

He was excited and anxious, now, to catch up with the young woman, put her in his truck and take her home to his distraught wife. He wouldn't even take her back to Sarah's, he decided; he'd dispatch a letter to her as soon as he got back to Cindy Lou and let them know all the details of finding her. If they wanted to see for themselves that Esther was alright, they could make the hours-long trek to Cindy Lou's, themselves.

He continued to follow the footprints down the road, speeding up occasionally, trusting they'd continue all the way back to Old Bill's house, eventually, but not confident enough to forego slowing to a crawl once in a while so he could see them clearly. As the day warmed up, however, and the sun heated the air in his truck, he grew tired and, anxious to get the miserable situation resolved; he drove too quickly for a long stretch of the road. When he realized his attention had wandered, he slowed, searching for the tracks, but they were no longer there.

Jimmy woke to an excruciating pain in his jaw and moaned loudly. Doctor Miles rushed to his side and helped him sit up, offering the broth he'd made, instructing him to suck on the tube he'd carefully inserted into the young man's nearly immobile mouth.

Jimmy did as he was told and was rewarded with the best tasting broth he'd ever had, filling his mouth. He closed his lips around the tube tightly and swallowed, then sucked in another mouthful. He was ravenously hungry, suddenly, though he hadn't noticed it before then. In seconds, however, his stomach felt full, nearly too full to stand, and he let the doctor take the tube away and tried to recall where he was and why his head ached so badly. Before he could work it all out, though, sleep overtook him again, and Doctor Miles went about cleaning him and changing his bed sheets, quietly congratulating him on having such a good appetite and promising he'd give him more of the broth when he woke again, in a few hours.

Doctor Miles finished his morning ritual; showering, dressing, and making his own breakfast, before going out to his washroom to do his laundry and Jimmy's. He was well pleased over his new patient's improving condition and calmer temperament. He couldn't be sure how much Jimmy understood about where he was, but felt optimistic for the first time since he'd brought the young man to his home, that he could undo, or at least mitigate, some of the damage he'd done to him in that moment of panic to save Old Bill so many weeks before.

    He didn't have any formal training to help him deal with such severe injuries as he'd dealt with recently, but he felt confident that teaching Jimmy how to work around his sightless eye and diminished appearance would be what gave the young man another chance at having some kind of life going forward.

Chapter 6

Cindy Lou paced the kitchen floor. It had been hours since Cory had left for Sarah's and she wondered now if he'd gone to find her sister for her, or if he'd just gotten away from her. When he'd stormed out, left, she'd been confident that he'd taken her dream as seriously as she did, even if he hadn't really believed her, and had gone to Sarah's farm to bring Esther home to her, to prove her wrong, but now she was worried.

She had told him she hated him and wished he was dead, after all. Fresh tears poured down her cheeks as she contemplated the affect her angry words might have had on her new husband. She did hate him for taking her Esther away like he had, so soon after their father was buried, and she was still quite angry that he'd taken Mrs. Wilcox away too, but she certainly did not want him to die; she'd only just nursed him back from the brink of death with her own hands.

Now, she felt sick and anxious that she might not have a chance to tell him she was sorry, and explain that she had been so angry, she'd spoken without thought when she'd said those terrible things, but that she hadn't truly meant them.

If Esther really was dead, and she felt sure in her heart she was, it wasn't his fault, she knew, but he'd treated the whole situation, and everyone involved, so rashly and hadn't even listened to her argument that the disruption was too much too soon, for all of them. If he'd only come off his high horse long enough to listen to her, she reasoned, her sister would be just fine, upstairs in their room, with Mrs. Wilcox to care for her, and he could have gone back to his supply store if he didn't want to be with them. Now, what little she had left in her world: her sister, Mrs. Wilcox, and Cory, were all gone and she couldn't talk to any of them.

She wandered around the quiet, still, house listening for any sound, any indication that she was not alone, as the sun went down. There was no sound to be heard, aside from her own footsteps. She went to her father's room, where Cory had been sleeping since her father's funeral and their unplanned, hurried, marriage ceremony, and stared at the rumpled bedclothes and the pile of soiled towels in the corner.

Her father had always had her and Esther to tend to his room, and it had never looked so shabby as it did now. Listless, and sure that Cory wouldn't be able to prove her wrong about Esther, she found herself picking up the towels and stripping the bed of its sheets and replacing them with fresh ones from the linen closet, then straightening the items, both Cory's and her father's, on the dresser, and dusting the window sill with her handkerchief, then the lampshade; cleaning as if someone would be sleeping in there that very night. She stared out the window, when the room was finally clean enough to suit her, at her father and mother's graves below, asking them out loud what in the world she was to do?

Almost at once, she felt exhausted from all the strain she'd been under. Feeling hopelessly lost, she laid down on her father's old bed and tried again to sort things out, resting her head against the feather pillow where her father had once rested his, and was asleep almost immediately.

As she slept, she dreamed most vividly of many sheets of writing paper filled with penmanship she did not recognize. In her dream, the papers were hidden under a bed, but she couldn't make herself reach out for them, to read what someone had scrawled on them.

She woke a few moments later, with a feeling that the papers she'd seen in her dream were very important, and that she needed to find them and discover what had been written on them.

She jumped off the big bed and knelt beside it to peer under, but she couldn't see anything. She turned her head this way and that against the floor, feeling even more urgency than she had a moment before, and a certainty that the papers were under there, somewhere. She reached a hand into the blackness, and finally her hand touched paper. She pulled them out and ran to sit by the fireplace so she could see better. The handwriting was as unfamiliar as it had appeared in her dream.

Her hands trembled as she scanned through the pages and when she set them aside, she felt heartsick. In those many lines of terrible penmanship, Cory had poured out his heart to her, told her over and over again, throughout, how much he loved her and how much, each morning when he woke, he hoped that that would be the day she relented and would speak to him again. One page after another he'd filled with his heartache and confusion, and his growing desperation that she would never love him, and maybe never had.

Near the bottom of the last page, she found, he'd told her he'd done all that he'd thought was right and best, and in-line completely with what her father, his dearest friend, had wanted, but he could see now that he'd done her and their marriage irreparable harm. He told her he couldn't imagine his life going forward without her, but was afraid to leave and afraid to stay, now, for fear of making things worse.

She was stunned. She hadn't dreamed her new husband had even the capability of having such thoughts. It frightened her a little to see, if secretly, how unsure of himself Cory had been those past many days, when he'd acted so brashly toward everyone and hadn't seemed to care for her wishes and feelings at all. The stack of letters made her feel so many emotions at once, she was overcome with tears - this time from shame.

Even more unsure, now, what she should do she sat, crying, in the still room, waiting, hoping Cory would come back, would prove that Esther was not dead, as she'd dreamed, and give her a chance to break the ugly spell of cruelty and silence she'd cast over her own home.

She could see now that she'd hurt Cory's feelings, hadn't given him the benefit of a doubt, and had somehow forgotten how deeply affected he continued to be over her father's death. Her tears dried in her eyes and she felt energy fill her again, energy more befitting a girl of her age, and more of it than she'd felt since her father had died.

If Esther truly was gone, she resolved to herself, she would not blame Cory for it. She would accept it as her own fault for creating such a terrible scene over his and her father's decision, rather than encouraging her older sister to see the bright side of a move to Sarah's, and consoling her that she and Cory would visit her frequently so she'd not ever feel alone.

While she waited, she decided, she'd clean the rest of the house as well as she had his room and set everything up appropriately so she could take care of her new husband when he came back. If he did not return that night, she'd go to his supply store in the morning, if that was where he'd gone, and convince him to give her another chance, she decided.

It was nearly midnight, and the house was spotlessly clean when Cory finally did return.

Sarah searched the sides of the road nearest her home until darkness began to settle in, and she had to turn back. She bit her lip to keep herself from crying as she made her way back home, stopping to call out for Esther at every noise she heard. She recounted her last confrontation with Esther in her mind, over and over again, then tried to convince herself that her sister's anger, and mean-spirited treatment of her, made her capable of walking away without a word, to return to her lover in Farmersville, quite capably and safely.

Lee met her at the door, feeling guilty for refusing to help her earlier, ready to console her and make her a nice dinner, to make up for not joining in on the search for her silly sister. He told her that Cory had not returned and she confirmed that she'd not seen him since he'd left, and they sat together at their kitchen table, trying to guess where Esther might have gone.

Lee assured her that Esther was quite safe, though he couldn't convince her of it, or prove it to her. He told her he felt confident that Johnny, Esther's lover, must have come for her in the night and taken her away to marry her, as he was expected to do, and advised her to stop worrying about the reckless girl; that they'd no doubt hear from her one day soon enough, that she'd run off and secretly married Johnny, had given birth to a healthy baby and had a fine home of her own, somewhere near Johnny's family farm.

Sarah wasn't inclined to believe Johnny would do any such thing, however, without a gun pointed at his head. He hadn't, according to Cory, even known she was in a family way, and he had no idea where she'd been taken. She pointed out to her husband that neither Johnny, nor anyone else in his family, even knew where they lived, but Lee stood his ground and insisted that Cory had certainly told Johnny's father where he intended to take Esther when he'd confronted him about her pregnancy.

He put his weary, depressed, wife to bed that night with the promise that they'd hear everything was fine and dandy with Esther within a few days. There was nothing they could do other than keep an eye out for her, and wait, he told her.

Cory pulled his truck into the driveway and turned off the headlights, but didn't make any move to get out, right away. He'd been racking his brains all the way there, to come up with a good answer for returning to Cindy Lou without her precious, troublemaking, sister.

From the moment he noticed the footprints he'd been following for so many miles, at such a fast clip, had ceased to exist, he'd searched the road behind him frantically. Hours later, when the sun had already set, he'd given up. Esther was not on the road, the footprints in the mud had stopped, and it would be too dark to see anything, soon, so he'd driven the rest of the way to Cindy Lou, hoping Esther would be there. If she wasn't, he didn't have any guesses as to where she had run to. He'd just have to confess that no one could find Esther, not at Sarah's house, nor anywhere else, yet, and deal with the consequences.

He wished he'd never gotten himself involved with Old Bill's family in the first place, at that moment. Had he left his dear friend to deal with his girls on his own, so long ago, he'd be worried about nothing more than running his supply store in town, now.

He sucked in a deep breath, realizing he might as well get it over with so he could get some sleep that night, and got out into the pitch darkness, hoping Esther was inside, or at least that Cindy Lou would be asleep, unable to question him about her sister and where he'd been. Cindy Lou was not asleep, though.

When he opened the kitchen door and stepped inside, she was not only awake, but coming right toward him, weeping as hard as she'd been when he'd left, hours before, with her arms stretched out to him like a young child. He grabbed her and held her tightly, confused. She looked dreadful, and sounded hoarse and exhausted.

He kissed the top of her head and rocked her side to side, trying to calm her so he could tell her all that he knew, but she just kept repeating that she was sorry; sorry for the silence, sorry for her accusations, and sorry for her tears, then begging him to tell her her sister was alright, that he'd spoken to her and that he'd let her come home now.

He guided her to a chair and sat in it, pulling her into his lap. He pressed her head to his shoulder and rocked her soothingly, while he told her he hadn't been able to find her sister. He told her of the search at Sarah's house and the road, and of the footprints he'd found and followed, then lost, and promised her he'd go out looking for her again as soon as it was light out, in the morning.

When he'd finished, Cindy Lou made no response. She'd been through so much in that long, horrid day, she'd fallen asleep in his arms, listening to him confirm her worst fears; her sister was gone. Even as she slept, tears continued to stream down her face.

He carried her upstairs in his muddy boots, not wanting to risk waking her to take them off. He took her first to her bedroom doorway, staring into the room where she'd remained since they'd taken their vows, and then thought better of allowing her to sleep, and wake up, in the room she'd shared with Esther for so many years, alone. Better, he decided, that she should sleep in her father's room with him, so he could comfort her if she had a bad night.

He laid her on the bed and covered her with a blanket, and sat in the chair next to her and took off his boots, then, leaving the blanket tucked in around her, undisturbed, he laid down beside her, covering himself with another blanket, hoping she wouldn't be furious with him when she woke up beside him in the morning.

As he drifted off to sleep, he felt her soft arm wrap around his chest and her head pressing against his shoulder. He couldn't help but smile with relief that, at least in her sleep, his new wife found comfort in his arms. He pulled her closer to him and wrapped a protective arm around her and fell asleep, praying that Esther could be located in the morning, alive, not the way Cindy Lou had dreamed her.

Morning brought banging fists and lots of yelling to Sarah and Lee's front door. Hoping it was good news about her sister, Sarah scrambled to make herself decent before her husband, so she could answer the door. Lee saw what his wife was trying to do and, feeling like there wasn't any good news to be heard from the shouting men at the door, ran, barely dressed, to the stairs and down to see what was going on, yelling back to her to stay upstairs until he called her.

She continued dressing frantically and, ignoring her husband's warning, ran down into the middle of a very excited group of young men who were each clamoring to be the first to tell her husband about the body they'd discovered on their way out of a field, a distance of twenty miles down the road. She fainted as soon as she heard the news. Lee ran to stop her from falling to the floor and ordered the men to silence, sending them into his study to wait for him, then he took Sarah into the kitchen, chastising her all the way and left her there to recover, while he went to talk to the men and find out about the body.

Minutes ticked by slowly after she roused herself again in the kitchen. She couldn't make herself move the whole while she waited for Lee to come back and tell her whether the body they'd found was Esther's. Finally, the men come out of Lee's study, and walked silently back out the front door. She started sobbing before Lee could cross the room to her to tell her the bad news; she already knew.

Lee sat with his tormented wife, holding her hand tightly while she wept for her sister, telling her over and over again how sorry he was, but that he was sure there was nothing anyone could have done to save Esther. He refused to tell her how they'd discovered her sister, or the way they'd described her face; it would have killed her to hear such details. So he told her only that her sister had most assuredly not suffered, and not seen her end coming.

The gun that the men had brought with them, he had put back into his gun cabinet, shaking his head furiously, worrying that Sarah had caught a glimpse of it when she'd first come down the stairs. He'd ordered the men not to breathe a word about finding his gun, with Esther's remains, before he'd sent them away to send a telegram to Cindy Lou, and take Esther's body to the Farmersville pastor, for him to take charge of until funeral arrangements could be made.

He was determined that no one should ever tell Sarah that her sister had stolen one of his guns; it would make no difference to her. To him, however, it was just proof positive that Esther had been nothing but trouble. She'd had little reason to hope to have a good life anyway, so she was probably better off dead, he told himself.

Doctor Miles woke Jimmy to give him more broth, in the early evening hours. This time Jimmy knew how to drink through the tube without any instruction, pleasing his doctor to no end.

When the bowl was empty, Doctor Miles explained to Jimmy, that he'd give him another dose of the strong morphine so he could sleep through the night, but that in the morning he'd give him a different pain reliever that would allow him to stay awake so they could talk a little, and get to know one another better. Jimmy seemed happy, if a little bewildered, at his words, but didn't resist at all when Doctor Miles gave him the shot in his arm. He fell asleep quickly, with Blasted by his side, sharing his bed with him, still.

Blasted waited, pressed close to Jimmy's side, until the young man was sleeping deeply again, then he got up to find his owner and beg to be let outside to run around a bit. When he was satisfied that no rival animal had been on his property, he allowed Doctor Miles to entice him back into the kitchen to eat his dinner, then he went back to sleep through the night next to Jimmy.

A little later, Doctor Miles looked in on Jimmy and said goodnight to his bed-hogging canine, before he turned in for the night. The next day would be a busy one.

If Jimmy could manage with just a pain reliever, starting the next morning, he'd be full of energy, hunger and, no doubt, questions. It was no use trying to plan out how things should go, as far as Doctor Miles was concerned; with a patient as volatile as Jimmy able to move freely, save his jaw for the time being, it seemed best to make sure only that they were both well rested, and let whatever might happen next, happen unplanned.

In time, he would know how debilitating, and how permanent, Jimmy's injuries were and by that time he'd surely know what living arrangements would best suit the young man: living in his own home, independent, or with him, cared for and protected at all times, with Blasted's help.

Cindy Lou woke with the sun warming her face. Unsure where she was for a moment, she scanned the room quickly before she got up. She'd become aware, at some point in the night, that she was not alone in her bed, but snuggled up tightly to a soundly sleeping Cory. Though his presence had startled her, in her exhaustion, she didn't move a muscle, but returned to her dreams feeling safe and warm. This morning, she felt entirely differently about the matter. She got herself into the hallway, quickly, trying not to wake Cory and face him at just that moment, and didn't let out her breath until the bathroom door was shut and locked behind her.

In front of the mirror, she gathered her wits about her. Her eyes were red and swollen, and her cheeks felt raw. She looked a mess and, before she could stop them, fresh tears began to stream down her face. When she'd pulled herself together somewhat, she went down to the kitchen and made bacon and toast, and a cup of coffee to help her wake up.

The house felt the same as it always had; creaking and groaning when the wind rushed around it, and then quiet and still, but Cindy Lou felt entirely changed. She felt old, tired, and miserably confused. All the joy had left her life, and her hands, once so soft and delicate, now seemed withered and ugly, to her.

She didn't have a thought to share when Cory woke to the smells of breakfast and came down to join her. Almost without will, she gave him a plate of bacon and toast and sat next to him, staring vaguely at it until he'd finished eating.

Cory didn't know what to say to his miserable looking bride. He was unsure whether her silence was from anger, resurfacing from the day before, or a new grievance Cindy Lou had developed overnight, concerning his decision to put her in his bed with him. He'd had no right to sleep with her that way, he knew, and he felt pretty certain, by the time he took his last sip of coffee, that he'd best be on his way, straight away, to resume his search for the missing Esther. So without a word, he pushed back his chair and made for the back door, grabbing his coat as he went. Once outside he glanced up at the sky miserably, and shrugged into his coat, and with a strong feeling in his gut that said things would not go well for him that day, he got into his truck and backed out onto the dirt road, headed toward Sarah's home, once again.

Sarah was inconsolable. Lee woke her early

that morning, but had not been able to coax her out of bed by pleading, cajoling, or even with the comforting odors from the breakfast he'd made her. The only thing he could think to do now was to leave her be for the day, to grieve and hope that by nightfall she would come around, to be held and re-assured that life would indeed go on.

Cory would no doubt return with Cindy Lou, when they heard that Esther's body had been found. Though he knew nothing about Cindy Lou or her new husband, he'd seen that his new brother-in-law cared deeply for Cindy Lou and would bear any burden to take care of her interests.

The money Lee had stashed in his safe; the money Cory had given him to pay for Esther's stay in his home, he'd now have to give back. Now Cory would demand it to prepare a proper funeral and burial for the girl.

He took the money from his safe after checking the hall for any sign that Sarah was up and about and, hearing nothing, locking his study door. He couldn't risk her, in such an emotional state, finding him fingering the small but impressive stack of bills he'd been given to provide for her sister and her baby, and mistake his miserable expression for a display of greed. Only he and Cory knew that Cory had gotten money from Esther's boyfriend's family to provide for her until the lover showed up to accept his responsibilities. Sarah, he felt, didn't need to know, and wouldn't understand if she did, what that money meant to their future, and wouldn't see him begin to try to cope with the idea of having to return it, so unexpectedly, without enjoying any benefit from it.

He only had until the moment Cory's fists banged on his door again to say goodbye to the plans he'd made to add not only to his farmland, a few acres, but a few rooms to his and Sarah's old farmhouse, as well. He wished he'd never had the money to begin with, now; wished Esther had never disrupted his happy life with Sarah in the first place; wished he could figure a way, some justification for keeping some or all of a stranger's hush-money.

There would be no baby now, he reasoned; no foolish young woman who could get herself into no end of trouble in the future, to protect, feed or support. A funeral service for Esther and burial on her own family's land certainly wouldn't cost even a tenth of the money that he couldn't seem to leave untouched on his desk.

There must surely be a fair way, he argued to himself miserably, to convince Cory that Sarah's need for the money, freely given by Johnny's father to compensate Esther's family for the damage done by his worthless son, surely outweighed any need he and Cindy Lou might have.

Cory was already an established, successful, businessman, and he and Cindy Lou had inherited her father's large and comfortable home. Lee and Sarah had gotten nothing from her father's home, aside from a few worthless mementos and a couple of pieces of furniture from Sarah's childhood bedroom, which they'd had and used as their only household furnishings for the first two years of their marriage.

The longer he looked at all that money and indulged his desire to discover a way to keep it, the more angry and indignant he became. He would stand Cory down, he fumed to himself, when the time came. If Cory thought he could just take back what he'd given, never mind the stress he and Sarah had suffered for having had Esther in their home and the fear, torment, and grief his wife was now bedridden with, over Esther's running away and dying, he'd be in for one hell of a surprise.

He re-stacked the money carefully, satisfied with his conclusion, and returned it to his safe. He put it in the chamber next to the deed to his land and house and locked the door on it, sealing it away, he told himself, from the greedy hands of Sarah's youngest sister and her already wealthy husband. He'd be damned if he was going to give it back when he and Sarah needed it and had every right to keep it!

Cory drove slowly down the dirt road, half-looking for Esther, half-trying to organize his thoughts and plan for the morning's search for Esther. He didn't register anything unusual about seeing Ralphie walking briskly toward him on the road.

He stopped his truck and waved the boy over to ask if he'd seen Esther that morning, since he was out and about the area already, and was horrified by Ralphie's response.

Ralphie gripped the window ledge of Cory's truck as he tried to explain, as quickly as he could, what he'd been sent to Cindy Lou's house to tell her. Cory put a hand on Ralphie's shoulder to steady him, and reassure himself that he wasn't really dreaming the boy's presence and devastating news about Esther.

Ralphie was so flustered and upset, Cory told him to get into his truck, telling him he'd drive him back to town and take away his awesome burden of telling Cindy Lou that her sister was dead. Ralphie scrambled onto the seat next to him and sobbed all the ride back into town with relief that he'd not have to deliver the terrible news to Cindy Lou, after everything she'd already been through.

He didn't like the spoiled rotten girl, but he wouldn't have wished this much suffering on an enemy. As soon as Cory stopped the truck a front of the post office, he opened his door and ran for the security of the small building. Cory didn't try to stop him. He wished he could do the same, and did in a way follow suit, except his hiding place of choice was his supply store apartment.

He wasn't in the right frame of mind to see Tyler just then, so instead of following the paved road through the rest of town, past Tyler's mill, then doubling back behind the buildings to park behind his supply store, where he usually did, he instead lurched across the empty lot between the post office and his store, parked where he stopped, and got inside quickly.

Once inside his store, he bolted the door and went upstairs to his apartment without even a peek at the sales floor. He'd imagined for quite some time what it would be like to walk back into the place, back into his old life again, but this was nothing like he'd ever pictured.

His apartment was the same as he'd left it many weeks before, except for a thick new layer of dust that covered everything in it. Without thinking he shook off a dishtowel that had been laying on his countertop and used it to switch off surfaces around the small room until dust filled the air around him, and caused him to choke.

He threw open his two small windows and tried to fan the dust out with his towel, but the wind fought him until he gave up in frustration, and fell into a chair. He knew he had to get back to Cindy Lou and tell her what he'd spared Ralphie of telling, but he couldn't make himself stand up again and go to her. How could he face her with such terrible news? How could he bear to hear what she would certainly say to him?

All he could think of, suddenly, was how he needed to get down the stairs into his store, to clean the cobwebs and dust off the life he'd once known, and open the doors once again to the townspeople. Before he knew what he was doing, he was following that plan of action.

He went down the rickety stairs and turned on the sales floor lights and used the towel he still clutched tightly, to bat at the shelves and their contents, the green rack, and finally the long counter. Feeling energized by the results, and even more determined and focused to rid the place of its musty smell and newly created dust cloud, he unblocked the back door and the one facing the street, and took a wide broom to the dirty floor, letting the wind he'd fought unsuccessfully in his apartment whip through the store from back to front, carrying the dirt and staleness out into the street.

Time escaped him as he swept and, entranced by the wind coursing all around him, his mind released the burden that weighed heavy on his heart, creating a gap in his memory just large enough to fill with all that had happened since his dearest friend, Old Bill's, death.

Tyler found his way into the supply store quickly, and Cory jumped with a yelp when he tried to still the store owner's frantic movements by putting a hand on his shoulder. The expression on Cory's face, when he spun around to face him, made Tyler flinch and eye the broom Cory held in between them, warily.

Unwilling to risk being struck by the wild-eyed shop owner, he deftly removed the broom from Cory's grip and tossed it aside, then he steadied Cory with a heavy hand on either shoulder and demanded to know what Cory thought he was doing.

Startled by the unexpected confrontation, and finding himself overpowered and unable to move out from under Tyler's control, Cory apologized and tried to explain his re-appearance in the supply store, and his desire to right the place for business. Then he tried again to turn and get back to work.

The deranged expression in Cory's eyes as he pled for help to get his business open again, made Tyler uneasy, and certain that something terrible had happened. He asked Cory who knew he was there in town, but even after stopping for a moment to think over the question, Cory could not get any response to come to mind; as far as he could recall no one knew he was there.

Tyler could see that Cory was getting worked up trying to answer his very simple question and, though he sensed things were not right in Cory's head just then, he decided it was best to help the man do what he was trying so hard to do, rather than upset him further with any more questions. He stepped over to the broom and put it back into Cory's hands.

With the broom back in his hands, Cory jumped back into motion, asking Tyler to help him out and wipe down the front windows and the door. Tyler did as he was asked, while Cory rambled almost incoherently about opening his store again, and how happy he imagined the townspeople would be to see things getting back to normal in town. Within the span of a couple of hours all that could possibly be done to prepare the supply store for business had been done and it was Tyler's lunch time.

Uncomfortable with the idea of leaving Cory alone in his peculiar state of mind, he suggested that Cory go with him to his apartment in the upper level of the lumber mill so they could eat some lunch and have a drink to celebrate the supply store's re-opening. Cory agreed and followed Tyler out of the store, pausing to stare at the town's buildings, all five of them including the supply store, before he secured the front door. No one was in the street and all was quiet as they walked down the paved road to the lumber mill. Neither spoke; Cory because he was overcome with emotion over getting his store ready to open again, and Tyler out of sheer discomfort over the bright gleam in Cory's eyes.

He couldn't be sure why Cory was behaving as he was, but the unease gnawed at Tyler's gut and made him feel he needed to stay close at hand, at least for this day, in case Cory's mental state turned violent. Something was seething just behind those oddly lit eyes that Tyler didn't want to see find expression. This man was certainly changed from the Cory he'd known for so many years.

As he heated biscuits and some gravy, left over from his morning meal, Tyler decided that whatever had happened to Cory and Old Bill, that had killed one of them and left the other in this peculiar mental state must have been far worse than even he had imagined when Cindy Lou had lied to him and said they'd come down with the flue, weeks before.

Cory kept up a steady stream of chatter until he and Tyler had taken their glasses of whiskey, from Tyler's still, down to the open doorway of the lumber mill, then he fell quiet drinking his drink, listening to Tyler recount all the town's major scuttlebutt since he had last been around. When their glasses were empty, Tyler rolled a cigarette, and as casually as he could, brought the conversation around to where Cory intended to live, now that he was going to reopen his store. Cory didn't hesitate a moment in answering. He would be staying in his apartment, of course, right where he always had before.

Tyler nodded, licked the edge of the thin cigarette paper and sealed the tobacco rolled within the cylinder. Cory, who hadn't seemed even remotely aware of the cigarette, brought out a book of matches, and by the time Tyler put the cigarette between his lips, was holding a lit match to it.

Muttering his thanks around a puff of smoke, Tyler rocked back on his heels and eyed Cory closely for a moment, inhaled, then exhaled with his eyes closed, trying to interpret what he'd seen and decided how he was to react to his newly married, fellow businessman announcing his intention to resume his former life, and living quarters, in town.

Since he'd noticed the door of the long-closed supply store standing open and billows of dust streaming out, and gone down to talk to Cory, he realized, Cory, nor he, had spoken a single word about Cindy Lou. He wisely discounted that Cory's present mental state was a reflection on his satisfaction, or lack thereof, with beautiful young Cindy Lou as his wife. Whatever was disturbing Cory was far deeper than a newly-wed quarrel. He made up his mind that he'd see Cory back to the supply store and help him finish cleaning, but as soon as he could, he'd get himself over to Cindy Lou's house and make sure she knew what was going on in town with her new husband.

By the time he'd ground out the remains of his cigarette, Cory was finishing off his glass of whiskey and searching out a safe spot to leave it so he could get back to his store. Tyler pointed to the window ledge, then walked with Cory back to the supply store.

Sensing, once Cory had opened the door, that his presence was no longer entirely welcome, he excused himself and returned to his lumber mill. He'd lock up, if no customers came around by the time a half hour had passed, he decided, and take the back way out of his mill, to get out of town unnoticed, and walk out to pay Cindy Lou that visit.

Time ticked by slowly, as it always seemed to in the afternoon, but finally he was able to justify shutting the place up for the day. He put on his heavy coat and made his way out, down the dirt road on foot, toward Cindy Lou's house.

Chapter 7

It was almost noon before Blasted could wait no longer for his owner to let him out into the yard to take care of his business. The big old dog had been up and down the stairs a half dozen times since he'd woken, and scratched insistently at the door to Doctor Miles' bedroom, repeatedly, to no avail. He'd leaned his body against it, but the latch had held firm, so he'd given in to howling and moaning, progressively louder, until Doctor Miles finally came awake and rushed to discover what was bothering his loyal companion.

As soon as he opened the door, Blasted rushed in against his legs and barked in excitement, until it registered that the dancing feet of his beloved companion meant he had to get the oaf out of doors, but quick. He grabbed his robe and ordered Blasted out of his room, then followed him down the stairwell, through the cold kitchen, and out the back door.

While Blasted explored and attended to his needs, Doctor Miles picked two good-sized hunks of wood from the pile, just outside the kitchen door, and carried them in to the kitchen fireplace. Before Blasted made it back, to eat his breakfast, he had a few good sized flames heading up the cold chimney, and a pot of water for his coffee on the stove over another quickly revived fire.

Aside from his own movements and Blasted's noisy eating, the house was still and restful, so the doctor settled himself with a cup of coffee at his kitchen table to join the day at his leisure. But leisure was not to be the order of his day, and his very casual attitude about it was corrected almost immediately by crashing's and banging's that shattered the quiet, from the hospital room and office side of his house.

He spilled his coffee onto the table as he jumped to his feet, his heart pounding and noises like a violent fight filling his ears. Despite his quick reaction, he found himself following Blasted's wide sturdy back down the short hallway to the hospital room's doorway. The door was open and Blasted rushed in to find his patient, but Jimmy Fenton was nowhere to be seen. Doctor Miles, when he reached the doorway and saw Blasted rushing back toward him from an empty room, turned with growing alarm toward his office door.

Sounds of breaking glass, furniture being shoved about, and cabinet doors slamming against one another made it clear where Jimmy had gotten to. Doctor Miles tried to open the door, get into his office and preserve whatever of its contents the young man hadn't already destroyed, but the door wouldn't budge. It was not locked, as he was always mindful of leaving it, but something was preventing it from opening, even when he threw his weight against it.

The noises of destruction continued to assault him until he realized that the only way left for him to enter his office, and stop the madness inside it, was to get outside and around to the only window in the room. He ordered Blasted to stay inside at his office door, and turned and ran for the back door.

When he was near enough to his office window that he could see Jimmy at his medicine cabinet, trying to pry open its doors and, he guessed, destroy the bottles inside it, he knew he would have to break out his own window and get himself in there, or watch his life's work be broken to bits before him. He quickly found a rock near the road, just larger than the palm of his hand, and without breaking stride, approached the window, climbed up onto the sill, and smashed the rock into it until enough glass was removed that he could push his body through and into the room. If he'd have given the plan a moment's thought he'd have seen right away the impossibility of accomplishing such a feat as he just had. He landed bottom first on the hard wood floor, in a sea of razor-sharp glass, and though he was quick to get onto his feet, Jimmy Fenton was much quicker to cross the room and get his hands on him.

In the afternoon Lee tried to wake Sarah again, and convince her to get up, if only for a little while, and come down stairs to have something to eat. She shrugged off his hand when he touched her shoulder, and cried for him to go away and leave her alone, at his invitation to join him for lunch. Hurt, but trying to be sympathetic to her suffering, he quickly withdrew from their bedroom and went back downstairs alone.

Accustomed to spending his time, in great part, out in the fresh air in his fields, the house didn't feel welcome, comfortable, or cheerful to him. Feeling alone in it with Sarah weeping into her pillow upstairs, he paced the hallway for awhile, trying to think of a way to cheer her up and get her back to normal, but he soon gave up and went to the kitchen to make himself something to eat. She couldn't stay in bed forever, he reasoned, while he warmed some leftover chicken he found in the ice box.

Sarah had been through so much so quickly, she hadn't had time to really accept one bad turn of events before the next one had come into play. He had tried to keep her busy, after she'd learned of her father's death, and he'd thought that was the right thing to do for her, but as the days had gone on, she had looked tireder and tireder, and seemed more irritable with everything he did or said to her, always looking on the verge of tears.

When Cory and her sisters had shown up, he had thought they'd cheer her up. They'd not only not cheered her up, though, the one had left right away and the other had moved in and treated her shabbily; hadn't even asked her how she was doing, just treated her like a maid, then had run off and gotten herself killed somehow.

The whole situation was unfair, he fumed. He had to find a way to get his wife on her feet again, excited again, and happy again. Today he'd let her stay in bed, but tomorrow things would be different. Tomorrow he wouldn't let her lay there, crying into her pillow in their bedroom with the curtains drawn and a door between them. He'd take her out for the day, over to the dairy in the next town if she wanted, just to pet the cows for a while. That had cheered her up after upsets in the past, why shouldn't it work now? And while he had her out of her hiding place, he'd point out the positives to her, like he always did, and remind her that he was still there, still loved her, and that they still had their whole lives ahead of them to do with whatever they liked. Surely he could bring her around, he consoled himself.

While he was eating the last of the chicken, he re-heated some meat stew to take upstairs for her. He heard doors open and close above him and quickly put together a tray, and took it upstairs to their room. She wasn't in their bedroom when he got there, so he quickly pulled the covers straight on the bed and opened the curtains, then sat on the edge of the bed with the tray in his hands, and waited for her to finish in the bathroom.

While he waited, he rehearsed a happy little speech about what they were going to do the next day. To him, everything should fall right into place and they'd be back to their old happy selves in no time. Then Sarah returned to their room.

She didn't register any surprise or interest on seeing him, or the tray of food waiting for her when she stumbled back through the door. Without any thanks, greetings, or explanations, she made her way straight to the window, shut the curtains tight, then trudged toward the bed holding her head in her hands and crawled back under the bed covers, crying.

Lee let out a grunt and felt around for the bedside lamp. As the room lit up, his wife's plaintive voice came from under the bed covers, begging him to turn it back off, complaining that the light was killing her, but he left it on. He told her to sit up and eat something, that lack of food was probably why she had such a headache, not to mention all her tears and a full day's lack of sunlight. Finally he gave up trying to reason with her and set the tray of food on her night table, and pulled the blankets off of her and the bed entirely.

This brought Sarah to a fully upright position quickly and, just as quickly, Lee re-adjusted her pillow against the headboard of the bed and propped her against them. Before she could move away, he placed the heavy food tray across her lap and demanded that she eat what he'd made for her.

Sarah picked up a crust of hard bread and threw it at him, but he didn't flinch or back off, so she picked up another and, after a moment's hesitation over whether or not to throw it too, she sighed heavily and dropped it into the hot stew.

Lee waited stubbornly beside her on the bed until she'd eaten her lunch, then he kissed her forehead and returned the bedcovers to her, helping her tuck them in all around her again. She'd be better tomorrow, she promised him tearfully, as he took the tray and turned the light off, leaving her to her misery.

Cory hadn't shown up, and neither had Cindy Lou, which made him feel relieved, but a little angry too. He didn't want to have a fight with them over the money he now intended to keep, but Cindy Lou hadn't even bothered to come to see how her sister was handling the unexpected death of their sister. He fumed to himself that he'd give her a piece of his mind when she did finally come around his house again. For the rest of the afternoon, however, since he'd checked all his fields the day before last and found them needing no attention, he'd work on fixing his tractor, maybe even getting the old tire off of it, this try, and roll it into town for repairs. He'd decided the money Cory had given him for taking care of Esther was rightfully his and Sarah's to spend, so he might as well start doing so right away, he decided.

Cory watched Tyler return to his lumber mill, relieved to see him go. It had bothered him that Tyler kept staring at him like he was a little nuts, throughout their lunch. He'd let the man help him straighten and clean up the supply store even though he'd have preferred to do it alone, and had spelled out as plainly as he could what he intended to do, but Tyler had just kept staring at him like he didn't really understand, or believe him.

Finally alone again, he could finish checking his stock and writing up orders to put in the next morning when the supplier showed up - if he hadn't given up on him after so long. If the man didn't come by, he'd just drive over to the grain mill after closing time, he decided.

As excited and anxious as he was to get back to business, he knew no one would come to town this late in the day for supplies from a store they'd become accustomed to seeing closed, so he didn't turn his sign in the window. By morning, he felt sure, Tyler would have spread the word around that he was back, had put the supply store in order, and would be open for business in the morning at nine o'clock sharp. He turned off the sales floor lights and climbed the stairs to his apartment, more tired from all the exertion of cleaning than he'd realized.

He searched his ice box for something to eat, but discovered nothing any longer edible in it. He rummaged through his two cabinets and found some jerky to chew on to keep his stomach from rumbling while he settled back into his new life in his tiny apartment, alone, with nothing but big plans and high hopes for tomorrow's re-opening.

Only when he finally laid down in his bed for some much needed sleep did pictures of Ralphie, looking pale, and crying, flood his mind, but he no longer had any idea why. The bourbon he'd drunk with Tyler after their lunch had probably been too strong for him after being sick and weak for so long, he reasoned. He brushed off the unpleasant images of Ralphie's troubled face, and he forced himself to go to sleep.

Tyler was the last person Cindy Lou had expected to find at her door, particularly that late in the afternoon. It had taken a second and third look just to recognize him when she'd first opened the door. She'd never seen him, and never expected to see him, away from his lumber mill and the paved road in town.

Tyler was uncomfortable out of his element. He felt too big and foolishly awkward, standing in Cindy Lou's doorway, and too far from the safety his lumber mill. He told her he was sorry he'd bothered her and turned to leave as soon as she said hello, but she'd insisted he stay. She wanted to know why he'd come, but all his thoughts were muddled suddenly and his fears about Cory's appearance and behavior in town seemed silly. But he tried to tell her all about it anyway; all he'd seen and said that day came tumbling out of his mouth incomprehensibly garbled.

Realizing he sounded as crazy as he was accusing her new husband of being, he again begged the girl to pardon him for coming, and tried to make good an escape, but Cindy Lou wouldn't hear of it. She insisted he come into the house and sit until he was calmer, then try to explain what he'd come for, again. She put a cup in front of him a moment later, and he gripped it in both of his calloused hands immediately, then jerked them away again as the heat from it registered, sloshing a little of the coffee onto the tabletop.

His face flushed a deep crimson and he stuttered out apologies while he used his sleeve to soak up the spill. More agitated and unsure of himself now than when he'd first arrived, he got up from the table again, eyes focused entirely on the door and started moving toward it. He stumbled around a chair, then into Cindy Lou.

Cindy Lou was as flustered as she'd ever been, but determined not to let Tyler leave her house until he'd explained all his ramblings about seeing Cory. If he hadn't thought he'd come for an important reason, she knew, he'd never have come in the first place. She put herself between him and the back door firmly and demanded that he tell her what had happened to her new husband.

Tyler's eyes widened in surprise, realizing she'd misunderstood him, and he assured her that no harm had come to Cory, nearly sure, now, that he'd overreacted to Cory's changed appearance, entirely. Cindy Lou let out a deep breath, relived at least to know this much, but she stayed in Tyler's path and continued firing questions at him until they were both thoroughly confused, then Tyler's head found clarity at last and he explained, despite his nervous stuttering, where he'd found Cory and what he'd been doing.

Cindy Lou listened patiently, but with a growing sense of unease. If what he was telling her was true, Cory hadn't gone, as he'd promised her the night before, to find her sister Esther; her new husband had left her. She was even more hurt when Tyler finished recounting the time he'd spent with her husband and claimed that Cory had not once mentioned her in all of it.

Tyler was so miserable in his stomach when he saw, at last, the look of embarrassed understanding take over Cindy Lou's face. He wanted to reach out and hug her, when her thin shoulders slumped forward and a dull, pained expression filled her eyes, but he didn't dare touch her for fear someone so large as he would break such a fragile creature at the barest touch. Instead he told her he was sorry, and accepted the rebuff without comment, when she shrugged his sentiments off.

There was nothing more he could think to say to her, and she didn't seem to notice he was still there anyway, so he quickly told her good-bye and slunk back to his lumber mill, cursing himself. When he got back to his apartment he was worn out. He poured himself a glass of whiskey and propped himself in front of his favorite window to glare down at the small town, vowing never to let himself get so worked up over someone else's problems, ever again.

When he'd been with Cory, he'd seen something greatly disturbing in his eyes, and he'd only intended to tell Cindy Lou so she could explain why her new husband was behaving so oddly. In the end, however, he'd done nothing more than tell the girl that her new husband had run out on her and gone back to the life he'd known before her. He hadn't asked her why; he'd only bluntly told her his conclusions, and hurt her deeply in doing so.

Only after a second strong drink did he finally determine, to his credit, that he'd merely told Cindy Lou what he'd seen and heard, and he'd helped Cory reorganize and clean the supply store as well, so whatever happened next was up to the two of them - none of his business and not his problem! Feeling better about himself with that conclusion, he finished off his bottle of whiskey and dozed contentedly, tipped back comfortably in his chair, in front of the window that overlooked Farmersville.

At the sound of shattering window glass, Jimmy Fenton turned from Doctor Miles' medicine cabinet, ready to do battle. His search for something, anything to relieve the terrible pain in his head, that had jarred him awake disoriented and desperate, he abandoned in favor of getting his hands on the only other human in the house who could help him.

Unable to get to his feet quickly enough to avoid the crazed young man, Doctor Miles found himself lifted from the glass strewn floor and carried to the cabinet where Jimmy had set his sights. He yelled at the young man and struggled to get free of him, demanding to be put down and be told what the hell he was doing barricaded in his office.

Between clenched teeth, his head still bound in the jaw-restraining bandages, Jimmy screamed "medicine!" and emphasized his demand by planting Doctor Miles' feet firmly on the floor in front of the cabinet doors he'd had been trying to pry open.

Realizing, suddenly, that Jimmy was pain-crazed, not wanting anything more than medicine he'd have given him by now, had he not overslept, the good doctor applied his trembling hands to the task of finding strong, fast-acting, morphine for his pain. Jimmy seemed to calm a little with his assurances that he understood and would give him a shot of morphine as soon as he could put his hands on a needle - one Jimmy hadn't broken in his mad search - and a vial from the cabinet. Rather than risking further misunderstanding he ordered Jimmy to go to his desk, where he'd find the key to the medicine cabinet and, only after Jimmy turned away from him to get the key, moved to the place on the counter nearest the door to search for a fresh syringe.

While he moved bits of broken jars and overturned containers with careful hands, he kicked the chair Jimmy had shoved in front of the door and sent it skittering across the floor toward the broken window. The door swung open and Blasted stumbled into the room with them, and headed straight for Jimmy with a menacing growl.

Jimmy made a terrified noise in his throat and froze in his tracks en-route from the desk, key in hand, and Doctor Miles whirled to face him, ordering his protective dog to leave Jimmy alone. Blasted obeyed and stopped short of jumping on the young man, but growled once more before positioning himself to stand guard between his owner and Jimmy.

Jimmy kicked at the great beast, to clear his path to the medicine cabinet, but Blasted would not be rooted from his position until Doctor Miles had found a usable needle and re-crossed the room to take the cabinet key.

Outraged to be pinned in, in such pain he could hardly bear it, under threat of even more severe injury if he so much as tried to move closer to his doctor and the medicine he so desperately needed, by a dog, Jimmy screamed at Blasted, though it made the shooting pain in his jaw even more intolerable to do so.

Doctor Miles ignored Jimmy's rage, concentrating his attention on selecting the right vial from the cabinet and measuring a bit of medicine into the syringe, then he turned his attention to his two warring companions, ordering Blasted out of his way and Jimmy to just sit on the edge of his desk and hold still. While he found a good vein in Jimmy's outstretched forearm, he calmed him and told him to leave the office as soon as he was finished; get himself back to the hospital room and into his bed, quickly, or risk the powerful medicine taking affect while he was still in the drafty, destroyed, office. If he lost consciousness, Doctor Miles told him, he'd have to lay where he fell until the drug wore off; he was too big to be moved.

Jimmy's breathing was ragged and gasping, and his adrenaline was still pumping frenzied energy through him when Doctor Miles motioned him toward the open door. He jumped to his feet and made his way toward his room with the doctor's help, Blasted leading the way. As soon as he was back on the mattress, on the floor of the hospital room, Blasted joined him and in an instant Jimmy was in a stupor. Doctor Miles pulled the blankets and bed sheets out from under the, now groggy, young man and, with many curses, covered Jimmy as he drifted off to sleep.

Having restored peace in his house, Doctor Miles found himself wanting nothing more than a place to rest as well. His hands trembled and he felt weak and sick, to the point he let himself sink to the floor beside the mattress and its two occupants, to gather himself and calm his racing heart. He held his head in his hands to stop a nauseating dizziness and slumped by his patient's side, unconscious, for several hours, while a strong wind coursed through the broken office window in the next room, chilling everything in the house.

Cindy Lou sat at her kitchen table long after Tyler had gone, biting her lip to keep from crying. What had Tyler meant by coming to her home so upset over Cory's activities in town? His story only added to her confusion. Her new husband had taken her into his bed with him the night before, then left her to go back to his supply store without a word of good-bye?

She replayed what Tyler had told her in her head, trying to stop herself from rushing into town on his heels to see for herself what "weird" look Cory had in his eyes, and hear for herself what peculiar thoughts her new husband had about where he planned to live, and how. Did he really intend to go back to his old life and leave her all alone without a word of explanation?

Then thoughts of Esther filled her mind and she resolved to herself immediately what she would do: She would find her sister, herself, then worry about Cory and what odd things he might be doing and saying in town.

Following that purpose, she quickly changed into a warmer dress and put on her coat and gloves, thinking the biting wind would have a struggle to get through all her layers of clothes to chill her bones. She found a lantern her father had always kept just inside the shed door and returned to the kitchen to light it from the fire in the kitchen, then she headed out into the growing darkness, down the dirt road away from town, toward her sister Sarah's house.

As she walked into the shadows of trees lining the road, the flickering light from her lantern cast moving shadows all around her. The further she walked, the more fearful she became. The road had initially been easy and relatively smooth, but the further she went, the more difficult it became to walk. The ruts grew deeper and the earth slicker under her feet, and she stumbled over rocks a time or two, then she slipped an errantly placed foot into a deep rut, and nearly dropped the lantern trying to keep her balance and stay on her feet.

The trees that had hovered over her so protectively gave way to short leafless shafts of rugged plant life, allowing the harsh wind to buffet her and cause her skin under all her garments to feel damp and cold. She swung her lantern to light up first one side of the road, and the ditch that ran alongside it, then the other, straining her eyes and her ears for any indication her sister was near. Rushing water several feet deep scoured the bottoms of both ditches, pushed relentlessly by the wind.

She was tiring quickly out in the elements and before very long she began wailing for Esther in despair. Pictures from her dream, of her dear sister's clearly dead face, antagonized her in the darkness and frightened her until all she could think of was to continue on along the dirt road until she reached a point nearly a mile ahead where trees once again folded their branches over her path. She promised herself she'd stop and rest most safely when she got there.

The goal calmed her somewhat and made her feel more sure and steady, and determined that she would find her sister. She began to imagine running into her Esther when she finally reached those protective trees to sit down to rest her feet, but by the time she reached the short span of the road where the treetops nearly converged she was almost hysterical.

She called out for Esther against the brutal wind, but knew that even if Esther were alive and standing quite near her she wouldn't have heard. The wind whipped Esther's name from her lips and deadened the sound of it almost instantly.

She started to cry, trembling from the cold and frustration. Her tears, chilled by the wind made her skin feel like wet paper, nearly frozen, and she tugged her long hair tightly around her ears and face, trying to stay warm.

She knew now that what she'd done was foolish. She realized she could have, and should have, gone to Doctor Miles' home and demanded that he take her in his car to find her sister. He would have gladly helped her, she knew, but it was too late, and too far, to try to go to him now. Feeling hopeless, she turned to retrace her path back to her house, knowing she'd failed to find her sister and knowing there'd be no one waiting for her at home to help her try again that night.

Nearly two hours after she'd dashed from the warmth and safety of her home, she trudged back through the kitchen door with her lamp, long since run out of fuel, with chills racking her body. She didn't take off her boots or her coat, right away; she was too weak to manage them. She slumped down onto a chair and put her head on the warm table, determined to rest there until she regained her strength; she fell into a dreamless sleep quickly, and remained there at the kitchen table, slumped in a heap, until morning.

Mrs. Wilcox was having her morning tea when she looked out and saw Ralphie putting a piece of mail into her letter box. She scrambled up from her table and rushed out to greet him, hoping to hear anything he might know about her girls, and Cindy Lou's brute of a husband. She brushed off the boy's rudeness when he ignored her "hello" and didn't hesitate to catch him by the arm to stop him from leaving so she could put her questions to him. When he whirled around on her, however, his expression, and the tears welling his eyes, gave pause. She quickly apologized for grabbing him and jerked her hand away from his sleeve, begging him to tell her what was wrong.

At her persistence, he lost his composure completely and shocked the one-time school teacher by stumbling back toward her, and falling into her arms. She held onto the weeping boy for a moment, speaking soothingly to him, then she turned him away from her enough for him to move alongside her, with her arms around him for support, and walked him into her house.

Once she'd maneuvered him into her warm kitchen, she pried him off of her and pushed him into a chair so she could have a better look at him, and interrogate him thoroughly. For a time, however, all her many and concerned questions were met only with great shoulder-heaving sobs. She sat down beside him, finally, frustrated and greatly worried, and held his hands in hers, trying to coax him to confide his troubles to her.

When Ralphie, finally wearied from his overwrought state, reduced himself to gasps and the occasional back-of-the-hand-supported snuffle, he told her the news Cory had, as far as he knew, spared him from having to break to Cindy Lou; Esther was dead and her body, by that very evening, would be returned to Farmersville, to Pastor Franklin's home, for burial.

Mrs. Wilcox was stunned. Her eyes filled with tears and she fell onto the table in a dead faint.

Not knowing what had happened to the woman so suddenly, Ralphie shook her shoulders and shouted her name until she opened her eyes again, then as soon as he saw she was alert and awake once again, he scrambled to get his mail sack and fled.

Mrs. Wilcox made no effort to stop Ralphie. The only thought she could form in her head was that she must get to Cindy Lou right away, no matter what the girl's foolish husband had said or done to her. She overturned the fire in her fireplace, snuffing the flames with ashes and hurried to dress herself warmly for the long walk to Cindy Lou's home.

Half an hour later she marched out her front door, headed for Farmersville, still stunned over the news that one of her two God-gifted, newly orphaned, girls had already met her end, blaming herself for not having found a way to protect either of the girls. She cursed herself severely for allowing herself to be so brutally removed from her place in their home without putting up more of a fight, and vowed most solemnly to herself she'd not leave Cindy Lou's side until death came calling for her, even if it meant death at Cory's hands, this time.

By the time she reached Farmersville it was late in the evening. Determined, and without any sensation of weariness to hold her back, she marched straight through the five building town, without so much as a glance at Tyler up in his window, and onto the dirt road that led to Cindy Lou's home.

No one answered her knock when she arrived on Cindy Lou's doorstep and no one, not even Cory, could be seen through the many windows Mrs. Wilcox peered through, on tip-toes. She sat on a front porch chair, resting briefly, then took off again for the road with a fresh head of steam.

Chapter 8

Mrs. Wilcox approached Doctor Miles' house thinking only that she might find a devastated Cindy Lou, coping with the shocking loss of her sister, there, where she'd lived for weeks until her father had passed away. She was relieved to see lights blazing behind curtained windows, but again her knocking went unanswered.

She stepped off the porch and began making her way down the front of the house, peering in windows as she'd done at Cindy Lou's, but found no one to let her in. Doctor Miles' office was clearly visible, and in complete disarray, she saw at last, through the open curtains that billowed and snapped in the cold wind. She stopped and clutched her chest in fear, and started to turn and run, but caught herself up quickly and marched herself toward the front door again.

She held her breath as she beat on the door, imagining, though she wished she wouldn't, all manner of evil waiting just on the other side of it to lash out at her. When she heard nothing, she twisted the cold doorknob and threw her weight against it. It didn't budge.

Unsure what she do, she stepped to the nearest window and tried in vain to peer through the thick curtains. It was no use, there was no seeing through them.

She gave a little gasp and hurried, with bravery she'd swear she didn't come by naturally, around to the back of the house, making for

Doctor Miles' shed, refusing to give into temptation and turn her head toward any window of the two-storied home, lest she should find some intruder standing there, watching her every move. She threw her weight against the shed door and it gave way easily. Feeling along the walls for the largest, sharpest, tool that might be leaning or hung by a hook there, though she couldn't see anything in the pitch darkness, she finally seized upon something heavy that satisfied, and rushed back into the doctor's yard.

She heaved a sigh of relief when, out in the better light, she stopped to see just how fit the weapon she'd discovered really was. The axe she held was long-unused, but quite sturdy and sharp enough to fend off any man or beast with whom she might become entangled, she felt sure. She held it tightly in her hands as she made a second approach on the good doctor's home, calling out for Cindy Lou or Doctor Miles to let her in.

She kicked the back door of the ominously silent house and yelled loudly, but got no response. At her wits end, but unwilling to give up, she started calling for Blasted, and that finally did the deed; Blasted came running.

It did no good, however, to have the attention of a dog on the other side of a locked door, and as hard as she worked on the freezing cold doorknob, with Blasted's barking support, the door remained shut tight between them. Even a blow from the heavy axe didn't change anything about their respective positions. Finally, she gave up on the door and, emboldened by her so far useless weapon, she strode to the front of the great house, to the shattered window of Doctor Miles' office. On tip-toes, she reached the ledge and tried to summon the doctor or Cindy Lou with more shouting and banging. Again she attracted only Blasted; he towered above her in the frame of the broken window.

Most intimidated at the sight of him, she nearly dropped her axe and fled. There wasn't any way she could see to get up to the window ledge, particularly if it meant coming face to face with the mass of fur and muscle in her path. Even if she could mount the shallow window sill, Blasted might, in foolish exuberance, push her right to the ground again, she fretted.

The situation seemed hopeless, but she felt most certain that she had to find a way into that house, Blasted or no Blasted to contend with en route. She returned to the front porch and set her axe in the seat of one of Doctor Miles' porch chairs, then hefted the chair in both arms and carefully made her way with it to the hard-packed earth under the office window.

Trembling violently from the cold and physical strain, she climbed up on the chair, set the axe on the ledge, and scrambled and clawed her way past Blasted into the doctor's office. Once she was safely inside, panting and clutching the axe in both hands again, she summoned her nerve and demanded that Blasted's take her to his master.

Blasted turned at once and padded through many scatterings of sharp window glass toward the door and, after looking back to see that the woman was following, led the way to the hospital room door and went in. He nudged his still slumped over owner, then resumed his most favored position on the bed mattress alongside Jimmy.

Mrs. Wilcox dropped the axe and ran to Doctor Miles' side, taking in the disaster of the man's office and oddly placed, door-blocking, bed mattress in the hospital room as she went. She fell to her knees and concentrated her full attention on reviving him, not noticing the young man who occupied the disassembled hospital bed, she was so singularly focused. She roused the doctor and demanded to know what had happened to him, and where she could find Cindy Lou.

While Doctor Miles was trying to right himself on the floor, gather his wits about him, and figure out why and how Laura Wilcox had come to be in his home, she finally noticed the bandaged figure next to Blasted. She screamed and jumped back toward the doorway, searching frantically for her axe. The jarring noise snapped Doctor Miles completely out of his fog in an instant, and he scrambled to his feet to get his hands on her before she was able to get hers back on the axe, explaining to her that everything was alright.

It wasn't at all easy to quiet the woman and make himself fully understood, but Doctor Miles finally managed to do so, convincing her, in the process, to go with him to the kitchen and leave his patient and Blasted to sleep on, undisturbed.

By the time he put coffee cups on the table and had stoked the kitchen fire to blazing, Mrs. Wilcox had fallen into tearful explanations for her visit, and when she told him of Esther's death, he too shed a tear, but he consoled his good friend that Cory was probably with Cindy Lou and would comfort her most ably until the next morning, when he could drive her over in his car.

Though he'd been unprepared to see Mrs. Wilcox, the doctor was happy to have her there. Living in his big house with violent and unpredictable Jimmy Fenton was trying, to say the least, and now that he had someone other than Blasted to talk to, he took full advantage of the   company.

They sat and drank coffee, as they'd done many times through the years, in the front of the kitchen fireplace through, almost entirely, the darkness of the night. After they'd caught one another up on all there was to know, both began to yawn discretely and shift uncomfortably in their chairs. Finally he reached for her hand and led her, unprotesting, up the stairs to his bedroom and invited her, with a suggestive chuckle, to spend the night with him.

Ralphie, feeling ashamed and exhausted for his emotional outburst at Mrs. Wilcox's home, had forced himself to carry on with the last of his deliveries upon escaping her, then found himself wandering, for the rest of the afternoon, aimlessly along the banks of the creek near town, trying to work up the courage he knew it would now require for him to face the townspeople again. Cory, he felt sure, would never call any attention whatever to the weakness he'd shown, bursting into tears that morning and confiding the news he'd been on his way to deliver to Cindy Lou. He knew the man could and would, keep the humiliating incident quiet, but he could think of no reason Mrs. Wilcox wouldn't tell anyone. Even as the shadows grew long and the wind chilled him to the bone, he struggled to fight back more tears over lovely Esther's death.

Esther had always been kind to him when other girls pretended he wasn't even alive. She'd told him of her dreams of running off to the big city one day, and confided in him all the unpleasantness she lived with each day, as the younger sister to bossy Sarah and older, ignored, sister of beautiful Cindy Lou, many times. He'd been in love with the girl for as long as he could remember and had told her so, once. She had only smiled and kissed him on the cheek, and told him he was far too young, but he believed she was secretly in love with him too. He didn't mind that she called his feelings for her puppy-love.

She'd said she was going to marry Johnny, no matter how bad everyone said he was, because she liked his wildness and the money he could give her - money that Ralphie would never have to offer. Even knowing this didn't dampen his spirits, however, or make him love her any less. All he wanted, when she finally had enough of Johnny, and enough money to run away to the city, was for her to let him go with her.

His family had never had much money and, he was pretty sure, never would. He'd worked for Esther's father, Old Bill, until he'd died. Old Bill had treated him fairly and paid him well, but not enough to put him in a position to support Esther the way she dreamed of. Johnny's family had lots of money and Esther was determined to get her share of it, no matter what she had to do to keep Johnny interested in her.

He had always hated that Johnny got to have more time with Esther than him, and he'd done his level best to never think about what his girl and the boy she claimed to be in love with, did in all the time they'd spent together, but he'd consoled himself that she always returned to him to talk about the future with. He wouldn't believe she didn't want him in it.

His dreams were shattered now, and he swore to himself that if he'd known the way things would end, he'd have stood up to Esther, told her how greedy and foolish she was being, and told her in front of every person in town how much he loved her and demanded that she marry him. Now she was gone and he hadn't even been able to say goodbye.

He didn't cross over the paved road in town until it was dark, to make his way home and cry himself to sleep in his bed.

Chapter 9

Pastor Franklin was surprised to see the two men waiting by their truck for him on the road that skirted the edge of his field, in the late afternoon. He didn't recognize them or their truck, but he'd hurried toward them when they'd called out to him, then stepped out to wait for him. He thought their demeanor was peculiar and felt a twinge of unease as he set down his armful of weeds and picked a path toward them.

    The two men argued quietly as the Farmersville Pastor slowly crossed his field. They were nervous, both to be out of their familiar territory and have been burdened to bring a Farmersville girl back to her home, dead. Neither wanted the responsibility of talking to the pastor and enduring the questions he'd doubtless have, and they feared the suspicion the body they'd come to give over would most certainly bring them. Finally, they agreed that each would tell a part of their news and both would do an equal share to uncover the dead girl's body, when the pastor finally reached them.

    Pastor Franklin hopped the ditch that gaped between himself and the two strangers neatly, and offered a hand toward the larger of them. The men shook hands with him uncomfortably and introduced themselves as Randy and Joe, from Louisburg, some 110 miles to the east of Farmersville. He showed great surprise and, as they expected he might, asked to know why they'd traveled so far in search of him.

    Joe, the shorter of the two men, stubbed the toe of his boot into a rut he'd been studying in the road and said nothing, leaving Randy to admit the purpose of their visit.

He explained to Pastor Franklin how they'd discovered a young woman's body the day before, when they'd been leaving a field with other workers, and how they had walked with several of them for many miles, knocking on farmhouse doors until they'd found some of the dead girl's family. Joe found his voice then, and carried on their tale of how they'd been instructed by the girl's brother-in-law to bring her body to Farmersville and deliver it to him. He told Pastor Franklin how they'd fought a powerful wind all the way to town, making their progress painfully slow, and before Pastor Franklin could question the men further, the both of them turned to the bed of their truck and lifted the heavy blanket they'd placed over Esther's body.

Pastor Franklin was shocked and sickened at the sight of Esther's very gray, very swollen face. He turned his head into the wind quickly and fixed his eyes on the sky, barking angrily to the two men to cover the girl back over. The men dropped their blanket and, growing more anxious by the moment to be finished with this unpleasant ordeal, tried to rush him through his shock and find out just where they were to leave their wretched cargo?

He shuddered, fighting mightily against nausea that threatened to drive him into the ditch. After a painfully long and uncomfortable moment, however, he was able to mumble to them to take him in their truck and he'd shoe them how to get to his home. Randy and Joe fairly ran back to the cab of their pickup and got in, leaving a length of the bench seat available for him.

When they pulled into the pastor's side yard, his wife, Millie, came running from her kitchen to see who'd come to call. She stopped short when she saw the truck and the two strangers lifting a bundle from the truck bed while her husband unlocked his shed door, then she ran after them, only to find the shed door shut abruptly in her face just as she'd prepared to step in behind them. Taken aback, she balled up her fists and set upon the wood door with a fury, demanding to be let in and told what the devil was going on in there.

Pastor Franklin, distracted with the task at hand, paid no attention to his wife's shouting and banging. The two men, having laid Esther's body on the table he'd pointed out to them, abandoned the shed, making a dash for their truck the moment he opened the door and caught his wife's flailing fists, telling her to be still and go back into the house straight away before he too lost his temper.

Millie was unimpressed by her husband's shushing, nor even his threat. She twisted her hands free and continued her barrage of questions about the two men who were, by then, making good their escape.

Seeing the two men leaving without any thanks from him, nor any dinner he'd have offered to have Millie stir up for them before they started back toward their far away home, infuriated
Pastor Franklin and he gave his wife an earful for it, before he turned on his heel and returned to his shed, again slamming the door in her face.

Left in tears and feeling quite abused, on their side lawn, Millie tried to decide whether she'd pursue her husband again, or return to her kitchen to weep. She chose the latter, but not before picking up a good sized stone and hurling it against the shed door.

Mrs. Wilcox was the last to rise in

Doctor Miles' house the following morning, and when she did she could hardly bring herself to move. Her legs ached as much as her back did, and for a long while she simply laid as still as she possibly could, staring at the ceiling, following the dancing shadows of leaves from the tree outside, on the exposed, rough-cut, timbers above her. She felt deeply sad and desiring only of a long hot bath to soothe her spirits and help start what she knew would be a long miserable day.

Doctor Miles had woken early and rushed down to the hospital room to check on his patient. Seeing Jimmy was still sleeping soundly, he'd called his dog off the mattress and taken him to the yard. He'd collected wood from the firebox, shivering in the cold, then went in and started a good blaze in the hospital room fireplace, and one in his kitchen. When Blasted pressed his nose to the door and gave a complaining bark, he let him back in to discover his bowl of food, while he started water to boil for coffee.

When the smell of fresh coffee permeated every room of the house, he checked once again on his patient, then headed upstairs with two steaming cups. He tapped on his bedroom door and waited patiently to be beckoned in, then he slipped in and re-joined Mrs. Wilcox on his bed.

With the bedcovers pulled up under her chin, Laura Wilcox propped herself up against the headboard, with a pillow behind her to ease the pain in her back. She took the coffee cup Doctor Miles offered her gratefully, but neither said much to the other in the chilly, but very bright, room until their cups were empty, then she asked if she could use his tub and hair comb to freshen herself up.

Doctor Miles jumped at once and went to prepare her a bath, then returned to his kitchen for another cup of coffee to take with him to Jimmy's room. He'd thought to sip on it by the hospital room fire until his patient woke up, but Jimmy was already tossing and turning, in the earliest of waking stages, when he entered. He stepped carefully over one edge of the mattress, trying to keep his cup from tipping as he went, and pulled a chair over to the fireplace, to sit in the warm glow and enjoy the last few moments of peace the morning had to offer.

Upstairs, Mrs. Wilcox slipped into a hot tub filled with bubbles, and relaxed her overused muscles with a deep sigh. But after a short while, she put her mind to the task that lay before her that day, distracted by memories of the night before, and the things Doctor Miles had told her, and the deeply sad and weary expression on his face, while they'd sipped their coffee in front of the fire. She had to struggle to keep her mind in the present, and only did so because she felt so uneasy for Cindy Lou and felt driven to go and be supportive of the poor girl. Finally, she made herself leave the warmth of the bathroom, and went down to the kitchen. Not finding the doctor there waiting for her, she refilled her own coffee cup, and sat to drink it near the kitchen fireplace, alone.

Doctor Miles heard the footsteps on the stairs and stirring about in the kitchen, but in hopes that if he gave Mrs. Wilcox time, she'd make him a grand breakfast, he kept still in his chair. Jimmy shifted his position and snored loudly, then tried to cough and woke himself with the pain of the effort. He jumped to Jimmy's side, pushing Blasted out of the way with a hearty shove, and while Blasted removed himself to the hearth a few feet away, Doctor Miles examined Jimmy and asked how he was feeling.

Jimmy rubbed his jaw with a wince and tried to answer, but Doctor Miles held up a hand and turned to sort through various bottles on a tall dresser nearby. He assured Jimmy he'd fix him up right and he'd be feeling no pain, in just a few minutes, and gave him a shot of painkiller.

Jimmy sat up and searched the room for his new pal, Blasted. While the doctor opened the bottle and placed two white pills in a bowl to crush, Blasted. Sensing he was wanted, Blasted lifted his head and turned to stare at him. Jimmy motioned for him to come back over to the mattress, but Blasted didn't move, so Jimmy crawled off his oddly placed bed, and crossed the room to sit by his comforting companion, and warm himself by the fire. He was fully awake by the time Doctor Miles brought him a glass of water and a tube to drink it through, and explained that the shot he'd given him wouldn't make him sleep the way the last one had.

He drank all that he could from the glass, hoping it would stop the pangs of hunger in his belly. He couldn't form clear enough words to express how hungry he was, so he resorted to pointing to his mouth until Doctor Miles burst out with the right words. He nodded and made excited noises in his throat when at last he'd gotten the message through and jumped to his feet unsteadily to follow the doctor, tugging Blasted by the scruff of his neck, out of the hospital room, down the short hallway, and into the kitchen, then he let out an unhappy grunt of surprise.

Mrs. Wilcox smiled up at him, despite the unfriendly greeting, and when Jimmy had steadied himself on a chair, she told him "Good Morning", but paid him no further attention.

Doctor Miles patted her on the shoulder as he passed by and, after the awkward exchange between her and Jimmy, and explained to her that his patient was starving.

He invited her to help him heat up some broth from the big stew pot, or cool a bit of coffee for Jimmy, in the windowsill, but she declined. She had it firmly fixed in her mind not to do what Cindy Lou had done; she would not assume any role, or accept any duties Doctor Miles might try to assign her while she was a guest in his home. Though she knew Jimmy could understand nothing of her attitude, she smiled and winked at him when Doctor Miles made noises of disgust behind her. When she had finished her coffee, she asked when Doctor Miles would be ready to drive her over to Cindy Lou's house, and helped herself to a piece of toast he'd made and put on the table for himself.

Doctor Miles ignored her question, fuming over her unwillingness to lend a hand and, when he noticed it, her rude pilfering of his very toast. He promised himself he was too much a gentleman to acknowledge the woman's gluttonous appetite as he made the liquid, that would be Jimmy's breakfast, warm over the cook stove and poured out a cup of coffee to cool in the window sill.

As a strained silence wore on, Jimmy grew agitated and was only calmed when Doctor Miles brought the drinking tube and coffee over to him, giving him a distraction. There was no such silence once he put his tube into the tepid coffee, however, and began slurping it up with only the slightest of apologetic looks in Mrs. Wilcox's direction. When the cup was empty, Doctor Miles replaced it with a bowl of beef broth and he kept up the disruptive noises until it too was gone, then he got up and returned to his room, with Blasted by his side.

Mrs. Wilcox giggled, after Jimmy was out of earshot and Doctor Miles swatted her with a towel to shush her, then he joined her at the table. He slid a plate with another piece of toast on it toward her, and kept a plate piled high with bacon for himself.

Jimmy didn't know what to do with himself in the hospital room while the horrid woman in the kitchen kept all of his doctor's attention for herself. He paced in front of the window until Blasted gave up following and returned to the hearth for a nap, then he stopped and stared at the empty bed frame and the mattress that still partially blocked the doorway. He decided the bed must certainly be put back in order, and assigned himself to the task of hauling his mattress back to where it belonged.

Once he'd heaved the unwieldy cushion up onto the bed frame, he set about stripping the sheets and blankets from it, then searched the linen closet for replacements and made the bed. He put the sheets he'd removed near the door, and went to the chair to rest and examine his handiwork from the fireplace side of the room. Blasted lifted his massive head and looked the hospital room over with him, then nudged Jimmy's leg until he was convinced to give his back a good scratching.

Feeling proud of the room's new, tidy, appearance, Jimmy pet his hulking companion, making happy noises behind his clenched teeth the whole while, then a memory of the day before returned to him and he pulled himself back up out of the chair: He couldn't recall, for certain, the location of the room he had been tearing up, when Doctor Miles had found him, the day before, but his pride would not allow him to rest until he had discovered behind which of the hallway doors lay the mess he now recalled creating, and cleaned everything up. Blasted, not wishing to be left behind, dutifully lumbered out of the hospital room behind Jimmy.

The first room Jimmy discovered was the bathroom, so Blasted waited patiently inside the door while Jimmy washed his hands, then they returned to the hall and quickly found the destroyed office Jimmy was searching for.

When he pushed open the door, an icy wind gushed past him into the house, so Jimmy quickly pushed Blasted back and slammed the door between them. Dismayed, Blasted leaned heavily on the hallway side of the door, whining, while Jimmy surveyed the damage he had done to his doctor's office.

Glass glistened all over the floor in the bright morning sunlight, and the curtains, as they'd done for so many hours, billowed inward with the strong cold wind. Jimmy didn't dare move and risk cutting up his bare feet, so he stood and searched all around him until he spotted a broom.   He plotted a route to it, and swept a path in front of him around the entire room, piling the debris in a corner near the door, then he applied himself to sealing the window Doctor Miles had broken. After exerting himself nearly too much he finally managed to grab ahold of both curtain panels and bring them together tightly, but once he'd done so he had no idea what he should do to keep them that way.

Doctor Miles, curious to see what Blasted was so upset about outside his office door, opened the door and peered in cautiously to see what Jimmy was doing. He realized at once the predicament Jimmy had put himself in and rushed to help him.   When Jimmy saw Doctor Miles he started, and nearly let go of the heavy panels, the strength of the wind behind them challenging every fiber of his weakened arm muscles. Doctor Miles ordered him to hang on long enough for him to clamp the curtains together under the window frame, and when they'd negotiated that clumsy task, he was exhausted and ready to take another rest.

Doctor Miles put an arm around Jimmy's sagging shoulders and looked his office over. He thanked him for cleaning up the floor, then led him back to the hospital room. He complimented Jimmy's fine work in the hospital room too, as he helped him into the bed, then he stoked the fire back to life and left him to take a much deserved nap.

Though he'd only been up and moving for an hour or so, Jimmy had done more work than Doctor Miles had imagined him yet capable of. He felt so encouraged by this show of progress and physical strength, his eyes danced with excitement as he told, and showed, Mrs. Wilcox how far progressed his unlikely patient was. Then, after looking in on Jimmy and giving a few instructions to Blasted, he happily agreed to leave for an hour or so, and drive her over to Cindy Lou's house to check on her condition. He escorted her out to his car in gentlemanly fashion and squeezed her hand affectionately as he pulled out onto the dirt road.

It seemed to him that everything was working out fine with Jimmy and Mrs. Wilcox, and he was glad for her company, considering that he must now go and console Cindy Lou for her loss, again. It would be much easier, he felt sure, with Mrs. Wilcox there to help him.

Chapter 10

Cindy Lou was startled to wakefulness by Doctor Miles' insistent knocking on her front door. She straightened her back and lifted her head to look around her, trying to figure out where she was and locate the clatter. After a moment she realized what she was hearing and went to answer her front door.

She stared at the doctor in confusion when, upon opening her door to him, he brushed by her into the foyer with Mrs. Wilcox close on his heels. She didn't understand the words of sympathy pouring from both the doctor and the former school teacher, and became even more flustered when Mrs. Wilcox began to cry, and Doctor Miles demanded that she tell Cory he wanted to have a word with him.

She put an arm around Mrs. Wilcox's shoulders and led the way to the kitchen, explaining to Doctor Miles, over her shoulder, that Cory had left her the morning before, to go get Esther from Sarah's farm, but had not returned and, at least according to Tyler, never intended to.

Doctor Miles stopped midway down the hall, shocked, thinking he'd not heard Cindy Lou right. Mrs. Wilcox cried harder.

Not noticing that the doctor was no longer following, Cindy Lou continued on talking and sat the weeping woman down on a kitchen chair, apologizing that she'd only just wakened and hadn't yet made a fresh fire or coffee, but would do both right away.

She stepped out the back door and grabbed up firewood, and returned to the kitchen to find

Mrs. Wilcox, still crying, at the table, alone. She asked where Doctor Miles had disappeared to, but the older woman could only shrug her shoulders in response, so overwhelmed to hear that the poor, dear girl had not only lost her sister, but her husband too, for what little Cory was worth, in her estimation.

Thinking Doctor Miles would be coming along shortly, Cindy Lou busied herself boiling water for coffee over the open flames in the fireplace. She laid a comforting hand on Mrs. Wilcox's shoulder for a moment, still wondering why the woman was so distraught, glancing around the hallway and foyer for Doctor Miles. She called out to him to come into the kitchen when she saw he was preparing to go back out the front door. He waved off the invitation, yelling back that he'd return in short order to talk to her, but that he first had to tend to some business in town.

Cindy Lou could tell by Doctor Miles' expression, when he turned to face her, that he was angry, very angry, so she didn't try to stop him. She went back to her kitchen to keep Mrs. Wilcox company and wait for her to calm herself enough to tell her what was going on.

Muttering furiously to himself as he went, Doctor Miles crossed the front porch and traced his steps through the yard to his car. He couldn't believe that Cory would dare leave Cindy Lou, a defenseless young girl, especially after he'd kicked Mrs. Wilcox out and her father and sister had just died. After everything she had done to care for him and nurse him back to health, this was how Cory had decided to treat Cindy Lou?

He would get to the bottom of things, Doctor Miles swore. He'd find Cory, give him the dressing down he deserved, then he'd bring him back to Cindy Lou and make him do right by her!

He drove toward town, so angry he could barely keep his car on the road, eyes blazing. He'd go straight to Cory's supply store, he decided, and see for himself if what Tyler had told Cindy Lou was indeed true. He raved to himself about what he would say to the shop owner when he found him, and what he'd say to Tyler if he found out that what the lumber mill owner had told Cindy Lou was untrue. One way or another he'd settle things, straight away.

Cindy Lou was too confused and groggy to figure out what had caused everyone to be in such an uproar. She made coffee and settled herself at the table with Mrs. Wilcox.

Mrs. Wilcox, after sipping her coffee a while, pulled herself together, somewhat, and wiped away her tears in anticipation of a long heart-to-heart with the doubtless devastated young woman. Cindy Lou sat staring blearily into the fireplace, showing no interest in talking, so the older woman struggled to her feet and hugged her tightly for a moment, then slumped back into her chair to wait for her to fall apart and cry out her misery over Esther's death. When the girl did nothing of the sort, Mrs. Wilcox began to pry, asking if Cindy Lou needed anything and assuring her that she would take care of all the "arrangements" with Pastor Franklin.

Cindy Lou mistook her offer to arrange things, thinking she was suggesting she annul her marriage to Cory, and she spoke harshly her for saying such a terrible thing.

Surprised, Mrs. Wilcox quickly explained herself, though, this time clearly referring to Esther's funeral arrangements, and finally Cindy Lou did dissolve into tears. Her shoulders heaved as

Mrs. Wilcox tried to sort out her confusion. She apologized for being so rude, but reminded the girl primly that the arrangements must be made, not realizing this was the first the girl had heard any confirmation of her sister's death.

Cindy Lou finally knew for certain that her dream had come true; her sister was dead, and worse, everyone seemed to think she'd already been told. When she found herself able to speak again, she interrupted a steady flow of confused apologies from Mrs. Wilcox, demanding to know where Esther was.

The question stopped the other woman cold. She stared at Cindy Lou for a long moment trying to remember what Ralphie had told her. Finally, she shook her head in frustration and confessed that she could not recall what Ralphie had said, other than that Esther was dead, and that he'd been on his way to tell Cindy Lou when Cory had stopped him and assured him he'd break the news to her, himself.

On hearing this, Cindy Lou jumped from the table, suddenly furious, demanding to know why Cory hadn't told her. Wasn't it bad enough, she yelled at the distraught woman, that he had abandoned her to go back to his silly damned store? Did he have to go without even telling her about Esther?

Mrs. Wilcox was, by now, so disconcerted, and so angry herself, she couldn't hold her tongue any longer, couldn't allow Cindy Lou's questions to go unanswered. She condemned Cory in all manner of speech, even calling into question his parentage, rather than trying to calm the grief-stricken girl.

Cindy Lou had never seen the woman so angry and hateful, and she was overwhelmed, suddenly. She was beginning to understand just how bad her situation had truly become.

Cory was opening his supply store door and turning the sign to "OPEN" with high hopes, and in good spirits. He'd slept well and wakened that morning with boundless energy, and a head full of ideas and plans to bring his supply store back to life; make it the center of attention once again, and make a fortune.

As he'd cleaned and swept the day before, he'd felt a growing dissatisfaction with his colorless inventory. The items every household needed seemed boring to him, somehow, and he set his mind to finding new, more exciting and extravagant, things to sell alongside the dull necessities.

He whistled happily as he searched the paved road up and down for his first customers, and finding Tyler standing out in front of his mill, staring at him, he threw up his hand and yelled a cheerful "Good Morning", then without waiting for a response, he went to sit behind his counter to sort through his catalogs while he drank his coffee. He couldn't keep his smile from his lips as he imagined how surprised and happy his first customer would no doubt be, to find the supply store finally open again and its owner inside just as things used to be.

He heard a car clunk onto the paved road outside, and his heart skipped a beat. He set aside his coffee and catalogs and ran to the door to welcome whoever had the money to own their own car, and entice them to shop in his store. He was surprised, but not at all apprehensive, when he recognized Doctor Miles' car. He waved at the doctor, to whom he owed his good health and great fortune, as he stopped his car, slammed the door and stomped toward him; only then did Cory, notice the deep coloration of the good doctor's face. He dropped his foolishly waving hand and proud, happy, smile and welcomed the doctor into the supply store, asking him with sincere concern what was so terribly wrong.

Doctor Miles ignored Cory's greeting and, without acknowledging his questions, he grabbed the younger man by the shirt collar and pushed him into the supply store, yelling as he went that he intended to do him great bodily harm, and stop only short of killing him, for what he'd done to Cindy Lou.

Taken by surprise, and stumbling backward, Cory knew the angry doctor had him at a serious disadvantage. He sputtered his protest, trying to stay on his feet and free himself of the older man's impressive grip. Finally, the doctor released his, now torn, shirt with another shove that caused him to fall backward and come to rest awkwardly twisted against his hardwood counter. He had no time to recover himself, however, before the normally good-natured doctor was yelling and cursing him roundly, for what he knew not; his face only inches from his the whole while.

He struggled to make heads or tails of the doctor's ranting and he tried to tell him as much, but his response only angered the other man more and the confrontation came to blows. Doctor Miles landed a bony fist against the side of his nose and without thinking he shoved the good doctor to the ground, kicking him with all the strength he could muster, as he fell.

Tyler, having seen the doctor push Cory into his store, ran to put a stop to the scuffle and find out what was going on. While Doctor Miles was struggling to get up, he lunged through the supply store doorway, and got his hands on Cory before he could do the doctor any further harm.

Cory didn't notice Tyler's appearance, he was

so singularly focused on his downed, but determined, opponent. He crashed to the floor under Tyler's much larger frame, believing the building had surely collapsed upon him, and he kicked and fought to get out from under the oppressive weight.

Tyler struggled to keep Cory pinned under him, and ordered Doctor Miles to get out of the store, while he could.

When Cory heard Tyler's voice above him, he stopped his fighting and concentrated his efforts on talking the man off of him. It took a while to convince him that he presented no further danger to the deranged doctor, but Tyler let him go, finally, and helped him back to his feet, watching him warily, like Cory had been the one who'd started the fight, and might attack him next.

Cory used the counter to hold himself upright, while he wiped blood from his lips. Then he turned on Tyler accusingly, and yelled at him for preventing him from defending himself against the doctor's unprovoked attack.

Tyler ignored Cory's accusations, checking himself over carefully for injuries. As he pushed down his shirt sleeves and brushed off his pants, he searched the store for Doctor Miles, hoping the man had run for safety while he'd distracted Cory.

But Doctor Miles had not run; he'd taken advantage of Tyler's unexpected appearance and made his way to the supply store's gun display cabinet. Now, he was standing, holding one of Cory's best rifles, aimed straight at Cory's back, positioned between two of the aisles.

Tyler was so shocked to see the seriousness of the fight he'd walked in on, he moved away from Cory quickly, toward the open doorway, sputtering at the two men and begging the doctor not to shoot him.

Cory spun on his heel when he realized what Tyler was trying to say, and he joined the terrified man in pleading with the doctor to put down the gun and talk sensibly with them, but to no avail. He tried to convince the angry gun holder to let Tyler leave, then he turned to Tyler and ordered him to go, but Tyler stood rooted to the spot, unable to make himself move, until Doctor Miles motioned him toward the street with a wave of the rifle barrel, then he bolted out of the store without looking back.

Once safely outside, Tyler ran, terrified, back to his mill, vowing not to leave it ever again, even if a fire were ever lit beneath him, to intervene on anyone's behalf in that community. He locked his door behind him and stumbled up to his apartment on the second floor, to hide from whatever evil had overtaken the people of his once quiet, pleasant, community. He gave no thought or consideration to the business he'd planned to conduct that day, instead turning to his whiskey bottle for consolation.

As he sat on his floor, drinking great gulps of his strongest whiskey, he lamented bitterly the death of Old Bill, feeling certain that his death had unleashed this madness between Cory and the doctor. If only he could turn back time, he swore to himself, he'd bring Old Bill back to the post office and everyone would go back to doing their level best to preserve all that was good in their town, instead of destroying it. Quickly overcome with the effects of the strong whiskey, he fell into a stupor, unknowing and uncaring any longer how the town's only doctor and newly returned supply store owner resolved their potentially deadly fight.

At the supply store, Cory and Doctor Miles continued to argue. Doctor Miles steadfastly refused to point the gun he'd found, and loaded, anywhere but at Cory.

Cory begged to know what had brought on this attack, but was disbelieving when the doctor told him what he'd done to deserve it. He could not make any sense whatever of the doctor's claims that he'd married his dearest, now dead, best friend's beautiful young daughter, Cindy Lou, evicted her sister and her caregiver, and then abandoned his wife like a coward, rather than tell her of Esther's death, and beg for her forgiveness.

Cory had no memory of, nor could he even begin to imagine himself capable of, such wretched and abusive behavior. He rejected Doctor Miles account of things outright and entirely, and demanded an apology, but the doctor was equally adamant that what he claimed was true.

They continued their standoff for what seemed like an eternity, before what Cory felt certain was his worst experience ever, grew still worse. Movement in the supply store doorway brought both the gun-wielding doctor and the desperate supply store owner back to reality, and Cory moved quickly to hide behind his counter; using the doctor's momentary distraction to escape and call out to whoever had come in for help.

Mrs. Wilcox followed Cindy Lou into the supply store, ready to take on the man who'd done her young friend, the girl she felt a motherly instinct for, so terribly and brutally wrong. She marched toward the sales counter Cory had run to hide behind, not suspecting that it was not her and Cindy Lou's arrival that had sent him scurrying. When Cory shouted for help, it gave her enough pause, however, to stop and have a look around the supply store. She screamed and fell to the floor in a dead faint when she took in Doctor Miles and the gun in his hands.

Cindy Lou, not knowing what had frightened Mrs. Wilcox to apparent death, fell to her knees beside the woman, and Doctor Miles quickly threw aside his weapon and ran to help his friend. Cory, hearing all the commotion so near him, peered over the counter at the scene on the other side, cautiously.

Doctor Miles, suddenly returned to a more normal state of mind, issued orders to Cindy Lou and her terrified husband with all his normal aplomb. He told Cindy Lou to get a cold cloth and bring it to him quickly, and sent Cory in search of a suitable blanket to prop up the woman's head, while he patted her icy hand and tried to rouse her.

Cindy Lou followed his instructions and ran for the stairs to Cory's apartment to find a towel. Cory forced himself to come out from the relative safety of the counter to cross the supply store sales floor and grab a blanket from one of the shelves, then to satisfy his desire to protect himself from any further threat he detoured, with the blanket in hand, to the aisle where Doctor Miles had recently stood and picked up the rifle.

He took the blanket and dropped it next to the doctor, then unloaded the weapon and replaced it, and the bullets, in the display cabinet, locking the cabinet before he turned back to see if there were any further assignment for him. He watched curiously as Cindy Lou came running down the stairs from his private apartment, wondering to himself how she had known where to find the towel she now carried. The picture of her coming from his apartment like she'd been up there before had a terribly unsettling effect on him, but, he reasoned to himself that everyone had been behaving irrationally since he'd opened his supply store just over two hours before.

He returned to the safe side of the counter and observed the quietly frantic scene before him, unable to figure out, or see, who the woman was who'd saved his life by her scream, and now lay being attended to by the man who would have been his killer, and is late best friend's youngest daughter, who the doctor claimed he'd married and since, abandoned. He shook his head and forced himself to ask if the woman would be alright.

Doctor Miles put the cold cloth Cindy Lou handed him over Mrs. Wilcox's forehead and told Cindy Lou not to worry, that she'd waken fully and be just fine after her heart recovered from the shock she'd had. He didn't acknowledge Cory's concern, nor give him any response whatever as he urged his lady friend to wake up and pull herself together. He told Cindy Lou to go find a glass of water, but Cory held up his hand to stop the girl from traipsing through his apartment, uninvited, again; he'd get whatever else Doctor Miles might require, himself.

Mrs. Wilcox reanimated quickly under the good doctor's ministrations, and fought valiantly to recover herself, and reconcile her last memory, with where she now lay on the floor. It took a thorough self-examination to prove to herself she'd not been shot, despite Doctor Miles' assertions that she'd only just fainted.

She tried to explain to Cindy Lou, grabbing the young girl's hands in her fright, that she'd seen Doctor Miles pointing a rifle at her, but Doctor Miles quickly distracted Cindy Lou from hearing any further details. He pried Mrs. Wilcox's cold, grasping fingers off Cindy Lou's, and sent the confused girl away in search of a stool.

Cory returned to the sales floor with the water and, after delivering it to the doctor, asked what Cindy Lou was up to now, dragging his chair from behind his business counter. He intercepted the confused girl at the far end of the counter, snatched the chair from her, taking it to Mrs. Wilcox and helping her get up onto it. When she'd steadied herself, a hand against the counter for extra support, he turned her care back over to Doctor Miles with a stony glare and brushed, unnecessarily, against the older man's shoulder as he made his way back around to his rightful side of the counter.

Cindy Lou, completely devastated by Cory's indifferent, almost hostile, treatment of her, and frightened by Mrs. Wilcox's desperate attempt to explain something about a gun to her, was overwhelmed, suddenly. Rather than waiting to see how things would progress inside her newly estranged husband's supply store, she fled, unnoticed by the others, into the street. She could no longer bear the company, as high-strung as everyone seemed to be, of others.

While Doctor Miles, Cory, and Mrs. Wilcox remembered their grievances with one another, and rekindled the fight Doctor Miles had started, Cindy Lou ran home. Once there, she searched the pantry for some food that could be heated and eaten quickly, and went to work over the cook stove. She ate her breakfast in front of the fireplace, staring into the flames absently, listening to the occasional hiss of steam escaping the not-quite-dry wood. Alone again, she felt almost calm inside, almost comfortable with the aching in her chest.

Chapter 11

Jimmy Fenton woke from his nap to the sounds of Doctor Miles and Mrs. Wilcox banging around, arguing in the kitchen. He rolled off his bed and made his way toward the irritable couple with a throbbing pain in his head, and food on his mind.

When he appeared in the kitchen doorway, the argument ended abruptly, and Doctor Miles remembered that his patient's next dose of pain reliever was long over-due. Rather than waiting for Jimmy to find a new destructive way to express his need for medicine, he set down the pot he'd been filling and rushed down the short hallway in his office. As he went, he told Jimmy to sit himself down at the table and let Mrs. Wilcox make him a cup of coffee.

Mrs. Wilcox bristled at the suggestion and followed Jimmy to the table instead, to sit and brood until the doctor returned. She muttered irritably about Doctor Miles' treatment of her, though she could tell her complaints were falling on uncaring ears. She harrumphed loudly enough to get Jimmy's attention, and when he glanced over at her, she fixed him, with an unpleasant glare. How dare this young man be told to expect her to play nurse-maid to him just because she happened to be there, she fumed. She was every bit as much a guest in the doctor's home as this murderer was! She'd give Doctor Miles a piece of her mind when he came back, she decided, but until then she'd sit right there at the table and enjoy a much needed, fully deserved, rest.

Jimmy stared back at Mrs. Wilcox, unsure how to respond. She reminded him, to her great misfortune, of his long-dead mother. His face warmed as she took out her bad temper on him and he was quite nearly too tempted to respond to her raving, by the time Doctor Miles bustled back into the room and put a glass of medicine and a drinking tube in front of him. He grabbed up the tube and quickly drank down the medicine, then shut his eyes to block out the unpleasant woman entirely. He clenched and unclenched his fists under the table, fighting against a powerful urge to overturn it and silence the miserable woman for good, but Mrs. Wilcox was either uncaring of the danger, or oblivious to it.

On Doctor Miles return, Mrs. Wilcox continued her tirade without missing a beat. She repeated her "how dare you's" and moved right on to the "if you expect me too's" without pausing for even a second to acknowledge the doctor's apologies.

Doctor Miles gave up begging for forgiveness, finally, and busied himself at the stove, nodding periodically and muttering under his breath while he made Jimmy a cup of coffee and set it on the windowsill to cool, letting his lady friend wear herself out with her complaints. When he'd given her and Jimmy the coffee cups, he finally got the moment of quiet he'd been wanting, and wishing for, for many hours.

As soon as Mrs. Wilcox put the cup to her lips, he launched into a voluble lecture of "now hear this!", which he concluded by marching out of the kitchen and slamming the door to his office behind him.

Getting no response to a few choice remarks she made to Jimmy, Mrs. Wilcox got up and marched down the short hallway in pursuit of Doctor Miles.

Despite her knocking and overly-loud pleas and demands she made through it, however, the office door remained firmly shut and locked before her, and nothing but the sound of silence returned to her from the other side of it.

She kicked the door mightily, adding injury to the insults she felt she'd suffered, and fell to the floor weeping over herself, fully expecting Doctor Miles to come at a run to help her. She cried louder and harder, and cursed him when he didn't appear.

Though she could now, from her position on the floor in front of the door, feel a cold draft, she wasn't able to figure out that Doctor Miles had, in a desperate attempt to find solitude, opened the broken window's curtains and left the wind to whip them once again, behind him. He had climbed out the window and dropped into the chair she'd left beneath it.

The chaos finally overcame Jimmy's ability to control his temper. When Mrs. Wilcox got herself up from the floor and returned to the kitchen, and tried to elicit the sympathy she felt she deserved, from him, he managed not to overturn the table, but he fixed her outrage by walking out the back door, giving it a satisfying slam behind him. He marched angrily around the back yard, shivering in his shirt sleeves, looking for a good place to hide for a while, in high hopes that the abrasive woman would give up and go home.

As he'd done in the past, whenever pushed beyond his limits, before he'd been taken in by Doctor Miles, he sought out a task that required great physical exertion: He went to the log pile behind the shed and used all the energy he had carrying wood from it to the back door box, careful not to jar his head in doing so, until the deep container was full, then he sat next to it, blocked somewhat from the biting wind, and let the sun warm him through. He determined that he'd remain right there for the rest of the day if he had to, to avoid hearing another word from the woman's foul mouth.

Cory, left to conduct his business only after Doctor Miles and Mrs. Wilcox had condemned him roundly, stubbornly refused to give in and close up his shop, even before it had been open again for a full day, and go back to the warmth and safety of his bed. The accusations the two had made against him outraged him and left him mightily confused. Not one, but both of them, had now made the distressing claim that he'd married, then abandoned Cindy Lou. He knew with all certainty that the things they'd said to him were patently false, unimaginable for a man of his stature, age, and reputation.

He stood behind his counter, waiting for one or another of the townspeople to come through the door and confirm how right he was, replaying in his mind the way Cindy Lou had behaved while in his store. He decided firmly that her attitude and treatment of him proved that even she knew that none of the terrible accusations were true. What bothered him most, and had seemed so odd to him, was that he'd had to stop the girl from traipsing around his store, and his apartment, like she indeed owned the place. Though he couldn't recall her ever doing such a thing before, he did his best to shake off the queer feeling.

No one interrupted his confused reverie, or came by to welcome him back. Though he went to the doorway and watched the road intently, only Ralphie seemed to notice. He'd waved at the boy when he'd seen him pass by, but no one else was around to be seen. Finally, he gave up and put the "CLOSED" sign in the front window and trudged up the stairs to his apartment feeling miserable and frustrated.

As he warmed a pot of stew, he gave himself a stern lecture, and set his mind on getting a good night's rest, getting up early the next morning and driving over to the next larger town to invest in some, more eye-catching, merchandise to sell in his store. He finished his dinner, checked each of his healing injuries, and crawled onto his bed, exhausted. He fell asleep promptly with only the most fleeting thought, that he could make neither heads nor tails of, of Old Bill's beautiful young daughter, Cindy Lou.

Cindy Lou was startled from her sad thoughts, by Mrs. Wilcox's banging fists on her front door. She sighed heavily and went to let the woman in, trying as she did, not to show her hurt feelings that this supposed friend had gone with her into town, yet once there, had forgotten her existence entirely.

Rather than complaining about no one noticing her leaving the supply store earlier, she simply poured a cup of coffee for Mrs. Wilcox and listened attentively to her new tale of woe.

She thought the woman, given enough time, would tell her what they'd said to Cory about the way he'd treated her, and how he'd responded, but Mrs. Wilcox was too excited over the rough treatment she felt she'd been subjected to at the doctor's house to let pass this opportunity to garner some feminine support and sympathy - which Cindy Lou gave freely, until Jimmy Fenton's name spilled out of the woman's mouth.

While Mrs. Wilcox related having marched out of the rude doctor's house and walked the distance all alone, on her sore foot no less, to Cindy Lou's; Cindy Lou's mind and attention were on other, most upsetting things like; how, after all Jimmy Fenton had done to her family, had he come to be living in Doctor Miles home?

The answer came to her in an unpleasant flash as she recalled her rushed marriage ceremony right there in her father's home only hours after her father had been buried. Cory had only married her because Doctor Miles had made him mad, and kicked him out so he could take care of Jimmy Fenton, she concluded.

She jumped up from the table and silenced the older woman with an hysterical tongue lashing. She ordered the astounded woman out of her house, and slammed the door on her heels when she finally gave up trying to defend herself and followed Cindy Lou's pointing finger out the door.

Cindy Lou stormed around her house, gathering her heaviest coat and gloves, then set out behind Mrs. Wilcox, though the older woman was, by then, out of sight, making her way back home. When she got to the footpath that led to Doctor Miles' home, from the dirt road, she turned her feet onto it and crossed over to Doctor Miles' road in record time.

Feeling perspiration trickling down her sides under her heavy dress and coat, despite the cold wind swirling around her, she tried to slow her pace. She knew such exertion was unwise and could make her very ill, but her anger drove her forward at an ever increasing pace til she reached Doctor Miles' back door, and found herself in the presence of her father's killer, who still sat, eyes closed in sleep, on the porch.

Seeing Jimmy Fenton sent Cindy Lou over the edge. She stomped right up to him and kicked him as hard as she could, in the side, then before Jimmy could register anything of what was happening, gave his upper leg a powerful kick, too.

Jimmy yelped and pulled his legs up to his chest, wrapping his arms around them reflexively. Not knowing who, or what, was attacking him, he rolled to his side and struggled to his feet, then lunged with all his might against Cindy Lou.

Cindy Lou screamed as Jimmy's weight drove her to the ground, and she continued screaming even after he recognized her and released her. She wasn't at all injured, but to hear her convinced Doctor Miles otherwise.

He rushed out from his kitchen and ran to her side, demanding to know what had happened. Hysterical, she accused Jimmy Fenton of attacking her.

Doctor Miles could see that there'd been a scuffle; Jimmy was still on his hands and knees, struggling to suck in air between his teeth, not more than two feet away, but he couldn't believe that the young man had attacked Cindy Lou. He knew for a fact that, only a few minutes before, the young man had been snoring. He wouldn't be convinced, even by the young girl's screams, that Jimmy had attacked anyone in is sleep.

Jimmy, finally getting air back into his lungs, propped his hands on his knees and steadied himself, trying to make the right words work with the right sounds to tell Doctor Miles his side of the story. The doctor wasn't interested though; he was busy picking the disheveled girl up out of the dirt and checking her over for injuries. He tried to get up, to run away from the doctor's house, sure that this scuffle with
Old Bill's daughter would most certainly spell out his doom, but Doctor Miles turned his attention to him

just then, and put a stop to his frightened thoughts, asking if he was alright?

Jimmy felt his ribs, wincing, but shook his head "no" and continued struggling to get to his feet. He brushed Cindy Lou's dusty footprints from his shirt and pants, not realizing that the good doctor's eyes were still on him. He looked up in unabashed surprise when he felt the doctor lifting him, helping him get solidly on his feet. His eyes bleared with tears the instant Doctor Miles spoke a few sympathetic words to him, and put his hand on his shoulder and ushered him, shooing Cindy Lou ahead of them, into the warm house.

Once inside, Cindy Lou's fury resurfaced and despite Doctor Miles ordering her to be silent, she screamed "Murderer!" in Jimmy's face. She wouldn't be stopped from having her say about the man who'd taken away her dear father, and her anger, further fueled by Esther's unrelated yet equally unexpected death, only served to make her more hateful, more determined, and more hysterical.

Doctor Miles pushed Jimmy forward toward the kitchen table, despite Cindy Lou's close proximity to it, and succeeded in getting him onto a chair and out from between himself and Cindy Lou, then he took the girl by the shoulders and forced her into a chair. At least, he determined, she could not any longer reach her intended victim with a flailing fist or vicious kick with the large, heavy table between them. He slumped into a chair, at last, and covered his face with his hands, elbows braced on the table top for support until Cindy Lou finally stopped her yelling and subsided in tears.

Before the doctor could make any move to stop him, Jimmy got up, got around him, and knelt down beside Cindy Lou's chair, to press a dishtowel into her trembling hand. Then, through tightly clenched teeth, almost incomprehensibly, he made quiet apologies to her.

Doctor Miles watched helplessly, too late to advise Jimmy not to do such a foolish thing, and was rewarded with a heartwarming surprise and relief when Cindy Lou turned her red, swollen, eyes toward Jimmy, but made no attempt to attack him again, despite his vulnerable position, near her feet. An eerie silence took over the kitchen while everyone took stock of their condition, broken only occasionally by a sniffle from Cindy Lou, muffled by the dishtowel.

The quiet, after such a loud and stressful day, finally got under Doctor Miles' skin. He got up and offered his chair to the surprisingly gallant young man, sliding it closer to Cindy Lou slightly, as he helped Jimmy onto it, then he busied himself in front of the stove, surprised, still, over the sudden change in the girl's temperament. He told them, over his shoulder, that he'd make them all something to eat, and couldn't help but indulge himself with a satisfied smile when Cindy Lou jumped up to help him.

It seemed to him that these two young people were actually quite comfortable with each other, like this was not the first time they'd met. And he had a mind to say something about his impression the next time he was alone with Cindy Lou.

Much as they'd been when her father and Cory had been his patients, Doctor Miles and Cindy Lou resumed their comfortable division of duties without any words between them. While he put dishes on the counter and dug around in the silver drawer, she gathered seasonings to add to the pot of stew she discovered on the stovetop. Doctor Miles brought in wood from the box outside his back door, thanking Jimmy for refilling it as he passed by the table, while Cindy Lou drew off a portion of the broth and set it aside for Jimmy, noticing the feeding tube on the counter and recalling Doctor Miles use of it to feed her father.

Tears welled in her eyes. To be in Doctor Miles' home again, preparing broth like she had so many times for Cory, and her father before he'd died, made her unwell, and she wished she'd never returned, never learned that Doctor Miles had replaced Cory, the night she'd agreed to marry him, with the man who'd killed her father. The routine at Doctor Miles' house was so familiar to her, though; preparing food and caring for patients came naturally to her, and she slipped back into her role in it, without hesitation.

Jimmy sat stone still at the table, his back to the doctor and the girl who'd, moments before, attacked him and accused him of killing her father. He knew he'd done it, he didn't need anyone, especially not Cindy Lou, who'd broken his heart just to please her old man, to remind him. He'd paid a heavy price for the fight he and Tim had had with the doctor and Old Bill. He had, after all, only barely survived the encounter himself, without anyone even caring for, let alone helping, him.

From the moment he'd resolved to himself, out in his fields, he'd never let another girl break his heart, or embarrass him the way Cindy Lou had, he'd done his best never to even think of her. When her father had walked her out of town, the afternoon they were to have had their first date, it had been the last he'd seen of her. He'd hoped he'd never lay eyes on her again. Now, he'd not only seen her, he'd comforted her, apologized to her even after her cruel attack on him. He could hardly keep his head from swimming to know that, just a few feet behind him, that same beautiful, hateful, girl was actually preparing his dinner.

He felt his rib cage gingerly. Then put his hand to his head, remembering the bandages there. He was humiliated that Cindy Lou was seeing him this way. Before he could prevent it, he was overcome with emotion and ran from the kitchen, letting his chair clatter onto its side behind him, and locked himself in his hospital room where Blasted lay sleeping in front of the cold fireplace. He fell to the floor next to Blasted and hugged him tightly, letting great hot tears spill from his face into the massive dog's fur. He hid his face in the scruff of the dog's neck and cried bitterly until Blasted freed himself enough to turn and lick his hands.

Doctor Miles was pretty sure that Jimmy would prefer to be left alone for a time. He knew the young man had had quite a hard day, as he had, before Cindy Lou had discovered him on the back porch. He also knew the young man's pride prevented him from admitting that little Cindy Lou had injured him, and hurt his feelings badly.

When she turned to him, he took her hand and guided her to the table, and sat with her and tried to explain why he'd decided to send Cory away and take Jimmy Fenton, secretly, into his home.

Cindy Lou wasn't sympathetic to Jimmy's plight, or his physical condition, and it took quite some time for Doctor Miles to get her to at least accept that he'd not taken Jimmy in to spite her. He told her what he'd seen out at the Fenton farm when he'd taken Jimmy there to leave him, or perhaps kill him even, the night of her father's funeral, and told her his heart could not bear, after picking up and burying Jimmy's brother's remains, to cause him any more suffering. With tears in his eyes and heavy emotion in his voice he told her he could understand how she must feel, but that he just wasn't the kind of man he'd have to be to do the young man any more harm.

When he'd finished speaking, Cindy Lou had tears on her own cheeks and found she couldn't argue with a man as pure-hearted as Doctor Miles seemed to be. Rather than even trying to put into words what she felt, she simply reached across the table and placed her hand on his for a moment, then got up and went back to the stove, hoping he hadn't noticed her crying.

Doctor Miles could see plainly, though Cindy Lou kept her back to him as she dished out two bowls of stew, that she was crying, and his heart ached to see her so miserable. He couldn't believe Cory had not taken care of the girl the way he'd promised to, and started to tell her how angry he still was about that, but stopped himself, knowing she'd been through so much more than that, that very day alone, and didn't need to be kicked while she was already so down. Instead he walked over and hugged her the way he imagined her father would have, and let her cry against his shoulder.

He patted her back and stroked her hair while she sobbed about all the unfairness, all the loss, and all the pain she'd suffered. And he offered her reassurances and when she told him how alone she suddenly was.

When she'd cried herself out, he led her back to sit at the table and asked her if she would stay with him for a few days rather than returning at once to her empty home. He told her he could use her help around the house and pointed out that that would keep her busy, and told her he hated to think of her all alone, especially at such a difficult time.

Cindy Lou didn't put up any argument, despite knowing that what would keep her busy there would be caring for Jimmy Fenton. She dreaded spending even another moment in her empty house, with nothing more to do than stare out her window at her parent's graves and wait for someone to bring Esther's body home to lay next to them. She didn't understand why Cory had left her, but didn't care to have him return and find her there just waiting for him, so she thanked the kindly old doctor for the offer and asked that he drive her home right away so she could pack a few clothes.

With that settled, and the air clear between them, Doctor Miles sent her to wait in his car while he had a word with Jimmy and gave instructions to Blasted. Once in the car, bumping over the ruts and rocks, he asked where Mrs. Wilcox had gotten off to and, for the first time that day, she cracked a smile as she told him how the woman had raved to her about him, until she'd finally ordered the woman out.

He chuckled a little, behind a concealing hand, then told Cindy Lou as sternly as he could that she was a bad girl to have done such a thing to the woman. Before Cindy Lou could defend herself from his scolding, however, he told her about the scene Mrs. Wilcox had made at his home earlier, before she'd called on her, and the two had a hearty laugh at the woman's expense.

Chapter 12

Mrs. Wilcox wasn't laughing over the raw treatment she'd received at the doctor's home or the rude send-off from Cindy Lou. She passed through the small town en-route to her distant home, fuming so loudly she hoped everyone would hear just how terribly she'd suffered that day. She limped dramatically, looking this way and that, hoping Tyler might poke his head out and offer her a sympathetic ear; she'd tell him all of Doctor Miles' secrets and some she now knew about Cindy Lou's new marriage, just for good measure.

Tyler would spread the word that these two weren't as charming and good as they appeared, then they'd know they shouldn't have messed with her; they'd be as unpopular as she always had been, she thought Tyler was not going to pop out from anywhere, though; he was still fast asleep.

When she reached the dirt road on the other end of town, she glanced around once more, harrumphed in disgust that no one had noticed her, then stepped easily onto the dirt road and, without the slightest limp, made her way home. A full two days in the same clothes, despite her bath the night before, had left her looking disheveled and, as she walked, she decided it was for the best that no one had seen her, after all, and as much as she'd hoped to stay with Cindy Lou to help her cope with the loss of her dear Esther, she was feeling quite relieved now that things hadn't quite worked out that way.

She could see, now, that adjusting to living in

the company of so many people, who could be so disrespectful, would not have been an easy thing for her. Quite some time would have to pass, she swore, before she'd accept apologies from any of them; no should dare to treat her this way. She was better off without any of them, she told herself, as she finally crossed through her doorway again. She hadn't been able to tell her tale of woe to Tyler, she thought, but she could just as easily cause the doctor and Cindy Lou trouble from this safe distance, the next time Ralphie came by with a letter for her.

Jimmy got up from the floor and tried to hide his tears when Doctor Miles had come to his door, and when he'd heard the doctor out, he couldn't conceal his surprise; Cindy Lou was going to stay there too? With him in the house? He couldn't believe it, but Doctor Miles had been in too much of a hurry to explain why. He'd said he would be back with the girl, and her things, in just a couple of hours.

After Doctor Miles' car crunched onto the dirt road, Jimmy battled with himself that he would not allow this girl, who'd embarrassed and hurt him so badly, to take care of him while his body was able. Only his jaw was still mending, he reminded himself, so there was no reason he should need her to take care of anything for him. He made noises of outrage in his throat and slapped his palms together to get Blasted's attention, then the two of them walked Doctor Miles' house from end to end, deciding what room was Doctor Miles' and which would best suit Cindy Lou, when she returned.

He chose a guest room nearest the bathroom on the second floor, and busied himself checking the linens and re-arranging the furniture the way he thought a girl might prefer it. He moved things around noisily while Blasted kept watch from the doorway, and when he'd finished, the bedroom looked as fine, to him, as his mother's room had looked when he'd been younger.

From the bedroom, he moved on to the bathroom and put out fresh towels, and livened the strongly scented bath soap he found, under hot water, between his hands in the sink. From there, he returned to the kitchen where he searched the pantry and cabinets.

He found potatoes and carried them out to the sink, checked the ice box and found several hunks of frozen meat, and set them on the counter to thaw while he broke the ends off a few handfuls of beans. He didn't really know how to cook, but he'd done all the things his mother had often made him and his two brothers do, confidently and quickly, then he had to stop and think about things, and figure out how best to cook all the things he'd prepared.

He was ready and waiting by the door when Doctor Miles returned with Cindy Lou, and before the girl could even put a foot on the ground, he was pulling her suitcase off the back seat and moving back toward the house. Though his head was beginning to pound, he muscled the heavy suitcase up to the room he'd prepared, and went back downstairs to the kitchen to look into the stove at the potatoes he'd put down in the ashes to bake.

When Doctor Miles saw the array of food covering his kitchen counters, he shrugged in confusion at Cindy Lou. Jimmy strode right past them, ignoring them entirely, to open the cook stove door and look inside, and Cindy Lou started searching the floor around the table and doorway for her suitcase. Unable to locate it, she finally asked Jimmy where he'd taken it.

Without turning from the stove, Jimmy pointed at the ceiling above him, and Doctor Miles helpfully interpreted that he'd taken her things upstairs. Then, while she went in search of her belongings, he quickly asked Jimmy just what he thought he was doing?

Jimmy made motions like a man eating and turned to the iron skillet he was heating on the stovetop. Doctor Miles, understanding the young man's intentions, if not the way he was going about things, kicked off his boots, and offered a few suggestions while he washed his hands.

He dropped a portion of the meat into the skillet and Jimmy followed his lead with the other two, then he turned one of the pieces with the fork and explained that Jimmy should turn the meat, as he'd just done, after it had cooked a while. Finally, he asked what Jimmy had put inside the stove, and Jimmy opened the door again and pointed out the potatoes he'd placed in the ashes. Doctor Miles chuckled at the sight and suggested they might be better boiled, then helped Jimmy get the potatoes out and wash them off. Since Jimmy hadn't done more than clean the handfuls of snap-beans, Doctor Miles took over their preparation, and by the time Cindy Lou returned to the kitchen both men were fully engrossed in making dinner.

She sat down at the table and a cup of coffee appeared in front of her, so she thanked the room, not sure which of the two had put it there, then returned to her own private musings, staring into the fireplace:

She'd been upstairs in Doctor Miles' house before, but didn't recall the bedroom where she'd found her suitcase looking as pretty as it did now. The bathroom too looked different from the way she'd last seen it and it smelled of strong soap. She'd taken her baths downstairs, but maybe Mrs. Wilcox had cleaned upstairs during her visit, she mused. If she had, she thought, she'd have been surprised. Mrs. Wilcox had certainly not acted like the thought would ever have crossed her mind.

She decided she'd compliment Doctor Miles on the new condition of things and let him tell her who'd done it, when he sat down to eat. She sipped her coffee, smelling the food cooking, and quickly developing a ravenous appetite, and ideas about a good night's sleep in that comfortable looking bed upstairs, as soon as she finished eating.

Dinner was presented to her at the table with a proud smile from Doctor Miles, directed, behind Cindy Lou's back, at Jimmy. The day had been long, painful, and tiring for his patient, he knew, but it seemed to him that the idea of having volatile Cindy Lou around intrigued and excited Jimmy Fenton. He had no idea how this new living arrangement would work out, but at least for the moment everything seemed to be going well enough. Even Blasted, he noticed, had quietly befriended Jimmy and attended him almost constantly. His old brute of a dog seemed to be a comfort to both his patient and Cindy Lou.

The three sat, with Blasted positioned strategically between Jimmy and Cindy Lou's chairs hoping for some scraps, and they ate with minimal conversation, Jimmy sipping a concoction he and Doctor Miles had created. When they'd finished, Cindy Lou would not allow either of them to get back up to help her clear the dishes. Rested, somewhat, she felt she should insist on doing her part and allow the two weary looking men to rest a while.

Doctor Miles jumped at the opportunity to avoid any more kitchen labor and went to his office

with a glass of water to make Jimmy's medicine,
leaving Jimmy to stare into the kitchen fireplace
contentedly, only slightly unnerved to have
Cindy Lou in the room with him, though she ignored
him completely. She was a married woman now,
according to Doctor Miles, but to whom, Jimmy
could not guess, and he wondered why she would
want to live in Doctor Miles' home, with him there,
instead of with her new husband in her own home.

He knew he couldn't speak well enough, with
his mouth clamped shut with the gauze, to ask her his
many questions, so he did his best to avoid inviting
any conversation with her. He'd try to ask the doctor
his questions, he decided, after Cindy Lou had gone
upstairs for the night.

Cory slept soundly until the wee hours of the
morning, then found himself unable to lie in bed any
longer. He showered and dressed, then slipped out his
truck for the long ride over to the next town. He
wanted to be back in Farmersville in time to open his
supply store early and, he hoped, generate some
business with whatever new items he'd been able to
find. He pulled out onto the paved road, hoping Tyler
would still be asleep and wouldn't notice his leaving.

As he left the pavement, he breathed a sigh of
relief that his leaving had gone undetected and
unhindered by the nosy lumber mill owner. He had
way too much to do to bring his business back to
profitable to waste any more time with Tyler.

An hour later, he stopped in front of The
General Store and parked his truck alongside two
others. The store wouldn't be open to customers for
quite some time, according to the sign on the door,
but he could see the owner conducting business with
a couple of men through the uncurtained display

window, so he went on up to the door and knocked to get his attention. The drive over had been moonlit, but it was now beginning to get light enough out so that Calvin, the General Store owner, was able to quickly recognize Cory, and he rushed from behind his counter to let him in.

Calvin remarked on his surprise to see Cory after so many weeks, and finished his transaction with the other men quickly so he could question Cory thoroughly about the recent goings-on in Farmersville. He had heard of Old Bill's passing and offered Cory sympathy for the loss of his dear friend, and shared Cory's confusion when he'd related what Doctor Miles and Mrs. Wilcox had accused him of, the day before. He assured Cory that he'd never heard a peep about anyone having married Old Bill's daughter, shaking his head in amazement to hear how far the town's doctor had taken things in Cory's supply store.

While they talked about Cory's new ideas for his supply store, they walked the isles together and Cory selected items from his list. Calvin showed him things he'd found to be good sellers in recent weeks, and they picked a couple of dozen more items, then Cory paid for everything and loaded everything into the back of his truck. When he'd finished, they said their goodbyes and Cory started back to Farmersville, anxious to get back to his store and create a grand window display he could now picture, with the new merchandise he'd found.

Tyler was opening the lumber mill doors for a delivery truck when Cory rolled back onto the paved road and parked his truck behind his supply store. With his time and attention occupied, he made no move to acknowledge Cory. He helped the driver unload rough-cut logs from his truck bed while Cory emptied his truck bed and unlocked the supply store doors.

Cory took large barrels, shovels and yard tools away from the supply store's front window and replaced them with a small rack of delicate headscarves, a stack of brightly colored hats and an array of carefully chosen ladies shoes. He piled bolts of fabric on a low bench to fill the rest of the window space, then stepped out onto the porch to check the effect.

Satisfied with the new look of things, he went back inside to re-arrange the rest of the store to ensure that its contents would please the ladies of the community. Before he could finish, his first customers strolled in, curious to see what was going on behind all the new frill in the front window.

Without a moment's hesitation, Cory welcomed the Simpson sisters into his store and guided them excitedly through the first few aisles, telling them all about the new items he'd brought in that morning and how much the talk of the town they each would be if they were the first to be seen in one of the lovely hats, or wearing a dress made of one of his new, fine, fabrics. The young women, greatly flattered by the uncommonly special attention Cory was giving them, agreed that the merchandise was lovely and each selected a few yards of one of the most expensive of the fabric's, and a hat and scarf they agreed would be most flattering with the new dresses they would make.

Accustomed to waiting for customers to approach him at the counter, he felt a little awkward to be shopping alongside the two, very flirtatious, young women, but he continued right along and even helped them select patterns for their dresses, before he found an opportunity to escape, and ran to hide behind his counter to await payment.

The sister's paid enough money between them to cover nearly all his cost for the extravagant new merchandise, and before they'd made it out the door they spotted the shoes he'd put in the front window and scurried back in again to pick a pair for each of them, and another pair for their mother. The balance they paid for the three sets of shoes made all of Cory's investment worthwhile, and he was smiling as happily as the sisters were by the time they waved back at him from his porch and rushed off down the street.

He beamed with pride as he filled, and refilled, his shelves throughout the day until, in the afternoon hours, he ran out of new merchandise to display. The Simpson sisters had spread the word that the supply store was open once again and it seemed that everyone in the community was determined to put in an appearance at his store, welcome him back, and buy at least one of the new items he'd brought in that morning. Though weary, Cory kept up a steady pace until closing time, assuring the ladies, who'd come too late in the day to find something they liked, that he'd bring more intriguing whatnots for them as early as the following morning. By the time he shut the doors on the heels of his last customer, he was exhausted and well pleased with himself. He counted the money in his drawer, dropped it into his safe, and dragged himself up to his apartment knowing he'd likely have as much to do tomorrow as he'd managed to get done that day. He ate his dinner on his bed, reliving his day, then set aside his dishes and fell asleep.

The following morning, Tyler watched from

his apartment window as Cory drove his truck out of town. He'd heard, from many of the townspeople the day before, confirmation that the supply store owner was as changed as the items he'd brought into his store, and that something peculiar lurked behind the well-thought-of businessman's eyes that made all who'd done spoken with him quite distressed.

He'd had a flurry of deliveries, interrupted on an irritating frequency, by townspeople who'd rushed down the paved road from the supply store, with bags and boxes in hand, to demand to hear what had happened to Cory and why he was behaving so strangely. He had answers for their questions, but his answers served only to startle and frighten them more.

Long past Tyler's normal closing hour, the townspeople had streamed steadily to him and he sent each away with a queer feeling. He told them with certainty that Cory had married, then walked out on Cindy Lou and had retaken his apartment above the supply store, but he hadn't been able to tell them what had prompted Doctor Miles to visit Cory's store in such a state that he and Cory should come to blows, and he couldn't, for the life of him, say what Mrs. Wilcox might have to do with any of it.

Some of the older ladies, upon hearing Mrs. Wilcox's name mentioned, unreasonably concluded that she must be the cause of all the upset. Amongst themselves they whispered that she must be up to her old tricks again, but that in going after Cindy Lou's brand new husband, Cory, or their stately town doctor, she'd gone too far and must be dealt with, right away.

After leaving Tyler's lumber mill, a handful of these ladies gathered in an overly-warm farmhouse kitchen to discuss what should be done about the former teacher they'd believed they were rid of, back when all of them had been relatively young. They discussed, at length, their each and every option, but admitted, to a woman, that none of them had the kind of physical strength to do what they ultimately wanted done.

Time was of the essence, they felt, and something must be done about the horrid Mrs. Wilcox quickly, or worse things would surely happen. The way Tyler had described the scene he'd walked in on, between Cory and Doctor Miles, at the supply store, convinced them that the good doctor had not gone mad, but rather; he'd gone to confront Cory with his affair with the very attractive, if older, Mrs. Wilcox and demand, with the backing of a high-powered rifle, that Cory get back to his home and new wife and do all that he could to make up to her for his dalliance. And, they assumed, Cory had attacked Doctor Miles for daring to challenge his decisions and the way he was treating his new young wife.

They shivered and shuddered at the thought of Tyler coming so close to losing his life in such a dreadful scene, and each imagined a unique set of horrors Cindy Lou must now be facing. And as the hour grew late, one of the ladies grew frustrated and announced that she would see to Mrs. Wilcox personally, provided the rest of them pledged never to say another word about the matter. The ladies agreed to hold their tongues, unhappily, and with that settled, their get-together came to an end, but upon their leaving, several of the ladies agreed they'd pay Cindy Lou a visit, soon, and reassure the young bride that things would be alright, that Mrs. Wilcox would soon be out of her husband's life, and their community, forever.

Cindy Lou crawled into the bed in Doctor Miles' upstairs guestroom, exhausted and full from the dinner the doctor and Jimmy had served her. She fell asleep almost immediately, completely unaware and unsuspecting of what the gentle-ladies of the community had concluded about her failed marriage to Cory, based on the scant but titillating information Tyler had provided them that day, or what one of them planned to do to Mrs. Wilcox.

In the night, she woke herself several times over, from nightmares of Esther. Images filled her mind, of men digging a deep hole next to her parents' graves and lowering her sister into it. By the wee hours of the morning she was wide awake and too miserable to try to get any sleep, so she slipped into a warm dressing gown and went downstairs quietly.

In the dark, she felt her way through the kitchen and started a roaring fire in the fireplace, then sat staring at the place on the floor in front of her where her father had died, letting tears stream unchecked down her face. She didn't want to recall the many hours and many days she'd spent here in Doctor Miles' home caring for her beloved father and trying to revive him, or the frustration and hardships she'd endured to keep Cory alive and bring him back to well, but the memories wouldn't leave her and the sadness of it all overwhelmed her until she could do little more than sob.

She wept for her father, and prayed that he'd been with her mother to welcome Esther to heaven. And while she didn't wish Cory any harm, she couldn't help but wonder why he'd been spared, instead of her father, her only living parent. She clenched her fists in her lap, and shook with anger that the one who'd been spared from the grave had caused her dear sister such anguish before she'd died so far away from her home.

    Blasted padded quietly into the kitchen and made her jump in surprise when he nudged her with his cold, wet nose. As soon as she realized it was him, she slipped from her chair to the floor beside him and threw her arms around him and continued to cry. The old dog sat firmly still next to her until she'd cried herself out and released him to lay down in front of the fire. With Blasted so close and the fire so warm and glowing, she soon felt comforted and sleepy, and dozed off where she sat on the floor, with her head upon her knees, until Doctor Miles woke her a short while later.

Chapter 13

Jimmy woke to the smell of coffee and sounds of movement in the kitchen, but his head hurt so badly from the position he'd slept in, he didn't make a move to get up. A long while later, Doctor Miles tapped on his door and came in with a glass of medicine and a tube, and helped him sit up against his pillows to drink it. He shut his eyes tightly after the doctor had taken the empty glass from him and waited to feel the throbbing in his jaw ebb away.

When the pain finally eased, he was anxious to get up. His room was cold and dark and Blasted was nowhere in it, but when he tried to lift his head from the pillow and swing his long legs off the side of the bed, his head swam and dizziness forced him to lay back. He heard a light tapping on his door and expected, with great relief, that Doctor Miles was returning - instead Cindy Lou walked in.

Not certain that she didn't intended to attack him again, his functioning eye opened even more widely and they quickly took on a threatening glint. To his surprise, she didn't come toward him. She went to is fireplace without a word and put together a raging fire for him. He followed her every movement with a cold stare, but couldn't make any move to take over her task and get her out of his room, fearful he'd fall or become violently ill from the exertion.

Finally, she turned and stared back at him for a moment, her hands busy with a towel between them, ridding themselves of ashes and soot. And when her eyes met his without flinching, he felt an unpleasant jolt pass through him and he made unhappy noises in his throat, increasingly loudly, until Doctor Miles appeared in the doorway. Alarmed to see Cindy Lou glaring at his prone, helpless, patient, he ordered her out of the room and rushed to Jimmy's bedside.

Cindy Lou burst out angrily, defensively telling him she'd only done as he'd asked and started a fire in Jimmy's room, but Doctor Miles ignored her protesting and pointed a finger at the open doorway until she gave up in frustration and stomped out through it, then he began to assess Jimmy's condition and try to decipher what the young man was trying to tell him as he adjusted the bandages that held his jaw shut and in place.

Cindy Lou flounced down the short hallway, back to Blasted, in the kitchen and busied herself furiously, fixing her companion a dish of food. She watched him clean out the deep bowl efficiently with his wide tongue, patting his back absently while she waited for Doctor Miles to return, planning to continue to defend herself when he did.

By the time he finally did rejoin her in the kitchen, she had a well-rehearsed speech prepared for him, but the expression of concern that creased his brow took her aback and she instead demanded to know what was wrong. He shook his head as he confessed he wasn't certain, but that it appeared that Jimmy had developed an infection. All thoughts of anger left Cindy Lou immediately and, despite her hatred for his patient, she asked the doctor what they should do?

Doctor Miles gave her instructions, then left her to decide whether she was willing to do what was necessary to save Jimmy. She didn't stop to consider, even for a moment, what a cruel position she was in now; burdened to help save the life of her father's killer. She started water boiling on the stove top and returned, resolutely, to Jimmy's room where, despite the hostility she could feel from him, she stood by his bedside and spoke to him.

As quickly as she could, though her voice faltered and her hands started shaking, she explained what the doctor had told her, and what he would need to do to cooperate with her, to get rid of the infection that might otherwise kill him. When she'd finished speaking she asked him to squeeze her hand if he understood and placed her small hand next to his on the bed.

Jimmy looked Cindy Lou in the eye and took her hand in his much larger, more calloused, one and squeezed until tears came to her eyes. She tore her hand free with a gasp and fled the room, searching the hall and office to tell Doctor Miles that, though she was willing to do what he'd asked her to do, Jimmy had made it clear that he would not let her.

Doctor Miles was furious when Cindy Lou told him what his patient had done. He left her to calm herself in the kitchen while he went to the hospital room to set Jimmy straight on the way things were going to be around there. He marched into the hospital room and leaned over the bed until his face was only inches from Jimmy's, and hissed violent threats he felt would certainly bring this patient into line.

When he'd finished, Jimmy only stared up at him, openly defiant. He shook his head in disgust, seeing he'd not only not gotten through to the desperately ill young man, but had now made him even more angry and mistrustful. He cursed Jimmy for not understanding how serious his condition was and appreciating that Cindy Lou was actually willing her help him survive, but Jimmy's expression remained fixed and foreboding.

In the kitchen, Cindy Lou took several deep breaths to stop herself from shaking and fight the anger welling up inside her. Only the knowledge that the man who'd just injured her might possibly die from infection if she didn't help take care of him, prevented her from gathering her things and leaving for the solitude and safety of her own home, straight away. She could not imagine allowing anyone, even Jimmy, to die, though, so she went back to carrying out the instructions she'd been given, and set about cleaning Jimmy's drinking tube and some dishes Doctor Miles had said he would be needing.

She filled a cup with the very hot water and took it, with the sterile tube, back down the short hallway into Jimmy's room; thinking to herself how odd it felt to be, yet again, caring for a desperately ill man, though this one was much younger, who rather than appreciating and welcoming her efforts, chose to fight her and hurt her in any way he could. This time, she consoled herself, as soon as this patient was well, she'd have nothing further to do with him.

Morning came too quickly for Mrs. Wilcox, and with it came a very distressing visit from one of Farmersville's most impressive ladies.

She'd been up and about and had finished her morning tea by the time Mrs. Sylvester had rapped crisply on her front door. She'd never been called on at her home by anyone, save Ralphie, and only him when she'd received a rare piece of mail. She wasn't dressed for company and had not bothered to fix her face or hair yet, but the persistence of the fine lady on her doorstep persuaded her to receive her as a guest, anyway.

Mrs. Sylvester had brushed past her without waiting for an invitation and, with an air of self-righteous purpose, marched into her living room and perched primly on a chair. She'd patted Mrs. Wilcox's sofa with her gloves and cleared her throat to interrupt her surprised excuses and apologies for her appearance.

Mrs. Wilcox fell silent on cue, and sat down stiffly on a chair opposite the woman.

Clearly not wishing to engage her in conversation, Mrs. Sylvester had come right out with her reason for dropping by: She was there, she announced, to make clear to her that, after breaking up Cindy Lou's marriage, she was unwanted and unwelcome in Farmersville. And further, that if she dared show her face in town again, she'd regret it; intimating with a wave of her hand that something dreadful would happen to Mrs. Wilcox's very home, as she spoke.

Without allowing for even a word in self-defense or explanation, Mrs. Sylvester rose and marched quickly out of the house. She was well out of the yard and moving down the dirt road toward Farmersville by the time Mrs. Wilcox recovered from the shocking threat sufficiently to run to the door; thinking to call out to her, to demand that she return so she could say a few words, herself. She didn't call out, however, when she noting how much distance the other woman had already put between them.

She slammed her front door and stomped to her bathroom, yanked a brush through her hair until her head was sore, then powdered her face and finished dressing as if she were preparing for the type of company she'd just seen leaving. Once she had made herself quite presentable, she didn't know what to do with herself, however, so she paced her small house, fuming, telling the walls all the things she'd been robbed of the opportunity to say to the woman.

She was mystified, and angrier than she'd been in many years to have such a haughty woman from such a horrid community dare to accuse her of interfering with Cindy Lou's marriage. The insinuation that she'd compromised Cory the, years younger than her, supply store owner outraged her even more and made her certain beyond all reason that she'd rip all the hair out of Mrs. Sylvester's very lovely head if she ever dared to come near her again. Finally, she began to tremble, as the seriousness of the woman's threats sank in; the idea that someone might destroy her lovely home frightened her to the core.

For the remainder of the day, she found herself moving in circles, unable to concentrate on any task she put herself to. A part of her was defiant, almost to the point of carrying her directly into town to prove to herself that no one would dare harm her, but another, bigger, part of her remembered every moment of the humiliating beating she'd survived on that main road through Farmersville, so many years before, when Darla Mae had caught her making love to her husband in their barn. The wounds the Farmersville women had inflicted on her had healed, but enough scars remained that she'd never forget what they'd done to her.

She told herself, through tears, that the things she'd done with those women's husbands had been their fault as much as hers, and that the accusations Mrs. Sylvester had made against her that day were utterly false and outrageous. To accuse her of having been found with Cory the way she'd been caught so many years before, with other men, was unfair after all these years. She wished with all her heart that the Sylvester woman would drop dead before she reached home for doing such a thing to her.

As for returning, in her lifetime, to Farmersville, she had had no intention whatsoever. The way Doctor Miles had treated her, and worse treatment from Cindy Lou, compounded by Esther's unexpected death, had already convinced her that the entire community had lost its collective mind. Particularly outraged to be treated this way after all she'd done to help Esther and Cindy Lou, the two girls who she felt she might consider her own daughters, she vowed that, threat or no threat, no one in Farmersville would ever be lucky enough to see her again.

Cory returned to his supply store with another truckload of new items to sell. He was in high spirits and hoped this day would bring him as much, if not more, in the way of business, than the day before. He unloaded everything quickly and opened the store, then went about creating entirely new displays with the colorful new merchandise.

Ralphie was the first person to come through the door, and Cory approached him with the same feverishly bright-eyed expression he'd startled shoppers with the day before, rapidly filling the boy in on all the new wares he had to offer. He didn't notice Ralphie's surprised expression, nor that the boy seemed really too anxious to purchase something, anything, and get out of the store.

When the boy was gone, Cory returned his focus to the new merchandise, not noticing that Pastor Franklin had come in.

Pastor Franklin had prepared Esther's body

for burial, fully expecting to receive words of instruction from one of her sisters, or their husbands, for her funeral service. After too much time had passed for him to excuse, he'd gone out to Cindy Lou's house to find out what was causing the delay. Finding no one at Cindy Lou's house to let him in, he'd driven into town to ask Tyler of her whereabouts, but had stopped short of the lumber mill when he'd seen Ralphie scurrying out of Cory's supply store.

He'd left his car where he'd stopped it, across from the newly re-opened supply store and, despite his surprise at seeing it so, had gone right in to have a word with Cory. Surely he would know when Cindy Lou would want to have her sister's service, he thought, and he might even be able to explain why no one had been around to see him since Esther's body had been so unceremoniously, and unexpectedly, delivered to his house.

When Cory turned around, and jumped in surprise to see him, Pastor Franklin quickly stepped forward and shook his hand, offering condolences as he did. When his eyes met Cory's, however, the next words he'd thought to speak died in his throat. Something was terribly wrong in Cory's eyes, and the icy-handed touch of the store owner's hand made him take a step backward and examine Cory more critically.

While he stood, dumbstruck, Cory greeted him and excitedly launched into telling him, oblivious to his discomfort, about all the new merchandise he'd brought in, trying to show him each new item he was positioning on the shelves nearest the door. Finally, he cut through Cory's chatter and asked him, with irritation clearly marking his words, what he meant by behaving this way and leaving him hanging about what he should do with Esther's body. He wished he hadn't done so, the instant he finished.

Confusion filled Cory's eyes and Pastor Franklin hastened to explain himself, but no amount of rewording seemed to be having any clarifying effect on Cory; he stood staring at the pastor for a moment, then demanded to know why he would be asking such things of him. Pastor Franklin was at a loss to explain himself. A lady entered the store, and he stared on in amazement as Cory reverted to his earlier, peculiar, persona, leaving him with jaw hanging in disbelief. Cory whisked the new customer around in much the same way, and with nearly identical chatter, as he had with him just moments before.

It seemed Cory genuinely hadn't known why he should be asked to give instructions for his sister-in-law's funeral. It was also becoming quite clear to him that Cory didn't seem to realize that he was still standing there. After another moment of confused hesitation, fully red in the face, he turned on his heel and left the store.

He walked first toward his car, instinctively trying to leave town, but caught himself before he could get in and turned instead toward the post office, thinking Ralphie might be able to explain Cory's odd behavior, or tell him where he could find Cindy Lou. He tried the post office door, but it was locked and a hand-scrawled sign informed him that Ralphie had gone out to make his deliveries for the day, so he forced his feet to take him back past Cory's supply store, to Tyler's lumber mill, where he felt certain he would be told just what was going on.

Tyler hem-hawed around a bit longer than usual in the office before he greeted Pastor Franklin, and seemed wary and hesitant to tell him what he was asking to know. He stalled until Pastor Franklin laid it clear to him that Esther's remains could not forever lie, without proper ceremony, in his shed.

Tyler gasped and turned pale. He scrambled to Pastor Franklin's side and told him everything he knew, begging him to return to Cory at once and, with him, demand explanations the entire town would be eager to hear. As he spoke, he shouldered the reluctant pastor out into the street once more, and they made their way back to Cory's store.

Once inside, he stepped to the side and pressed Pastor Franklin toward Cory, urgently, and for a second time, Pastor Franklin found himself demanding funeral instructions from a man who seemed more confused than himself. This time, however, when Cory turned to face him, there was neither a trace of familiarity, nor sanity, in the man's eyes.

Pastor Franklin froze in his tracks, all thought fleeing from his head, and while Tyler looked on in a state of high anxiety himself, he and Cory stared stupidly at each other struggling to find words to say, and a route of escape. Cory's eyes blazed when he finally spoke. He pointed toward the door and ordered the two townsmen out.

They had gone mad, Cory swore, and he could not abide having them destroy the possibility of any further sales that day with their hostile and accusatory presence. He'd not tolerate the coward hovering in the corner of his storefront any more than the crazed man of the cloth who'd, twice now, tried to make him accountable for funeral arrangements for one of Old Bill's daughters. He'd not be pressured to take on another's rightful responsibilities. He'd not raise a hand to either of them, but he'd see them both out of his store for good, right then, and hear no excuses as he did!

He marched forward and Pastor Franklin marched backward in step with him, fearing he'd collide with Tyler, who must certainly still be behind him, but he was unwilling to tear his eyes from Cory's to assure himself of a clear path of retreat. He needn't have worried for Tyler's position in this matter, however, as Tyler was, though indeed behind him, well clear of Cory's store by then; taking himself straight away to the safety of his lumber mill.

Fearing the worst from Cory, Pastor Franklin finally abandoned all reason and turned and ran blindly for his car in the street, afraid, like he'd never felt cause to be before, of the supply store owner. Unthinking, he got himself into his car and drove away in the direction his car was facing, no matter that his home was in the other direction entirely.

As he sped off the paved road and put his tires into the well-worn ruts on the dirt road, he couldn't force himself to even look back to see whether or not Cory was pursuing him. He didn't care. He was leaving Farmersville either way. To look back now, he feared, would be to scorn fate.

Cory did not give chase. He was satisfied seeing the two men leaving. He returned, almost immediately, to his work and the musing he'd been doing before Pastor Franklin's return; wondering why the pastor had insisted, twice now, that he give him instructions concerning Esther's burial. He'd had no idea that the girl was even dead, he fumed. The entire town, he declared aloud, had gone decidedly mad.

In two days' time, he'd been accosted by not two, but three of the town's most respectable men, men he'd once considered friends, and he'd been accused of deeds he felt all certainty he'd had no involvement in, nor responsibility for. How they could make such accusations and attacks against him was baffling to him, and made him hesitant to even keep his store open for the remainder of the day for fear that one, or all, of them might return, but his determination to re-open his store and make it an even better success than before resurfaced before he could shut the doors. He renewed his resolve to let nothing stand in his way, or inhibit his new business plans.

      Pastor Franklin's car roared down the dirt road in the direction of Doctor Miles' house, but only when his sensibilities and a bit of calm returned, did he come to realize that the house he was rapidly approaching was not his own. Trembling as he was, he made himself turn his car into Doctor Miles' side yard, to sit for a moment and collect his thoughts.

Chapter 14

Doctor Miles looked up from his book, hearing the deep roar of a car motor. It was Pastor Franklin's car, he knew, by the time it came close enough for him to see it out in front of his house. Pastor Franklin's visits were rare enough to evoke some level of alarm in the good doctor. By the time the car turned fully into the side yard, he was on his feet, heading for the door. He walked out to the pastor's car briskly, fearing the delivery of another patient to his already quite filled home, but as he neared the car and noted no passengers in it, he grew concerned that some illness had befallen the pastor himself. He called for Cindy Lou to come and help him, then opened the pastor's car door and drug the man out, demanding to know what was the matter.

    Cindy Lou rushed to take the pastor's arm and helped Doctor Miles guide him toward the house, and when they'd settled him onto a chair in front of the kitchen fire, the pastor was still rambling about her sister's body, and her husband's bizarre treatment of him. She slumped into a chair with tears overwhelming her sight, to hear her dear sister spoken of, and worse, hearing details of how her body had been delivered to the pastor's home.

    Pastor Franklin righted himself with a start and shut his mouth quite suddenly when Doctor Miles touched his shoulder and pointed at Cindy Lou. Realizing at once that he'd been in her presence, telling Doctor Miles all that had happened and all that he knew, he regained his composure and, with great shame, begged the girl to forgive him; Cindy Lou could not respond.

Hearing all the commotion, Jimmy quickly followed Blasted from his hospital room and discovered Cindy Lou crying in a chair at the table. Though his fever was hot and his head swam, he fought back a body-wracking chill and once again knelt beside the girl and tried to make comforting noises to her.

Pastor Franklin stopped, shocked at the sight of Jimmy Fenton, with his head wrapped tightly in gauze and only one steel-blue eye visible under it, stumbling down the short hallway toward Cindy Lou. He looked in horror to Doctor Miles, expecting him to intervene and protect the girl, but the doctor held a finger to his lips and motioned for him to follow as he stepped quickly and silently past Jimmy and Cindy Lou, toward the his office.

Pastor Franklin followed, unable to tear his eyes from Jimmy until he reached the hall and forced himself to turn and enter Doctor Miles' office. Once in the small room, he turned again to stare back at the shocking scene playing out in the kitchen, until Doctor Miles shut the door and pointed him to a chair.

Doctor Miles sat down behind his wide desk and waited for him to process what he'd just seen and find the words he wanted to use to express his conclusions. At length, the pastor finally burst from curiosity, into a full barrage of questions.

How had Jimmy come to be re-injured? He wanted to know, and how could the good doctor allow the murderer to come so close to the daughter of his victim? What on earth was he thinking? The pastor demanded, jumping from his chair to pace the room.

Doctor Miles answered all that Pastor Franklin demanded as best he could, but the pastor shook his head in disbelief throughout his explanations, and railed at the very idea of allowing such a volatile, dangerous man so much as a moment's opportunity to harm Cindy Lou further, accusing him of madness, not unlike the madness he'd seen in Cory's eyes just a few minutes before.

Doctor Miles endured the challenges without comment, but when the pastor declared his intention to put a stop to what was happening in the kitchen, and moved toward the office door, he crossed the room swiftly and barred access to it with his body. He'd made his own observations and evaluations and it was his own judgment on which he would rely, not that of a very harassed and hysterical minister. Pastor Franklin backed away and fell into a chair, deflated, unwilling to create more trouble for himself by further angering the good doctor.

When he felt sure the pastor was convinced not to pursue his ideas of rousting Jimmy from his house, Doctor Miles returned to his seat behind the desk, and urged the man to calm himself and explain to him what had happened in town that had so convinced him that Cory was crazy.

Pastor Franklin stared at him across the wide desk, expressionless for a moment. Had this doctor no sound reason? That he should have chosen to, rather than kill, take the murderous Fenton boy into his home, had seemed the ultimate in compassion, he'd thought, but to permit Cindy Lou to believe herself safe from such a monster, enough to be under the same roof, regardless of her plight, was sheer stupidity!

He would not quarrel with the good doctor, he resolved to himself, but he'd not leave Cindy Lou behind when he departed either. He had a home and a good wife in it, to provide shelter and comfort for the girl, and in his home she'd deal no more with the man who'd killed her father.

    Feeling quite settled on this, he proceeded to confide in Doctor Miles his version of what had just taken place in town; explaining that he'd merely gone to Cory for instructions for Esther's burial and describing, in elaborate and terrifying detail, the reaction he'd been met with. Doctor Miles heard him out from the edge of his seat, then alarmed the man further; relating his most recent encounter with Cindy Lou's new husband. The two quickly lost themselves trying to find some way to explain away the terrible change they'd both seen in Cory.

    While they talked, Cindy Lou was beginning to recover from the shock of Pastor Franklin's outburst, in the kitchen, and realized who was with her, holding her hand.

    She turned her eyes from the fireplace when she felt her hand being lifted into another's and, at first, assumed it was Doctor Miles, or the pastor, offering comfort, then she saw Jimmy's calloused hands and jerked free. She moved away from him, startled; knowing only that he'd not been there a moment before, where Pastor Franklin had been. She was exceedingly disturbed to find herself alone, with him by her side.

    It took a moment for her to realize what seemed so wrong with Jimmy's presence in the kitchen; he was supposed to be in the bed, in the hospital room, resting while his body fought off the infection, she finally realized. She rushed from the kitchen, calling for Doctor Miles, and grabbed a blanket from the bed in Jimmy's room. She negotiated the short hallway with Doctor Miles and

Pastor Franklin, getting back to Jimmy before them, somehow, to wrap the blanket around him.

Doctor Miles and the pastor quickly took over and whisked the young man away to his room, with Cindy Lou and Blasted on their heels. When they'd gotten Jimmy back into his bed, Blasted pushed his way between them and took up his position on the bed beside his patient, and no amount of ordering, coaxing, or outright shoving, would convince him to come away from Jimmy. When he bared his teeth at the pastor and his owner, at last, Cindy Lou begged the men to leave the great beast be, and go find more blankets to heap on Jimmy.

Doctor Miles started to argue against Cindy Lou's aggressive pleas, but Pastor Franklin, taking restock of his opinion, tugged the doctor out of the hospital room by the sleeve, reminding him as he did so, that he'd been the one who'd insisted that Cindy Lou was a more than competent nursemaid to the very sick young man. Doctor Miles harrumphed and jerked free of the pastor, and the two men carried out the girl's orders, arguing the whole way.

When they returned, with several blankets each, Doctor Miles insisted on taking charge again. He sent Cindy Lou to the kitchen for a bowl of cold water and a towel, while the two men piled blankets over Jimmy and his canine protector. He gave Jimmy a thorough examination, and when Cindy Lou returned, he assured her that everything would be alright, and advised the pastor to take her to the kitchen so they could speak privately about what Cindy Lou wished for Esther's burial. Cindy Lou didn't resist Pastor Franklin's guiding hand on her shoulder.

Once in the kitchen, Pastor Franklin sat at the table, close to the fire, while Cindy Lou made coffee and asked him her questions about Esther. He told her that once Doctor Miles had seen to her sister's examination, he could hold a service for Esther and have her buried with her parents.

She agreed, rather distantly, to all the pastor said, but when he turned the subject to her leaving with him, to stay in his home until she felt she was able to return to her own, her demeanor changed and she became quite engaged with telling the pastor how thoughtful her decision to return to Doctor Miles' home, especially with Jimmy Fenton's presence, had been.

By the time Pastor Franklin took his leave of Doctor Miles home, just over an hour later, he was most thoroughly convinced that Cindy Lou was either the most gracious young woman he'd ever before seen, or that her mind was breaking down under the tremendous stress of the past few weeks. He felt as confident as Doctor Miles had been that he wouldn't ever fully understand the dynamics between Jimmy and Cindy Lou, but saw that indeed some chemistry existed, of such an apparently powerful nature that nothing could convince one not to show compassion for the other.

He shook his head when he thought of it as he drove back through town toward his home, and passed Cory's supply store once more, slowly, staring through the front window glass at the display Cory had made since he'd been there earlier. When he came to the post office, a light shining from within caught his eye. He stopped his car and went inside to talk to Ralphie.

Ralphie was just putting on his coat to leave when he went in. Despite the boy explaining that it was well past time for him to be going home, he insisted that he stay and talk with him, so, unhappily,

Ralphie invited him into the back office and perched on the side of the desk, impatient to lock up for the night.

Pastor Franklin asked him, straight away, if he'd indeed been notified of Esther's death, as the two men who'd brought her body to him had claimed and if he had, why had he not told Cindy Lou as was expected of him; he was the current Post Master, after all.

Ralphie quickly defended himself and told him how Cory had come upon him in the road, on his way to deliver the terrible message, and driven him back to town, promising he'd break the news to his new wife, himself. He was distraught when the pastor explained that the message had not been delivered as promised, and he demanded to know what he was to do; should he go directly to Cindy Lou's home that evening and tell her of her sister's death? How was he to explain the delay? Ralphie wanted to know.

Pastor Franklin assured him that no such thing was necessary, that Cindy Lou had been made aware, quite accidentally, by Mrs. Wilcox and Doctor Miles, following his seeing Mrs. Wilcox and sharing the sad news with her. Ralphie was visibly weak with relief. Realizing how distressing the entire situation was to the boy, Pastor Franklin quickly stood and excused himself so he could close up the post office and go home.

All the way out the door, he offered the boy reassurances that no one blamed him in the least for the delay, and seeing that this lifted the boy's spirit's a little, he offered to drive him home, but Ralphie refused. As he locked up the post office, he told the pastor he'd send condolences to Sarah, and they parted company; Ralphie to walk home and the pastor to drive himself home to his wife, Millie, who was ready and waiting for him.

Millie Franklin was standing in the doorway, when her husband returned in his car. She glowered at him, sidestepping his kiss, and crossing her arms boldly when he'd taken off his coat and turned a full circle in their kitchen, searching for his dinner plate; which lay in tiny, food-encrusted, pieces by her side, in the trash can.

Pastor Franklin took in the vision of his angry wife, finally, and followed her eyes to the trash can, before nodding unhappily. Understanding immediately where he would find his dinner plate, he sighed and sat down to explain himself, knowing that if he could make her understand what he'd been through and seen that day, quickly, she might show him a little mercy, just this once, and not make him try to sleep through the night without any dinner.

It took him handing over each of the smallest details of his day, and a good many well-placed sighs, to convince Millie to fire up her stove once more, so late in the evening, and make him another plate of food. He devoured two heaping plates of her meatloaf and potatoes, while she put a multitude of unanswerable questions to him.

Between mouthfuls, he assured her that he'd told her all that he could think to know of the situations he'd encountered that day and, in order to pry a piece of pie out of her kitchen window for his dessert, he heaped lavish compliments on her appearance and fine cooking, and promised that he'd not ever make himself so late for dinner with her, ever again. He went to sleep at last, full, but still confounded over the goings on in town, in the guest bedroom.

Millie hadn't felt quite forgiving enough,

despite her husband's harassed day, to overlook his being late to dinner, again. While he snored in the next room, she sat up in her bed, for many hours, applying herself to figuring out what had brought about all the strange happenings in Farmersville, and to its people. She was up well before him, and waiting for him in her kitchen, ready to quiz him all over again, the following morning.

Pastor Franklin refused to repeat all that he'd told her the night before, and assured her that he had come up with no answers in his sleep. He reminded her that Doctor Miles would come by later in the morning to examine Esther's remains, while he made his way to all the neighbors Cindy Lou had specified, to announce Esther's funeral service, to be held the following day. He told her she'd have to prepare the chapel, and make the notice of Esther's death to post in town that afternoon, then leave him alone so he could prepare his service. The day would be difficult, and he was as weary as his wife, but the delay had been long already and Cindy Lou, and the community, needed the closure only a service and burial would give.

Sarah and Lee received notice in their mailbox, that Esther's funeral service was to be the following afternoon, and quite an unpleasant fight between them quickly followed: Sarah collapsed, overcome with grief, but when Lee tried to console her, she lashed out bitterly against him, then she informed him that she'd changed her mind and demanded that he take her to Farmersville so she could be there to see her sister buried.

Lee was furious. He'd done all he could to distract his wife from her mourning and had thought the matter of Esther's funeral was settled, but his peace of mind, over the money secreted in his safe, was shattering. Sarah was determined, now, to see her sister buried, but if he gave in to her demands, he would be forced to deal with Cindy Lou's husband. He was very sure he didn't want to give up all that money from Johnny's family, but not quite as sure that he was ready to live with the consequences, so the last place he wanted to go was Farmersville.

It had been nearly a full week since they'd received word of Esther's body being discovered. They'd agreed, or so Lee had thought, that they should let Cindy Lou and her husband take care of all the arrangements and the funeral, that they would wait for Cindy Lou to come to them when it was all over, and tell them how everything had gone, in order that their poverty didn't become an issue between Sarah and her remaining sister.

She had agreed that they couldn't afford to go, he reminded her; she'd even admitted that Esther had not been a good sister to her, and was owed nothing. Why, so suddenly, had she changed her mind? How could she be angry with him? He demanded.

He had still not told her about the money Cory had given him for Esther's care and he dare not mention it now, or ever let her discover it, now that attending Esther's funeral had become such an issue. He'd loosened the purse strings a little, since hearing of Esther's death, and Sarah had seemed to be grateful for it, but there was no way he was spending any of it to go to Farmersville.

Even seeing his wife's state of mind didn't cause Lee to waver. He had already decided what would be best. After all, what good could come from his wife seeing her wretched sister buried. She would only come away more bitter that he'd not been able to afford to take her for her father's funeral, if she would come away at all from her childhood home again. He'd not risk losing her to her father's home and her one remaining sister; he needed her more than they did. Surely she would see reason, he thought. But she would not. Despite his best arguments, she insisted that he go and find a car that evening and have it ready to leave in the morning.

He slammed the front door on his way out and slunk down the dirt road away from his house, swearing he'd stay out late enough to make Sarah worry for his safety, but return on foot. He'd rather live with her fury for a few days, than give up the small fortune in his safe for the sake of seeing Esther be buried.

While Sarah packed her bags to return to Farmersville the following morning, and Lee sat in a distant field biding his time til the sun went down.

Chapter 15

Cindy Lou told Doctor Miles what Pastor Franklin needed him to do the following morning, in order to have a proper death certificate for her sister, while they ate their dinner in front of the fireplace in the kitchen. They talked about what Esther's funeral service would be like, and agreed that she should stay with Jimmy until he returned from the pastor's house, then both fell silent, each contemplating what they must do the next day.

When their plates were empty and she had finished tidying the kitchen and settled herself at the table with her coffee again, Cindy Lou asked if she could take his car, after he returned the next day from examining Esther's body, to drive out to Sarah's farm and bring her back for the funeral. He told her "no!" but she pleaded with him, that her sister and her husband would no doubt know, by now, of Esther's death, but didn't have a car or money to borrow one and put gas in it for such a trip. She reminded him, when he gave her a grave look, that Sarah had not been able to come to their father's funeral, and put it to him plainly, that she would think very poorly of him if he turned down such a reasonable request after all she'd been through, and done for him.

Finally, he relented and promised he'd consider her request overnight and give her an answer in the morning. It was after all, he reminded her, very important for a doctor to have his car in case someone needed him. If anything should happen to it, the community would suffer a great deal.

Well after dark, Sarah sat on a small stool near her front door, wringing her hands with worry. Lee was to have been back already, unless he'd not been able to borrow a car and had had to walk home, or if something terrible had happened to him.

She'd searched the road for any sign of him from the front porch, until the bitter wind had driven her back inside. All she could do was wait and pray that he'd come home soon.

Lee had left in such a fury, he hadn't put on his heaviest coat, or his warmest boots, and as he sat in a distant field, with the wind growing colder by the minute, he began having feelings of guilt over what he'd done. For a long while, he rationalized to himself that he was doing what was best for his family, but his conscience bothered him still. Several times, he'd jumped to his feet to truly go and find a car to borrow, but each time the thought of having to admit that he had the money to put gas in it, to Sarah, stopped him in his tracks. He knew, if he gave in to his wife's tears, he'd be in quite a spot.

The clock chimed midnight and there was still no sign of Lee. Sarah wailed, pacing in front of the door, throwing it wide at every sound, then slamming it against the cold night air, disappointed. As the hours ticked by, she grew weary from the stress of it all and crumpled to the floor next to the door, and cried herself to sleep.

Around four in the morning, Lee forced his frozen fingers to turn the knob on his front door. He stepped over the threshold and stumbled over Sarah. Falling to the floor beside her, he held her tightly for warmth, and told her all the lies he'd come up with to explain not having returned with any borrowed car, through chattering teeth.

Sarah was so relieved that he was back, and safe, she begged him to forgive her for sending him out like that. She pushed the door shut and struggled to get herself and her and him off the floor and upstairs to their bedroom. She tugged off his boots and clothes while he told her stories of rejection upon rejection, and he damned the whole selfish community as she tucked blankets and bedcovers around him and got into bed beside him, snuggling close to help him get warm.

Several hours later, they woke to someone banging on their front door.

Sarah urged Lee to stay under the covers and rest, while she put on a warm robe, and padded down the stairs. Blinded by daylight when she opened the door, she stumbled backward and dragged Cindy Lou with her through the doorway, and slammed the door, throwing them into darkness she couldn't see through any better.

Cindy Lou grabbed Sarah's arms to steady her until she could focus, and the two hugged. They went to Sarah's kitchen, and when Cindy Lou had a cup of coffee in her chilly hands, she explained how she'd come to be there and why. Sarah was so relieved she began to cry, and told Cindy Lou how hard Lee had tried to find a car to borrow.

Lee struggled into his clothes, noting the lateness of the hour, and went down to see who'd come by to pay them a visit. As he passed by the front window at the bottom of the stairs, however, his heart skipped a beat. He couldn't believe his eyes, or his bad luck. Someone with a car had come to call and he could only hope no one he'd mentioned having visited the night before had bought a new car, or he'd be in real trouble. He made himself walk into the kitchen, but nearly cursed out loud when he saw Cindy Lou sitting at the table. This was even worse, he thought; if Cory had driven Cindy Lou over, then he must certainly be waiting for him in his den, waiting to demand that he return the money he'd given him.

He said hello to his young sister-in-law, and ask where her husband was hiding. All his efforts the night before, he swore in his head, were wasted. He got himself a cup of coffee and nearly burned himself badly when she claimed she did not know, and explained that she'd driven out to their farm by herself to take them to Esther's funeral.

Lee was flabbergasted. He choked on his next, more cautious sip and sputtered apologies to his wife and her sister.

Hearing her husband's coughing fit, Sarah immediately and guiltily assumed that he had become sick after the long night out in the cold. She ordered him back up to bed, despite his protests, and took his coffee cup away from him. Cindy Lou agreed with her sister's diagnosis, that he looked very pale, and he was helpless but to throw up his hands in defeat, and return to bed.

Sarah and Cindy Lou followed him upstairs, insisting that he was ill, but Lee only stopped his protestations of perfect health when Sarah told her sister that he could not possibly go with them, in this condition, to Farmersville. Then he realized that this was the solution for the spot he was in, and began a new, entirely faked, coughing fit, to further his wife's assertion. His acting sealed his fate, as far as the sisters were concerned and, without further arguments, Lee got back into bed, sick.

When Sarah and Cindy Lou finally left him

tucked under many a warm blanket, to rest and recuperate, a short while later, he smiled wickedly to himself and rolled over to get some more, much needed, sleep. He'd not have to deal with any trip to Farmersville, nor any run-in with Cindy Lou's new husband after all. Because he'd staged the brilliant ruse the night before, he had his wife's sympathy, all that money, and wouldn't have to suffer through a moment of anyone's depressing funeral.

Cindy Lou and Sarah argued for a while, in the kitchen, over whether or not Sarah should go with Cindy Lou, or should she stay home and miss yet another family funeral, to nurse her husband back to health. Finally, Sarah agreed that she'd only go with Cindy Lou if Lee didn't have a fever, and if Cindy Lou would promise she'd drive her all the way back, as soon as Esther had been buried.

Cindy Lou promised, hoping against all hope that Doctor Miles would agree to let her drive his car so late at night, and the two tiptoed upstairs, once again. Lee was sleeping soundly.

Sarah checked her husband's forehead and felt no heat, so she woke him gently and asked if he felt well enough to be left alone long enough for her to go to her sister's funeral and return. He feigned doziness to cover himself while he mulled over the question. He knew that if he let her go, Cory might demand the money from her, and cause him not only his wife's trust and affection, but the money as well, so he moaned a miserable moan he felt sure would impress her, then whispered that she should go; he could take care of himself. Sarah teared up immediately and looked pleadingly at Cindy Lou.

Lee kept his eyes tightly shut and rubbed his temple, grimacing slightly as if he was in pain. Sarah caught sight of his display and wiped the tears from her eyes resolutely, telling Cindy Lou, as she did, that she could not go. The sisters agreed that after he had done so much to try to find a way to get Sarah home for Esther's funeral, and become so sick because of it, it wouldn't be decent or fair for Sarah to leave him to fend for himself, even for a short while.

After Cindy Lou drove away, Sarah returned to her, once again sleeping, husband and sobbed into her pillow. Lee knew nothing of her tears; he slept soundly, relaxed, now that he felt sure he'd at least postponed having to give back, or even admit to having, all that money. A smile crept over his face as he dreamed about the many acres of land he would buy with it, but Sarah was too distraught to notice.

Cindy Lou pulled Doctor Miles' car back into his barn a few hours later. Her eyes were red-rimmed from all her crying on the drive home. Though she'd not ever confess it to Doctor Miles, she'd had to stop the car twice from going into the ditches along the roadside, her tears had been so many. She dreaded having to explain why Sarah and her husband weren't with her, as she'd planned, because she knew she'd cry all over again when she explained how her sister's husband had come to be so ill. She whispered a prayer for Lee as she got out of the car and made her way into the house.

Even Blasted, she noticed, seemed to know she shouldn't have come back alone. When he met her at the door, he peered around her, whining as if he expected to find someone behind her. A moment later, Jimmy came in and Blasted followed him, tail wagging, through the kitchen, down the short hall and into the hospital room. Jimmy had only nodded as he'd passed by her.

The doctor seemed quite relieved to see her back. He accepted her being alone with sympathy, and patted her on the shoulder supportively as he invited her to sit with him.

She sat and stared into the fireplace while he poured them coffee, then he returned to sit with her looking as if he meant to say something important. Instead got back to his feet and crossed the kitchen, and moved her coat to a different peg than the one she'd chosen, kicking her discarded boots out of the doorway, then he sat back down with a grunt.

They sipped their coffee silently for a moment longer, then he glanced furtively down the short hallway toward Jimmy's room and, satisfied that Jimmy couldn't hear him, he asked Cindy Lou if she'd seen him when she'd driven up. She shook her head "no", so he explained to her rather hurriedly, that nearly two hours after she'd gone, while he'd been sleeping, Jimmy's fever had broken. A short while later, he'd gotten up and searched the house for her. When he had explained where she'd gone, he said, Jimmy had returned to his room and sat staring out at the road from his window, then about ten minutes before she returned, he had walked out of the house and seemed to be waiting for her in the side yard.

Cindy Lou assured the doctor that she had not seen Jimmy until he'd come through the door behind her, but since he'd only nodded to her as he'd gone by, she didn't believe what Doctor Miles had observed was of any importance to her.

Doctor Miles shook his head in frustration, realizing the girl didn't understand, or didn't want to understand, the point he was making. He felt bad, suddenly, for having mentioned any of it to her while she was dealing with so much already. He'd gotten excited to learn something new about his patient, he chastised himself; he'd forgotten how meaningless such a discovery would be, to Cindy Lou in particular. He promised himself he'd not forget himself again, as she got up and started making dinner.

While she was busy in the kitchen, he stepped quietly down the hall to Jimmy's door to see what he was doing. Jimmy was in his bed, with Blasted by his side, sleeping again. He watched him sleep for a moment, from the doorway, then moved on into his office to do a little musing until dinner was ready.

Long after they'd eaten dinner that evening, Cindy Lou sat by herself in Doctor Miles' kitchen, staring into the dying embers of a once raging, once warm, fire. Blasted had found a warm spot, next to Jimmy, on his hospital room bed, and was snoring softly, and Doctor Miles had gone up to his room early, hoping not to dream of young Esther's swollen face and featureless form that he'd had to examine earlier, in preparation for her burial.

Cindy Lou didn't cry as she stared into the ashes, she couldn't even bring a single thought to mind. All that existed for her in those many quiet moments was emptiness.

Jimmy dozed fitfully, an arm wrapped tightly around the fury mass beside him, twitching and jerking from time to time as a dream carried him back in time to a large rock on the edge of a field, where he sat, once again, with Cindy Lou so close to him he could smell the soft lavender scent of her skin.

His dreams would not allow him to recall, this night, how miserably things had turned out for him. In his dreams, he didn't recall the hours he'd spent preparing for his first date, the interminable wait in the sweltering heat, leaning against the lumber pile in front of Tyler's mill, staring at the post office door, or the humiliation he'd been rewarded with. All memory of the treachery and misery those two encounters with the beautiful girl had resulted in, blissfully eluded him.

Cory, in his apartment above the supply store, felt dejected and frustrated. His efforts to create a whole new supply store, filled with exciting merchandise for the ladies of Farmersville, seemed useless and wasted. How was he to be successful if the townsfolk persisted in making such terrible accusations against him, disrupting every attempt he made to attend to his customers by picking fights with him over Old Bill's youngest daughter?

He wished, as he sat at his kitchen table with his head in his hands, that Old Bill was still alive, still his loyal, sane, friend. He needed the old man's advice and help like he'd never before needed them.

Only Old Bill had known where he'd come from and how he'd come to be the owner of the supply store. As Cory saw it now, most clearly, the rest of the town had never known him; he'd never been anything more than a stranger to them. He was just the man who sold them what they needed to go on living in this otherwise desolate landscape; farming, raising their families and fighting to maintain what life they felt they deserved. Not a single one of them cared for him, or made him feel a welcomed member of the community and now that Old Bill was gone, not a one of them cared a wit whether he was there or not, he felt sure.

Such sympathy he felt for himself that it seemed, to him, the only resolution of the matter was to sell his supply store and return to where he'd come from, to Will and Darla Mae's home, far away from this place and these people, to start a new life. The very idea of leaving Farmersville gave him relief at once and, with lighter a spirit, he set to work organizing and packing his belongings into crates from his stockroom.

    Late in the night, when he'd finished loading the crates into the back of his truck, he stood silently for a long while on the stairs, looking over the dark, still, supply store sales floor, mentally adding up the cost of all the merchandise below, adding a small margin of profit for himself, and fixing what he felt was a fair price for all that he owned in Farmersville. Then, though it was nearly daybreak, he went up to his apartment for a couple of hours sleep, feeling satisfied with his decision, and at ease enough with his conscience, to lay his head on his pillow and sleep.

Chapter 16

Sarah spent the nighttime hours somewhere between tears and sleep. Her worry for her husband nearly overshadowing her heartache over missing her sister's funeral on the morrow. Feeling she'd done what was right, at least by her husband, in sending Cindy Lou back to face the funeral alone, kept her from worrying too much what affect her decision might have on her relationship with her only remaining family member. It was all a matter of time, and she hadn't enough of that to care for her husband in his time of need, and her sister in hers.

Getting to sleep, for Lee, had been easy, but staying in that solitude proved a bit more challenging. Through the long, dark, hours he woke many times with a start, fearful and unsettled, reaching out for Sarah each time, to console his fretting mind that his nightmare had not come to life, and that his wife was still there. He nearly woke her more than once, to confess his guilty conscience to her and beg her to go to her father's home, no matter the cost to him, but the money stashed in his safe loomed before him, threatening to disappear if he spoke a word of truth to his miserable wife. He'd sigh, rather than wake her, and drift off again, eventually, into another disturbing dream.

There wasn't a soul outside Farmersville more heartsick and frustrated than Pastor Franklin was when he finally dropped off to sleep that night, rehearsing the solemn words he planned to speak the next day at Esther's funeral. He still carried an odd feeling in his chest over Cory's behavior. And the sight of Cindy Lou and the monstrous Jimmy Fenton, locked away in secret at Doctor Miles home, only served to distress him more. Everything about what had happened recently disturbed him deeply, but it seemed there was nothing he could do about any of it.

Though he'd heard Doctor Miles' reasoning for allowing the Fenton boy such close contact with such a vulnerable child as Cindy Lou, and had agreed not to disrupt the diabolical household arrangement while there; he'd had the time enough since to convince himself otherwise.

It was his responsibility, he chastised himself, to rectify this terrible, very dangerous, situation. As Farmersville's pastor, he had a role to play in the community, a title he must live up to. It was his job to protect the weak and the helpless, and not just go along with whatever idea appealed to one of the townspeople in order to keep the peace. He had to see to it that the young girl's virtue and reputation be preserved during a time of such deep sorrow. Cindy Lou simply could not be left in Doctor Miles' home, he concluded; she must either retake residence in her father's home with her husband, or live in his home, with Millie to care for her. These were the only right solutions for her, he felt certain.

Even while he'd prepared Esther's service, he'd resigned himself to confronting Cindy Lou with the facts of the matter, right after he buried her sister, and taking the afternoon to relocate her to whichever place, her home or his, she wished to move to.

The following morning, Ralphie woke early and rushed to town to deliver whatever mail had come in to the post office. He was determined to finish his route in time to attend Esther's funeral service. As he opened the post office door he noted Cory's truck leaving the paved road, heading the other way, out of town, and wondered whether Cory would be at the service later, or if he was making his escape early to avoid any more scenes with the townspeople?

He shook his head as he took up his mailbag, stuffing the few letters that had come in into it, plotting the fastest route to the homes he must deliver to as he relocked the door, and walked up the paved road past Tyler's lumber mill. He imagined, with so very few stops to make, that he would have no trouble at all getting to the church on time. He waved a hand at Tyler as he passed him, but the other man didn't notice him, and didn't return the greeting.

Tyler had a great deal on his mind that morning. Like Cory, he'd spent many hours of the previous night thinking his future, and where it would most profitably, and happily, be. He'd weighed his every idea against his bottle of whiskey and had come to the same conclusion Cory had, before he'd fallen into his bed. It was time to move on, to leave Farmersville and all it had become to someone else, someone who would accept the people of this community for what they had become, rather than mourning who they'd once been. He'd decided to send off an ad to each of the larger cities in the state and claim a handsome price for his, no longer fun, nor rewarding, lumber mill.

Though he'd seen the notice the pastor's wife, Millie, had placed on the post office door, setting the time for Esther's funeral service, and despite his assurances to her to the contrary, he had no plan whatsoever to attend the young woman's funeral.

He'd never cared for Esther, he justified to himself, and there'd be no finer opportunity to leave this God-forsaken town without a lot of hoopla, than when everyone else was tucked away in the church, unable to witness his exit.

That morning, he put all his cherished possessions onto a log truck he'd just finished repaired, and tied everything down carefully. He locked the door to his apartment one last time, then put himself in a chair by the large door to the mill, to wait, impatiently, for the appointed time of Esther's service.

When all the townspeople had passed by his post and found him behaving just as he had every other day for so many years, they would go into the church, unsuspecting, and he would climb into the log truck and leave forever. He'd not have to explain himself to anyone this way; he'd simply post a sign announcing that the building was closed, and disappear.

No matter what success of failure he found outside of Farmersville, he swore to himself, he'd never put foot in the town again. It wasn't a pleasant place to be, anymore.

Jimmy Fenton woke first, that morning, and shoved Blasted off his arm as he got up. He moved about the room, quietly dressing, then snuck down the short hall, with Blasted trailing him, and out the back door, past Cindy Lou, who was still asleep with her head on her arms, on the floor near the kitchen table. He shooed Blasted off into the yard and took up some firewood from the box on the back porch, then when Blasted returned to him, they went inside and Jimmy built up the fire in the kitchen.

Blasted nudged his leg as he worked to get the

fire going, nearly knocking him over, anxious to eat and get to his napping in front of the fireplace. Jimmy rummaged the pantry until he found what Blasted was hungry for, then slipped back out into the cold morning.

In his waking moments it had already begun to bother him that he wouldn't be permitted, or wanted, at Cindy Lou's sister's funeral service. Though he understood why, it made him intensely angry. He wanted to be with Cindy Lou, especially on such a trying day. What if she needed him? he fumed to himself, as he took up Doctor Miles axe and set to work making small chunks of the logs piled in the back yard. The whole situation was entirely unfair.

In a few minutes time, he'd amassed a weeks' worth of fireplace logs and woodchips enough to fill every wood box in the house, but his temper raged on. He sunk the axe blade in the chop block and strode angrily back and forth from the woodpile to the back porch, then, making no attempt to be quiet any longer, he went inside and filled all the wood boxes, except the one in Doctor Miles' room, waking Cindy Lou in the process, then locked himself in the downstairs bathroom.

He stared at his bandaged head in the mirror for a long moment, angry at his own reflection. In seconds, he'd unwrapped them and stared in disgust at his much changed face. Deep lines from the bandages remained imprinted on the side of his face and his functioning eye widened at the collapsed state of the other side of his face, entirely evident despite his wildly overgrown hair and beard. He felt sick and cold with sweat.

After taking in the nightmare those many layers of bandages had concealed from him, he frantically, but skillessly, re-wrapped his head. It was far more bearable, he decided, to hide behind the gauze, than endure the reaction others had to seeing his horribly changed appearance. His tears streamed into the gauze as he retied it, and he gritted his teeth to keep his jaw from trembling until he could finish. It was only a matter of time, Doctor Miles had told him, before his bones healed, but considering what the rest of his face looked like now, he wasn't sure he cared.

With the bandages haphazardly replaced, and still crying, Jimmy slipped out of the bathroom, crossed the hall, and hid himself behind the door in the hospital room. Despite the chill, he didn't build himself a fire, but instead sat with his knees to his chin, arms wrapped tightly around his legs, crying bitter tears for himself. He wouldn't take the bandages off again, he swore angrily; he'd go to his grave in them, but he'd never live without them.

Cindy Lou stretched her aching back and stared blearily at Blasted, then at the blazing fire, then, startled, out the window. Finally it sunk in that the night had passed already, leaving her no more time to escape reality. She got to her feet and called out for Doctor Miles, but he didn't answer.

She put water on the stove and rekindled the fire in it for coffee, then left it to go up and dress quickly in her room. She heard noises of doors opening and closing downstairs as she brushed out her hair in front of the mirror, and knew Jimmy was awake, but Doctor Miles' door was still shut when she made her way back down to the kitchen. She made coffee for herself and retook her seat at the table, looking perfectly incapable of getting through the miserable day ahead of her.

When she'd found the bottom of her cup, she

refilled it and took it up to her room with her. She had packing to do, though not much of it; she'd made up her mind that it was time for her to go back home.

She would take her suitcase with her when Doctor Miles drove her to the funeral, then have him leave her at her house after Esther was buried. After all, she reasoned, he didn't really need her help to take care of Jimmy any longer, and Jimmy behaved so strangely around her lately, unless the aging doctor had only imagined that he'd gone out to wait for her, in the cold, the day before.

No matter what, she told herself, she couldn't avoid going home forever. She wouldn't have the townspeople worrying over her and drawing untoward conclusions about her living with Doctor Miles, rather than in her own home. It was only a matter of time, she knew, before tongues started wagging unflatteringly about her, just as they once had about Esther.

By the time Doctor Miles woke there was such a miserable feeling in the house he wished he could just spend the day hiding in his room. Guilt drove him down the stairs quickly, however, to see what he could do to make things easier on Cindy Lou. He was startled to see her suitcase by the back door, but tried not to show any reaction when she set a cup of coffee on the table for him and announced her intention to return to living in her own home after her sister's funeral. Her tone left no invitation for comment, so he drank his coffee quietly, thinking of the many arguments he'd have liked to make against her going home just then.

In silence, they finished their coffee, then while he went upstairs to dress, she slipped down the short hallway to Jimmy's door, thinking to step in and say her goodbyes, but he didn't answer her knock.

She knocked harder, and waited a moment, then, becoming alarmed, she called out for Doctor Miles and pushed her way into the hospital room, searching for Jimmy.

She located him quickly, where he still sat, huddled on the floor.

When she approached, he lifted his head, making little attempt to hide his crying, and she saw the condition of his bandages; she knew what he'd done in an instant. She called more urgently for Doctor Miles, then dropped to her knees in front of the devastated young man.

Jimmy dropped his head again, but she put her small hands to work quickly, removing all the twisted gauze and setting it aside so she could see if he'd done himself any harm. He covered his face with his hands and refused to move them until she finally gave up and ran from the room to find the doctor. She collided with Doctor Miles midway up the stairs and tugged him by the hand, the rest of the way down and into Jimmy's room, explaining the whole way what condition Jimmy was in, and what he'd done.

Doctor Miles was furious when he saw that Jimmy had disregarded his orders to leave the bandages alone until his jaw was fully healed, but when he saw his broken state of mind, he stopped yelling and set to work with fresh gauze, re-wrapping the young man's head, warning him again as he did, not to take them off again and to stop his crying before he made himself even more embarrassed in front of Cindy Lou.

Cindy Lou stood and watched from the doorway. She didn't know what to think or say about what she knew Jimmy was feeling. She knew he would not believe her if she tried to tell him he didn't look that frighteningly bad, so she just stayed silent until Doctor Miles had finished, then excused herself to finish getting ready to leave.

There wasn't much time left before the service at the church was to start, but Cindy Lou wasn't as concerned as Doctor Miles was about getting to the church. She dreaded with every aching fiber of her being, stepping into the crowded church once more, so soon after she'd done so for her father, and face the townspeople who'd treated her sister, the one she must now see buried, so cruelly.

Though she knew it had been Esther herself who'd created such a disgraceful stir in the small community, she didn't see how she could bear facing them all as they paid final respects to the girl they'd shown no respect for. She'd go through the service and burial without protesting, though, she resolved. The townspeople would only be there to show support for her; she would be there entirely for her sister; she owed it to Esther, especially since Sarah would not be there.

Unable to really calm Jimmy, Doctor Miles finally talked the young man into getting up on his bed and taking a sedative to make him sleep for a while. He couldn't justify leaving with Cindy Lou while his lone patient wept inconsolably on his hospital room floor. He felt it would be safer to have him rest comfortably, under Blasted's guard, until he returned.

As soon as Jimmy was settled and he'd assured himself that his patient was truly asleep, he called for Cindy Lou, loaded her suitcase into his car, and drove toward town, both of them thinking, but not speaking of, Cory.

Tyler checked his watch as he said "Good-day" to one of the townsmen who'd stopped to chat with him on his way to the funeral. The only car he had watched for all day was Doctor Miles' and it hadn't appeared yet. He was getting antsy to be on his way and had been keeping a wary eye on the storm clouds that had been building steadily, and were moving rapidly to shut out the sun above him. It might be a treacherous escape if he waited until the snow started falling, but he felt he must wait til he saw the doctor pass by, before leaving lest he should pass him on his way out and feel compelled to explain his leaving. He liked the good doctor, much as he'd liked all the townspeople, til recently; he didn't want the added burden of bidding them farewell, personally.

Finally, he spotted the dust cloud rolling steadily toward him and planted himself once more in his chair. Only minutes remained now of his life in Farmersville, and his heart raced mercilessly as he waited for the doctor's car to pass by him and disappear out the other end of town. He waved as friendly-like as he could muster, as the car came to a stop in front of him.

Doctor Miles rolled down his window and asked him if he'd like to ride with him and Cindy Lou to the service, but he leaned back on two legs of his chair and casually lied that he'd be along shortly, then waved them away. He saw the doctor shrug at Cindy Lou, who hadn't acknowledged him, or even seem to notice they'd stopped, as he drove off toward the church.

He jumped from his chair and picked it up to carry with him to the log truck, as soon as the car was out of sight, and felt a sharp pain in his chest as he tied it down with the rest of his possessions. He forced himself to walk back through his eerily silent lumber mill once more, in case he'd overlooked something and, seeing nothing he wanted, locked all the doors securely and posted the sign he'd made. Then he climbed into the truck, sadly, and drove off the paved road, away from Farmersville, without looking back.

Chapter 17

Esther's funeral service was a blur, wasted entirely on those who'd gathered in the church to say final good-bye's to another member of Cindy Lou's family. While some fretted away the hour wondering what the weather would do, other's couldn't keep their minds from straying to memories of Old Bill's recent funeral and all that had happened that day; still others, along with Cindy Lou, searched the small group of faces repeatedly, wondering where Johnny had gone off to and why his family hadn't come to pay their respects.

Very few tears fell when Millie played everyone out of the church. No one even seemed particularly touched by anything Pastor Franklin had said about the young life that had been lost. Everyone was numb. Old Bill's recent death had been such a blow to the community they could not cope with, or really comprehend, this additional tragedy.

The townspeople hugged Cindy Lou and offered their sympathies, out in front of the church, but only the pastor, his wife, and Doctor Miles would continue along to see Esther buried. The rest blamed the on-coming storm for needing to start their walk home right away, and Cindy Lou assured them all that she'd be fine, feeling relieved that it would all be over soon so she could just be alone.

No one asked her about Cory; word of his leaving her had spread quickly, and no one wanted to be the one who brought up the whole heart-breaking mess to her, but they speculated amongst themselves as they drifted away in small clusters. Angered that he hadn't even shown the decency to attend Ester's service by Cindy Lou's side, they concluded resolutely that Cory should be dealt with severely, at their next cooperative meeting.

When everyone had gone, Cindy Lou climbed back into Doctor Miles car and waited there for him to finish helping Pastor Franklin put her sister's body into the his car for her final ride home. Tears welled up in her eyes as she waited, but none fell, and she couldn't even tell for whom she might cry at that very moment.

Doctor Miles got in behind the wheel and pulled onto the dirt road behind the pastor's car. He asked how she was feeling, and offered sympathy that the storm would prevent the others from seeing Esther buried, but Cindy Lou only nodded in response; she had something else on her mind.

When she could see her house in the distance, she felt confident enough, suddenly, to ask the good doctor the questions she'd been trying to answer for herself: Would Esther get to go to heaven, and if not, where would her baby go?

Doctor Miles was shocked and couldn't think how he should answer her. He'd pondered the same issue when he'd examined Esther's body in Pastor Franklin's shed, the day before, but he hadn't asked the pastor for his opinion, not wanting to make the other man and, through him the rest of the community, aware of Esther's pregnancy. After a long moment, he confessed to the girl that he couldn't say he knew for sure.

She accepted his answer without response, continuing to stare out the window at the frozen fields until they arrived at her father's house. She got out of the car, staring at the large mound of dirt, piled there the day before by the two men who now stood waiting, beyond it, to finish their work.

As if in a dream, she watched Pastor Franklin pray over Esther's casket once more, then give a nod to the grave digger and his helper to lower the casket. The two men came forward and solemnly placed her sister in the earth next to her mother. Then, overcome by the sight of it all, Cindy Lou began to wail and fled into her cold, empty, house.

After giving Cindy Lou a few moments alone in her family home, Doctor Miles gathered some wood from what had once been a sizable woodpile, and went inside to light a fire in the kitchen fireplace. He could hear her crying from some other room, but didn't try to find her.

Pastor Franklin came in shortly thereafter, explaining that his wife was anxious to get home before the snow started and was waiting for him in their car, and they chatted briefly, and quietly, about the way the service had gone, but the pastor was clearly agitated about something else, and Doctor Miles could sense it.

The pastor fell silent for a moment, seemingly contemplating the scene they'd been discussing, back at the church, but then he burst out, forcefully announcing his intention to either take Cindy Lou home with him, right then, or see to it that she stayed where she was, in her rightful place in her father's home. He told the doctor, quite forcefully, that he'd not allow her to return to living with him and the Fenton boy.

Doctor Miles' response was not what he'd expected. Rather than taking up his arguments to the contrary, the old doctor merely shook his head, and sadly informed the well-intentioned pastor that

Cindy Lou had already made a decision on the matter; she would be staying in her own home.

At this news, Pastor Franklin ran from the house to usher Millie in from their car. If Cindy Lou was to stay here, he informed the good doctor as he went, there was much to be done in preparation.

He bustled a cold and protesting Millie in, and sent off to search the house for Cindy Lou, when he returned, and instructed the doctor to check all the cabinets and the pantry, to make sure there was enough food stuffs in them to keep the girl alive til they could return with more. Then the two of them tromped back out into the cold and, despite a heavy, wet, snow falling all around them, worked up a sweat chopping wood to fill all the boxes in the house.

While the men split logs in their shirt sleeves, out in the cold, Millie tried her level best to convince Cindy Lou to take pity on them all and agree to go home with her. Cindy Lou wouldn't hear of it, though.

She dried her eyes, put on one of her father's heaviest coats and went outside to gather the wood, and brought it inside by the armloads while Millie fretted and wrung her hands in hopeless frustration.

When the wood was all in, Cindy Lou made coffee and settled the exhausted party at the table to rest a while. When they'd all had a cup, she reminded Doctor Miles that he had things to attend to at his own home and thanked the pastor and Millie for helping to get her settled in, dismissing them all.

The three stood to go, promising to return the next day with food and other necessities, and Doctor Miles went to retrieve Cindy Lou's suitcase from his car while the pastor drove his wife away to their home. Feeling guilty, the doctor stayed a few minutes longer, hating to leave the girl alone in the large house, especially after what she'd been through that day, but she chastised him for leaving Jimmy alone for so many hours already, and convinced him he must go before the storm made it too unsafe to drive.

He drove back through town slowly, thinking to stop in and try once more to get through to Cory that he was needed desperately, and absolutely must return to his young wife and take proper care of her. He stopped his car and, though he noted the "CLOSED" sign on the door, knocked until his hand hurt. He looked through the display window at the dark interior of the store and called out for Cory, but saw no signs of anyone stirring about and no lights burning inside.

He walked around the building angrily, noting the snow beginning to collect on the ground, but when he got to the back, he could see that Cory's truck was gone. He cursed and stomped back to his car, deciding he'd stop at Tyler's and have him address Cory about his wife's needs as soon as Cory rolled back into town.

He stopped his car again in front of Tyler's lumber mill, and noted the sign on the main bay door, but he knocked anyway, until his hand genuinely pained him. He yelled for Tyler at the top of his lungs til his voice cracked and the blowing snow made it hard for him to see, but Tyler didn't appear.

Furious now, Doctor Miles returned to his car and took up pencil and paper. He scribbled a curt note to Tyler and then slipped it under the door to be sure he would see it as soon as he returned. He'd wasted too much time in getting home, already; to return to the supply store and leave Cory a note too, so he got back in his car, bristling with anger, and drove himself home, barely able to see the road before him the whole way.

Even when he got into his own house and out of his wet, cold, clothes, his temper hadn't dissipated. When Jimmy came out of his room, he raved to the young man about having to leave Cindy Lou all alone in her father's home, completely defenseless and alone, while her husband gallivanted the countryside feeling no compunction to take responsibility whatsoever. Jimmy listened, growing angry himself, over Cindy Lou's plight.

Still able to do little more than make noises through his clenched teeth, and equally unable to control his temper at hearing what the doctor had done, Jimmy smashed his fist against a wall, startling Doctor Miles to silence. His one eye stared with such an evil glint, Doctor Miles regretted his outburst immediately, but he couldn't undo the impact of his words, and he couldn't get between Jimmy and the back door quickly enough to prevent him from storming out into the blizzard.

Doctor Miles gave chase for a short distance, calling out desperately for Jimmy to come back, to at least put on a coat, anything but risk further injury like he was, for the sake of his evil temper, but Jimmy was quickly out of sight and did not respond. He slammed the door, cursing, then realized that Blasted too was gone.

He searched the house for his dog, then put his coat back on and went out into the yard calling for him, but Blasted was truly as gone as Jimmy was, and he could only hope the two were together. He prayed they'd come to no harm out in the storm, so late in the day there was hardly any light left to see by, as he trudged back into his house, not knowing what else he could do.

The road had been so hard to see, when he'd

driven it a short while before, he had no hope to believe he'd accomplish more than stranding himself in a ditch if he dared do it again. He forced himself to sit and think things through more calmly, more rationally, and hope they'd return while he was deciding what to do.

He couldn't be certain whether Jimmy's anger had been directed at him for leaving Cindy Lou at her home alone, or if he too was angered by Cory's lack of concern for the girl? Either way, it settled in his weary mind, Jimmy had almost certainly gone to her. What he should do about that, he had no ideas. His only consolation lie in his hope that Blasted was indeed with Jimmy and would protect him from the storm, and protect Cindy Lou from Jimmy if he should become unhinged when he arrived, if they made it to her house safely.

Pastor Franklin drove Millie home, enduring hysterical accusations. She couldn't understand how he and Doctor Miles, knowing how young and fragile Cindy Lou was, could agree to leave her on her own in that huge house during a blizzard with hardly any food in her pantry. She tearfully demanded, many times over, that he turn the car around and get the girl, but he drove steadily homeward, feeling that at least Cindy Lou was finally out of harm's way, clear of the murderous Fenton boy.

By the time they were home, Millie was in such a state she refused to budge from the car, wailing that she'd rather die in the cold than have the girl face all manner of evil in that house, alone. Pastor Franklin calmly got out, crossed to his wife's side of the car, picked her off her seat and carried her, under a barrage of flailing fists and scratching fingernails, into the house.

Once inside, she resorted to flinging pots and pans at her beleaguered husband until he fled for the safety of his study, behind a locked door. Then she wore herself out beating and kicking the study door and finally gave up to go weep in front of the fire in her now highly disorganized kitchen. She was certain beyond all reason that her husband and the good doctor had made a terrible mistake, and that poor little Cindy Lou would suffer the consequences.

Chapter 18

Cory sat in front of a blazing fire in Will and Darla Mae's overly-warm living room, telling them all about the happenings in Farmersville of late, and of his decision to leave his supply store to come home to them. Darla Mae was thrilled, but Will was taken aback by the odd feeling he got whenever Cory's eyes met his.

He could use the extra, skilled, hands on his small farm, Will assured Cory, but only if he was sure of his conclusions about Farmersville and truly wanted to return to them. Cory answered him by showing him that all his possessions were with him, in his truck, ready for a new home and a new life.

Darla Mae and her youngest daughter, Lisa, made up a bed for Cory while Will told him all about his oldest daughter's recent marriage, then Cory explained that he'd not slept much the night before and took himself off to bed.

Will and Darla Mae sat up by the fire, talking, until late in the night, Will trying to explain the uneasy feeling Cory gave him. But Darla Mae dismissed his concerns, reminding him of Cory's obviously very long, very stressful, day. She would hear nothing of her husband's concern for her adoptive son's mental state, and assured him that time with them on their lovely little farm would do Cory a world of good and set any possible mental unrest he might be suffering right again, in no time. Will wasn't convinced.

Will couldn't shake a nagging worry that Cory

was keeping something important back from them, though. It didn't seem plausible to him that everyone in Farmersville, except Cory, had lost their minds at the same time. He decided he'd drive over there and find out, in Cory's truck, under some pretense, as soon as the storm had passed and the snow had melted down some. Already it was several feet deep outside and there was no end in sight. He could only hope, in the meanwhile, that whatever had put the odd look in Cory's eyes was fixable; he prayed Darla Mae was right about it only being exhaustion.

    Cindy Lou sat in her father's study, staring out the window at the great white flakes of snow falling and blowing in the wind. The fire crackled and popped and the wind wailed as it swept over the house. She felt curiously peaceful, all alone, with no one to bother with, free to dream of the happy life she'd once had.
    She imagined her mother and father, and Esther and her baby, all sitting and talking together happily on the other side of the room from her, passing the wintry evening together. She didn't feel like she'd imagined she would when she'd decided to pack her things and leave Doctor Miles' house. She felt almost giddy and intensely curious about everything in the house that, at the same time, felt so comfortable and familiar.
    She'd not yet moved her suitcase from the spot where Doctor Miles had put it in the kitchen; she'd do that later. For now, she was content to sit and watch the driving snow, enjoying the solitude of the big old house.

    Jimmy followed, as best he could see it, the road into Farmersville. Blasted ran along beside, keeping stride and a watchful eye on his patient. When they finally reached Tyler's lumber mill, Jimmy beat on the door, shivering from the biting cold, his bandaged head soaked through with the driving snow. After a moment, he gave up trying to rouse Tyler and moved on to Cory's supply store up the street. He started at the back door, though he could plainly see Cory's truck was not there.

Getting no reaction to his pounding fist, he led Blasted around to the front of Cory's store and in utter frustration, kicked the door open. Blasted ran into the dark supply store, searching and sniffing every reachable area before bounding up the stairs to Cory's apartment. Jimmy followed, thinking the dog must surely detect Cory cowering behind the door at the top.

He kicked open the apartment door, fists clenched, ready for a fight, but there was no one there to fight with. The apartment was empty, had been cleaned out, and its owner was long gone.

He was too keyed up to give up making sure Cindy Lou was properly taken care of, if not by Cory, he decided, then by he himself. He returned to the sales floor, found some heavy boots and a thick coat and put them on, then he went back out into the raging blizzard and marched on toward Cindy Lou's house. He'd go there, he decided, and make sure she had whatever she needed, then he'd protect her for as long as she needed him. Blasted trotted alongside him, his faithful companion, yelping excitedly as they left the paved road.

Sarah and Lee spent the day in their bedroom, Sarah crying every time she thought of Esther's funeral. She worried aloud to Lee, when he could be roused from his sleeping, and fretted to herself over her younger sister having to take care of all the arrangements by herself.

She sat down and penned her sister a long letter, pouring out her heart to her about the losses they'd suffered, and asking what she planned to do about Cory. She sealed the letter and addressed it, then noticed it was snowing rather hard out, and cried over the delay the snow would cause.

Lee, not daring to face his wife, especially on this day, and risk falling prey to his guilty conscience, decided he'd best continue to contrive illness and get some rest. As he tried to sleep, he noted in frustration that he'd never before known a body could cry so much as Sarah did and not run dry. His guilt turned to irritation and anger more and more each time she woke him to wail tearfully about some new worry she'd come up with, concerning Cindy Lou, and Esther's funeral, or her father's before it. He snapped at her, finally, and she'd snuffled a bit, then turned to her pen and paper, leaving him to hope she'd tire of her misery and leave him alone.

Time seemed to stand still for Cindy Lou as she stared out at the white blanket forming beneath the window and on the window ledge, outside. Peaceful weariness took her over and her felt warm and drowsy. Time was passing, however, and with every tick of the clock behind her, Jimmy was getting closer and closer to her house, with Blasted tromping alongside him, enjoying the adventure, unable to contain his excitement.

Jimmy swore venomously as the storm grew more intense. Small bits of ice pelted him, mixed with the snowflakes the wind flung at him. Several times, he wished he'd not bothered to walk all the way into town, realizing it would have been far faster to have taken the small, rugged footpath to Cindy Lou's house from Doctor Miles'. The anger that had carried him out of the warmth and safety of the doctor's home hadn't dissipated, with the added aggravation of not being able to clearly see his way on the old dirt road.

Blasted danced around his feet, knocking into his legs and otherwise making a loud nuisance of himself, but Jimmy was glad he was there. The dog would make it a certainty that Cindy Lou would allow him to come around her father's home.

Unable to find Cory and force him to go home to Cindy Lou, he applied himself to figuring out how to do for her what might be needing done. He couldn't commit his undivided attention to the matter, however, between Blasted's yelping and having to stomp his feet, painfully hard, with each step to find firm footing and keep sensation in his toes.

The cold seemed to fill him with sharp pains that nearly drove him to his knees. Before he had passed half way down the road from town toward Cindy Lou's house, all his mind would allow him was to follow Blasted's wide back as it moved and bounced, and veered through the snow.

Cindy Lou started from her dozing at the distant, hollow, sounds of a barking dog. Suddenly, the night took on a different feel and the snow storm seemed more a danger than a thing of beauty. Her heart leapt in her chest, alarmed to realize how treacherous this storm would be for a dog without any shelter.

She ran to the kitchen and listened at the door. Again she heard the barking, so she put on her coat and boots, quickly, and opened her door to call out to the dog. She whistled as loudly as she could, but everything seemed insulated and still. She stopped to listen, but heard nothing.

She called out again and again, crossing the deep snow in the yard toward the road, and finally, she heard the barking again. It was coming from the road, and she turned toward it and whistled long and loud, not considering for a moment that it might be a wild, dangerous creature, only worried that it would soon meet its death in the snow if she couldn't get it inside and warmed by the fire.

The barking came loud and close, a moment later, and Cindy Lou suddenly felt alarm she might have felt sooner, had she given her own safety a moment's thought before leaving her house. Before fright could carry her back to her warm kitchen, however, Blasted appeared and she fell onto him, sobbing with relief. She turned to guide him back to her home, talking excitedly to him, not seeing or sensing that he was not alone.

Jimmy's voice startled her so badly she nearly fainted. She whirled back and searched the road.

Jimmy appeared and took her arm quickly, startling her further. She screamed and tried to flee, but Blasted, not understanding what had caused such alarm, pushed his body into her legs, holding her upright and preventing her any escape for the split second it took her to realize who had ahold of her.

Seeing it was Jimmy gave her pause, but only for a moment. She could see he was in no condition to be out in the cold and knew he couldn't last long unless he too was taken indoors. She ordered him to hold onto her arm tightly and guided man and beast back to her house, demanding to know where Doctor Miles was.

Once inside her warm kitchen, Blasted took

himself directly to the fireplace, while Cindy Lou helped Jimmy out of his purloined coat and gloves and led him to a chair, then she ran to her father's study and poured out a glass of liquor from her father's bottle.

Having no tube, as Doctor Miles had, to get the warming drink into Jimmy, Cindy Lou did her best to help him drink it down, spilling much of it on his bandages and shirt front as she did. There wasn't any helping it, she told him, when he recoiled and grunted in embarrassment. If he was to get warm ever again, he must do whatever it took to drink some of it down, she told him.

This wasn't at all the way Jimmy had imagined taking care of hapless little Cindy Lou, but he felt so chilled so deep in his bones, and such excruciating pain in his jaw, he could only do his best to continue to understand and follow her instructions, and worry about the rest when he could think clearly again.

All he wanted, at that moment, was to drift off to sleep, but she wouldn't let him. The liquor burned his throat and he choked on a small amount of it while another minute quantity headed for his stomach, burning a path all the way down, but within minutes his hands felt steadier, and he was able to take the glass from her.

Cindy Lou turned her attention to Blasted, rubbing his back to generate some warmth in him, then she stoked the fire and put water in a kettle over it for fresh coffee. Jimmy, noticing her shivering, made noises until she turned back to face him, then he held out his glass to her.

Not understanding his offer, Cindy Lou brusquely instructed him to finish it all and turned herself onto the chair beside him, but Jimmy persisted, making grunts and half-words she finally came to understand, then he handed her the glass. She took a small sip and gasped; it was hotter, somehow, than anything she'd ever before drunk. She coughed, understanding suddenly, Jimmy's reaction only moments before, but he urged her to drink more and she did. Finally, she handed the glass, nearly empty, back to him and he finished it off, half by drinking, half by spilling.

Satisfied that her visitors would survive, she demanded to know what Jimmy thought he was doing, coming out to her home with Doctor Miles' dog, then it occurred to her that Doctor Miles might have sent them to her. She whirled from making the coffee to ask, but Jimmy shook his head "no" and pointed a thumb at his own wide chest in response. She shook her head, scolding him and Blasted, in turn, for the unexpected call.

Now that he'd made his destination, Jimmy began to realize how poorly thought out his plan had been. He took the cup of coffee Cindy Lou gave him, uncomfortably, and warmed his hands around it while he watched her search the cupboards and find a piece of rawhide to offer Blasted.

The big dog licked Cindy Lou's hand then took the gift she offered and eyed Jimmy over his shoulder, for a moment, before turning his attention to the rawhide, leaving it to Jimmy to explain their presence and purpose. Jimmy just stared at the dog, feeling overwhelmed by a tiredness that had crept up on him.

Cindy Lou sat down at last, in a chair across from Jimmy's. She was a little irritated that he'd disrupted her first night back at home, but she did her best to hide her feelings behind a courteous smile.

He wished he could disappear, fall asleep and wake in the morning, hours from now, to find himself in the hospital bed once again, at Doctor Miles' place. All his plans to take care of Cindy Lou seemed lost in his head somewhere, unable to surface and give him reason for his presence.

No matter his intentions, he'd done nothing more, in Cindy Lou's opinion, than chase down his weary nursemaid, seeking further care.

Jimmy was disgusted with himself, but he could not speak clearly enough to explain his high intentions. He pulled himself back to the moment to find the girl staring at him with what he took to be a tolerant, almost sympathetic, smile.

Angered greatly by the unexpected turn about in his plans, he got himself on his feet and made to put his coat and gloves back on, pointing her attention to the fire, now burning low on old logs, to explain his intention to bring in more wood. Before she could protest that the wood box near the fireplace was already full, he was back out in the blizzard, sucking in deep breaths of the cold night air.

Cindy Lou shrugged her shoulders and asked the distracted dog what Jimmy was thinking, then assured him, though he showed no interest or concern, that she'd go out in a few minutes and bring him back in where it was warm and dry.

Thought it occurred to her that she should, for the sake of propriety, send Jimmy and his canine companion directly out of her house, despite the lateness of the hour and never mind the brutal storm, but she would not. While Jimmy collected unnecessary wood for the firebox, she went up to the room she'd shared with Esther and made up what had once been her bed, for Jimmy to sleep in that night. She'd send the two on their way in the morning, when daylight could show them the way back to the good doctor's home, she decided.

Jimmy searched the yard, and shrugged his shoulders to force his coat collar to cover his neck fully and to block out the bitter wind-blasts. Several feet away from the porch where he stood, snow concealed the wood axe where Doctor Miles and Pastor Franklin, had left it, sunk neatly in the chopping block. The porch wood box was only barely visible at his side, so in an attempt to make his escape worthwhile, he scooped off the snow and took up a few large pieces in his hands. He kicked at the door frame to clear his boots of snow, then a couple more times to bring Cindy Lou to open the door for him.

Upstairs, working quickly to change the bed linens, muttering to herself, it took an extra-long moment for Cindy Lou to hear and understand all the banging going on downstairs. When she realized she was being summoned, she stamped her foot angrily, tossed the blanket she'd been trying to place on the bed, and stormed down the stairs, only barely disguising her upset by the time she threw open the door for Jimmy.

As he passed by her with his arms laden with logs for the box, he muttered thanks to her, soothing her riled temper a little for the effort. She closed the door and leaned against it, sucking in a deep, calming, breath before she thanked him and started back toward the hall stairs to finish making the bed.

Jimmy dumped the logs on the floor next to the box, already filled with firewood, feeling a little better for having done something he could call helpful. He stacked the wood he'd brought in, neatly, then turned to pat Blasted on the head, looking around for Cindy Lou.

She wasn't anywhere he could see, so he

picked up his glass from the table and went into the hall in search of the source of liquor Cindy Lou had given him a short time before. He found Old Bill's study behind the first door he opened and, though he hesitated momentarily, not sure how Cindy Lou might react to him roaming around her father's house, he went into the fire-lit room with a shrug.

The study was warm and comfortable looking, as nice as his own father's study had been when he had been a young boy. The chairs were made of fine, rich, leather, and sturdy polished wood that gleamed softly in the flickering light. The same gleaming wood made up a small table in a corner of the room, and on it, sat a row of glass bottles with liquor in them.

He looked the room over as he crossed to the table and poured out another glass. The walls were lined on two sides of the room with book shelves. He strode around the room, looking more closely at its contents while he sipped and spilled the liquor from the glass. Finally, he set it with the others he found on a table in front of the couch.

The room was more pleasant to be in than his father's study had ever been. He sat down on one of the chairs, when he came to them, and stared absently into the fireplace to wait for Cindy Lou to reappear.

Cindy Lou had expected to find Jimmy in the kitchen where she'd left him, when she'd finished preparing the bedroom. She'd intended to tell him to take Blasted with him and go to bed for the one night she'd permit them to stay under her roof, but the sight she beheld when she came down the stairs and passed by her father's study stunned her to complete blankness of mind. Jimmy was sitting in her father's chair.

He turned when he heard her come in, and upon seeing the expression on her face, got quickly to his feet and wavered there, uncertain where to take himself. He motioned her toward the other chair, separated from the one he'd chosen by a small table, then sat again, once Cindy Lou had slipped into it. They sat silently for a moment before it occurred to Jimmy that she did not have her coffee with her. He left the room quickly to get it for her, leaving her alone to work through the feelings the scene she'd walked in on had evoked. He returned a moment later, followed by a curiously polite, almost hesitant, Blasted, and stood holding the cup out to her for a long moment before she realized he was there. She thanked him, but much to his dismay, didn't seem interested in it at all. She was too distracted by the large dog who'd stopped as if awaiting an invitation, just inside the doorway.

    Jimmy re-crossed the room and shut the door behind Blasted, shooing him toward Cindy Lou and the fireplace. He recovered his glass from the low table and refilled it, then stoked the fire til it blazed, and retook his chair.

    After slopping a bit of the liquor again on his nearly soaked through bandages, he finally mastered the necessary curve of lip to avoid any further waste, or embarrassment. Cindy Lou took no notice, staring absently at Blasted's wide back as he circled around the space of rug directly in front of the fireplace and set himself down with a huff, resting his massive head on his front paws, turning only his eyes back and forth to stare at Jimmy and Cindy Lou.

    Doctor Miles was too weary to keep up his pacing as the night wore on. He could hear no response to his repeated calling, from his dog or

Jimmy, and as the fire burned low in his kitchen, he slumped, dozing fitfully, in an unforgiving wooden table chair. Every few minutes he'd wake with a start, thinking he'd heard some cry for help, or a muffled bark, enticing him to his door and a few feet out into the snow, to call out again for the young man who'd disappeared with his faithful companion.

Those who'd made it out to the church to hear Pastor Franklin give young Esther back to her maker were tucked under many piles of blankets, with cozy fires keeping the chill out of their homes, sleeping until the morning light came. Many feet of snow blew and piled up on and around their homes as they slept, unknowing and uncaring that two very important men had, that day, departed from their small town and that Cindy Lou was, at that very time, alone for many hours, in her father's home with her father's killer, the doctor's dog, her only source of protection.

Darla Mae and Will went to their bed, long after Cory had begun to snore loudly from their daughter's room; one relieved and happy to have Cory back home and the other wary and disquieted by the younger man's unexpected return, and very changed demeanor.

Their daughter, Lisa, tossed and turned at the foot of their bed, on the makeshift bed Darla Mae had made for her. She'd not rest easy with the chill that swept through every crevice in the walls and floor, not much hindered by the thick blankets swaddled around her.

She had no memories of Cory, the man who'd appeared that day in her parent's home, asking to stay with them. She'd been only a small child when he'd come to live with them before. Though he seemed familiar in the most vague sense, she couldn't really think of him as a brother.

To her, this handsome man's appearance was a remarkably good turn of events. Seldom had she seen such a man, younger than her father, yet older than her sister's new husband by several years, anywhere. To have Cory visit at the most dull time of the winter dreariness seemed almost like a Christmas gift, to her way of thinking.

As she tossed and turned, her dreams carried her into morning, into her room where the handsome, older, man slept in her bed, carrying hot coffee and warm biscuits, to wake him and invite him to take her out with him into her father's barn to talk secretly and quietly, and perhaps hold one another's hand.

Cory's sleep was filled with dreams that brought with them little peace of mind. The excitement over returning to Will and Darla Mae's home began to wane as soon as his head met the lumpy down-filled pillow. The sights and smells of the home he'd loved and appreciated so much as a teenager now seemed unsuitable and vaguely uncomfortable.

He could sense some change in Will he hadn't anticipated, and it made him uncertain of his decision to leave Farmersville and the comfortable life he'd known there for so many years. He'd thought the aging man would be pleased to have another strong back to help him carry out his day-to-day tasks on the farm, but Will seemed cold, almost unfriendly with the idea of having him around.

By the time he drifted off to sleep, he'd nearly made up his mind to leave when the sun came up the next morning, never mind the snow outside. As he slept, however, he revisited days long past, and the night his father's men had nearly killed him, then followed his own life into unfamiliar and disconcerting memories of Old Bill and his daughter, Cindy Lou.

As his life unfolded before his mind's eye, his mind rebelled against him and closed off the most recent of events. Only blackness of thought and sight came to him following a hazy picture of Old Bill dying in his beautiful daughter's arms, before a fireplace in Doctor Miles' home, but in that blackness, his heart raced in his chest and a sense of dread overtook him, until even the memory of last seeing his dear friend faded.

Chapter 19

Jimmy drank down the liquor he'd poured himself, slowly, his mind restful, enjoying a feeling of utter peacefulness inside where there had been only misery and torment before it. Without turning his head, he could take in the scene around him and the beautiful girl in the next chair, and an unfamiliar feeling of warmth and belonging made him wish to sit all the more still so that feeling would not ever leave him.

When Cindy Lou's cup clinked against the table, he finally forced himself to turn toward her. There were so many things he wanted to ask, and explain, but fearful he would not be understood if he tried, he kept silent to let her speak, if she would.

After staring back at him without expression for a long moment, she finally found her voice, and her legs. She stood up abruptly and, trying to block out the images she'd become entranced by, she told Jimmy quietly that he was to sleep in her old room where she'd prepared a bed.

He struggled to his feet, nodding, and Blasted raised his head attentively, but did not stir from his spot in front of the fire. Confused, Jimmy pointed at Cindy Lou and tried to ask where she would sleep if he took her room.

She giggled uncomfortably, realizing how her invitation had come across, and explained that she'd be in her father's room, then she turned, quickly, so Jimmy couldn't see her face redden, and led the way upstairs to the room she'd shared with Esther. As she reached the top of the stairs, she heard Blasted's toe nails clicking on the treads, far behind her and it struck her at once how very different her family home had become, so quickly, since her father's death.

It suddenly felt, as she led the young man up to what had been her bedroom, like the eyes of her parents and older sister were all watching. She felt a sharp pain in her chest and stopped for a moment to grip the door frame, and stop a sob in her throat.

Seeing the tears in Cindy Lou's eyes, as he came to the landing, Jimmy took a hesitant step toward her, then turned and retraced his steps back down the stairs. Blasted, passed in the other direction, stopped his lumbering climb and stared up at the landing, then after Jimmy, in confusion. He continued up to the top when Cindy Lou slumped to the floor where she'd stood, and provided his furry neck for her tears.

Jimmy returned straight away to the chair he'd only just vacated, feeling anxious and at odds with himself over what he should do now. Staying put where he was, he decided, was best. Only physical distance between them could prevent him from at least trying to take the beautiful girl in his arms to comfort her. His own tears fell, but he did nothing to stop them. He was monstrous now, he knew, and no matter how badly he wanted to erase all the hurt in Cindy Lou's eyes; seeing him, particularly in her father's home, was certainly only bringing her more unhappiness.

His life, and his terribly changed face, and all that he'd suffered, didn't make up for what he'd done to her, and it was not his place, nor his right, he knew, to comfort and protect her. She was married now, to Cory, not him, and it could and should only be her husband who cared so much for her. He swore in frustration and banged his fist on the chair arm.

Cindy Lou and Blasted were startled by the noise from Old Bill's study, and her tears were forgotten as she jumped to her feet and descended the stairs. At the study door, she was again struck by the sight of Jimmy sitting in her father's chair and she couldn't decide, from the crush of conflicting thoughts on the matter, whether to order him never to sit there.

He had killed her father, and his parents, people said, had been responsible for her mother's death, yet as she stared at him, all she could hear ringing in her head were the words Doctor Miles had spoken on his behalf. She couldn't feel her own rage or the hatred she'd so recently felt, for Jimmy.

She went back into the study and sank back into her chair next to him. Morning would come, she knew; what difference could it make if they stayed together, if neither of them went to sleep?

Blasted resettled himself in front of the fireplace, huffed once, then took up his napping again while Jimmy and Cindy Lou wallowed quietly in their own miseries, each resolving to be rid of the other forever, when morning came and the storm had passed.

Millie woke early the next morning with Cindy Lou on her mind, still. She went through her larder and pantry, piling various food items high on her kitchen table to take over to the young girl she'd been forced to leave to fend for herself on such a horrid night. All her banging around quickly roused her husband and brought him to her side, fearful that she'd suffered some sort of accident.

Pastor Franklin was relieved to see Millie upright and uninjured. But seeing the kitchen in disarray, he demanded to know what she thought she was doing with their winter supplies. He only nodded patiently as she explained, with great irritation, her plans to take food to Cindy Lou, straight away, then he pointed her toward the snow-covered kitchen window in response.

Millie stared at the window for a moment, then dissolved into tears, and found her way to a chair to sit and weep out her frustration. Pastor Franklin comforted her with a hug, then opened the door to see just what conditions lay between them and the girl his wife was so bent on rescuing that day.

A heap of snow collapsed into the kitchen, followed by a blast of frigid wind, forcing him to throw his weight against the door to reset it against its frame. With the cold shut out once again, he set himself to scooping up what snow hadn't been forced out by the door and removing it to Millie's sink. When all that was left was a puddle, he flicked his hands in his wife's direction, spraying her with icy droplets as he passed by her to stoke up the kitchen fire, laughing.

Her angst for Cindy Lou suddenly forgotten, Millie leapt from her chair, screaming, and shoved her husband as hard as she dared, complaining volubly over her suffering. The pastor recovered his balance quick as a cat, and continued laughing at his severely outraged wife until she stamped out of the room in search of a blanket to warm herself and recover from the rude shock.

No one in Farmersville, nor anyone in nearby communities would be going far this day. Though the storm had passed, the cruel and biting wind had not, and feet of snow obscured the landscape all around, piled even to the roofs of some of the local's homes, and there wasn't any call for man or beast to try to dig out until the bright sunlight melted down the insulating blanket. Only those with livestock to tend to would brave the elements this fine morning and them, only to satisfy their minds that their livelihood had not and would not suffer for this terrific storm.

When Millie shuffled back to the kitchen, somewhat calmer and fully wrapped in a bed blanket, Pastor Franklin assured her that Cindy Lou had plenty of food on hand to last her a few days and promised her he'd drive her, and all the food she'd set out, to the girl's house as soon as it was possible.

Though unhappy still, she didn't argue the issue any further. Deciding she'd not speak to her husband, in repayment for his chilling her to the bone. She huffed and set about making a new, neater, pile of the food items she'd set out on the table.

Seeing he'd not win any battles with her that morning, Pastor Franklin poured himself a cup of coffee and escaped to his den to take up his reading, and pretend he didn't notice his wife's silent treatment. He'd get his own breakfast when he decided the dull ache in his body was indeed hunger, but he'd not leave the safety of his den a moment before then, he determined.

Millie continued brooding and rooting about in her kitchen, even after he'd escaped, until she decided that her best method of pay-back lay in ground sugar cubes, spread evenly upon the sheets of her dear husbands side of their bed. Once she'd fixed this, she felt better about things, almost happy as she pictured what his reaction would be that night when he laid down to sleep.

She drank her coffee alone, smiling wickedly, then made herself a fine, full, breakfast of smoked ham and eggs, which she felt certain would make her husband's mouth water to smell, and ate it all, not sparing him a crumb, as noisily as she could on a chair outside the door of his den.

Cory woke to find Lisa, Will and Darla Mae's daughter, stirring around noisily in his room. When he opened his eyes, she was holding out a cup of coffee to him. Alarmed, he pulled his blankets up under his chin and ordered her out, unnerved by her prancing about his room before he was awake and decent. He cursed her roundly when, startled, Lisa dropped the hot coffee onto his bed, near his arm, and fled the room in tears.

The plan had not come off nearly as she'd imagined in her dreams the night before, and Lisa was outraged. She made no attempt to conceal her disappointment, but instead ran directly to her father, seeking explanations and reassurances.

Astonished by his daughter's outburst, and the reason for it, Will felt even more concern over Cory's presence in his home. He calmed his daughter as best he could and sent her to her mother to help with breakfast, then finished dressing and went to find Cory, to talk things over and devise some new plan for Cory's immediate future.

Darla Mae made it to Cory before Will had finished dressing, however, and complicated matters greatly in doing so. She made apologies for her daughter's innocent flirtation, then quickly expressed her pleasure over his return once more. She told him how Will's health seemed to be suffering in recent months and begged him to stay on with them and tend to their land so Will could rest.

Cory was swayed by his surrogate mother's pleas and quickly assured her, throwing out his plan to leave entirely, that he'd stay as long as she felt he was needed. He made his own guilty apologies for yelling at her daughter, and promised he'd try to be more understanding and tolerant of her sensitivities, then he excused himself, sending her out so he could dress.

Unaware of his wife's conversation with Cory, Will entered his room after only a sharp rap, moments later, and while Darla Mae chastised her daughter, between giggles, over her crush on Cory, Will talked himself in circles, trying to convince the younger man that he should make better plans, elsewhere, perhaps return even to Farmersville and his supply store, rather than linger about in his old home, causing a ruckus for him and his emotional, teen-aged daughter.

Cory would hear nothing of leaving, no matter how artfully Will told him he must. For every reasoning he could offer, Cory countered with promises that he felt it wiser to stay on right there, tending to things Will had long since grown too old to tend to alone. And he assured him he'd treat his most sensitive daughter with such proper courtesy, she'd have no cause for further compliant against him, just as he had, only a few moments before, promised Darla Mae.

Will could not find any advantage over Cory's arguments and finally, weary of trying, he gave up and left him to finish dressing. He found Darla Mae and Lisa, whispering and giggling together still, in the kitchen and huffed irritably as he got himself a cup of coffee and took in what the blizzard the night before had left piled nearly to the very top of the kitchen window - many, many feet of tightly packed, snow.

Cindy Lou woke suddenly in the cold, dimly lit study, unable to fully identify where she was. She saw Jimmy slumped in her father's chair in the dim light and rushed to see if he was alright, catching up to the day in a flash.

It was terribly cold in the room. The fire had gone out, and she realized the muted light was coming from the sun as it fought to break through the snow, packed tightly against the windows on the far side of the room.

She shook Jimmy's shoulder and called out his name until he roused fully and looked around him trying to get his bearings. His jaw ached miserably and his muscles were stiff. While Cindy Lou pushed Blasted out of the way and rebuilt the fire, he sorted out where he was and how he'd come to be there.

When Cindy Lou slipped out to the kitchen, he wandered out behind her and Blasted followed behind him. He stepped into the small bathroom near the stairwell and stared at himself in the mirror for a long moment before using his fingers to deliver fresh cold water to his dry, chapped, lips. The gauze beneath his mouth was discolored and smelled sickeningly sweet, but neither the odor nor the stains from the liquor he'd spilled on them the night before would be removed. He pressed a hand towel to the stains to soak up at least the icy water before it froze the gauze to his flesh. The whiskers that had overtaken his face dripped with cold water under the bandages, irritating his already raw chin.

He made his way to the kitchen, finally, and accepted Cindy Lou's offer of coffee, then remembered Blasted, prancing excitedly by the back door. He opened the door, but a wall of snow met him, unmoving. He shut the door again, unsure how to get the big dog out into a yard twice as deep as he was tall with packed snow.

Blasted grew impatient and barked excitedly, urging Jimmy to be quick about letting him out.

Jimmy led him to the front of the house, to try the front door, hoping that the porch roof had protected enough territory for Blasted to escape and take care of his business. The snow was high, but manageable, outside the front door, and Blasted plowed into it as soon as Jimmy got the door open.

Jimmy felt awkward to be in Cindy Lou's fine home. He didn't know where he was welcome to be, or quite certain how to act, so he returned to the study with a snow-encrusted Blasted, to warm himself by the fire and hide. But the sounds and smells of the food Cindy Lou was cooking soon enticed him back to the kitchen. He made himself comfortable at the table and watched the sleepy girl make breakfast for the three of them.

Cindy Lou set out plates for the two of them and made more coffee, then helped Jimmy feed himself crushed bacon, eggs, and a biscuit. While she finished eating, she looked the other way til Jimmy had finished slipping Blasted his plate, then she crumbled an extra biscuit into a pan and set it on the floor for the great beast.

Jimmy tugged uncomfortably at the damp gauze under his chin, drawing Cindy Lou's attention to the condition of it, and she, without a word to him, disappeared up the stairs and returned with one of her father's clean white undershirts, torn into strips, a few minutes later. She explained how she intended to use them to replace the gauze around his head, and after slapping away her hands a time or two, unhappily, Jimmy let her remove the soiled gauze, cringing the whole while, dreading what her reaction would be.

She showed no reaction whatever as the last of the bandages fell away, merely asking if he'd like to use her father's razor, upstairs, before she re-wrapped his face. Jimmy nodded and jumped to follow her up the stairs and into the icy cold bathroom and she left him there to clean himself up. She returned to her kitchen, feeling oddly lighthearted, almost happy to have him and Blasted in her big home, with her.

Doctor Miles woke with a pain in his chest and a weight so great in his body he couldn't lift himself from the table chair. His breath showed white in the cold morning air and only a few embers remained of the once roaring fire before him. He tightened his grip on the edge of the table and tried to force his back to straighten, but the damp cold had set deep in his joints and none of his muscles would be governed by his will power.

He gasped to fill his lungs with fresh air, but as he did the pain in his chest overpowered him. Unconscious in an instant, he fell onto the table top and struggled no more against the pain.

Chapter 20

When Sarah woke to find snow piled high outside her window, the morning after her sister had been buried, she felt like the world had renewed itself. She woke Lee, excitedly, and as soon as she'd satisfied herself that he was well enough, urged him to pull her around the yard on an old sled they kept on the back porch, in hopes that there'd be cause to use it.

They played in the snow like children, pelting each other with snowballs. Then they forced their way back into the warmth of their kitchen and drank their coffee between sniffles and giggling.

Sarah felt as if she was free, finally, from all the sorrow-filled days gone by. She was happy for the first time in a long while and Lee was relieved to see her that way.

Still feeling the burden of his trickery of her as they relaxed by the fireplace, later, he broke down and told her about the money Cory had entrusted to him for Esther and her baby's care, until Johnny returned, and begged her to forgive him. Sarah was shocked.

Unable to re-bandage his head when he'd finished shaving his wildly overgrown whiskers, Jimmy had no choice but to leave the safety of the bathroom and give Cindy Lou another opportunity to faint dead away at the sight of his mangled head. She heard him come down the stairs, and found him a moment later in the study.

Instead of turning away even, she took his

misarranged face in her hands and told him what she'd dreamed of telling him in the night before: that she thought she loved him. Then, before he could get his stunned mind to let him say a word, she put her lips against his for a breathtaking moment.

Jimmy's mouth moved, but no sound came. He cleared his throat and tried again to speak; he didn't know what to do, or what he might say, so he let her move away in embarrassment. Before she could run from the room, however, he grabbed her hands and pulled her against him, trying to tell her he loved her. She melted against him, certain she knew what he was trying to say.

For a long moment, Jimmy held Cindy Lou tightly to him, murmuring noises into her hair, feeling a lightness in his heart he'd never felt before. It was unreal to him to have her so close, suddenly. He pulled her into his lap and cradled her there, more happy than he'd ever imagined himself capable of being.

Blasted, unhappy to find himself left out, made his way over to the chair and pressed his cold nose against Jimmy's arm until he'd made room for his massive head. Cindy Lou giggled and patted the persistent dog's head, then sighed contentedly, resting her head on Jimmy's shoulder, breathing in the lingering scent of her father's strong soap on his skin.

For a time, in the quiet old study, Jimmy felt as he had so very long before: consumed with the idea of having beautiful Cindy Lou all for himself. She wasn't his, though, he realized with an unpleasant jolt. The gentle, lovely girl curled up like a harmless kitten on his lap, breathing softly against his neck, was a married woman and she wasn't married to him. He was stealing time with her, and the idea of it suddenly made him recoil from her.

Jimmy didn't try to explain what had occurred to him, instead he pushed her out of his lap. Blasted ran to retake his place in front of the fire while Cindy Lou jumped to her feet, demanding an explanation.

Jimmy's chest ached and anger made his face grow hard, bringing a menacing glint to his eye. The idea of being in such a position with another man's wife repulsed him. Even though he had walked out on her, to Jimmy's way of thinking, Cory remained Cindy Lou's rightful lover and protector.

Refusing to let her leave the study without explaining himself, he pulled her to her knees in front of his chair and painstakingly formed the words necessary to make it clear to her that her husband was on his mind. As he forced the words through his clenched jaw, he dropped her hands in disgust with himself for being so easily tricked again by the beautiful girl, angry with her for even thinking to hurt him again, as she'd been so happy to do before.

Cindy Lou protested his accusation that her love wasn't any longer hers to give anyone but Cory, now that she'd married him. She argued tearfully that she'd never loved Cory, or felt the feelings Jimmy made her feel, but Jimmy only shook his head, glaring at her reproachfully.

Hearing such convincing words from the girl he loved so dearly only made him more angry. He cursed her and flew into a rage as she ran from the room. He chased after her and grabbed her arm as she tried to climb the stairs, and pulled her back down to where he stood, almost effortlessly, crushing her arm in his hand.

Cindy Lou struggled to free herself, crying even harder now, still trying to make him understand that she'd not, in truth, married the man she loved, telling him she regretted having gone through with a marriage he didn't understand at all. She cursed him back and threw herself against his chest, still fighting to get her arm free, but he wouldn't let her go.

Blasted, upset by all the commotion, ran quickly to protect Cindy Lou, but Jimmy was immovable, even for the massive dog. He barked and jumped, teeth bared, at Jimmy's back, but Jimmy was too tall and too strong himself, now, to be moved. He ordered Blasted to go back to the study, but Blasted stood firm, growling menacingly, ready to wound him badly for upsetting Cindy Lou.

The noise was deafening, suddenly, and Cindy Lou begged both man and dog to be still, finally getting through, at least to Jimmy. He flung her hand away and stormed into the study, slamming the door behind him.

Cindy Lou, with Blasted on her heels, fled to her father's old room, nearly catching the poor dog's tail as she slammed and locked the door behind her. While Jimmy paced Old Bill's study, grunting and cursing, she laid face down on her father's big bed, weeping. She was so tired from the long stormy night before, she cried herself to sleep, in minutes.

Managing to control his anger enough not to destroy the room around him, somehow, Jimmy tried to work through what had just happened. It hadn't been right, he knew, to have been with Cindy Lou the way he had only moments before. He slumped into a chair and fumed that he'd done nothing more than take advantage of her when he'd intended only to take care of her, since her husband would not.

He replayed what she had said, in his head, as he stared wearily into the fire. What had she meant when she'd said he didn't understand her marriage at all? Had she not really married Cory? Had he never lived with her? Shared a bed with her?

Curious now, and a bit more calm, he searched the rooms upstairs until he discovered the locked door. He tapped lightly and called out to Cindy Lou, waking her. Though speaking with jaw clenched tightly was difficult and his words hard to distinguish through the solid door, he made himself clear enough, to the exhausted girl on the other side of it, to convince her to open the door.

He stood in the doorway putting his questions to Cindy Lou while she returned to sit at a distance from him on her father's chair, but the answers she gave didn't meet his high hopes or expectations:

"Yes." she'd contemplated marriage to Cory for a time. "Yes." she'd known how serious it was that she'd followed through. "No." circumstances had not forced the issue, but "Yes." Cory had, once, shared a bed, the bed Jimmy was staring at in fact, with her. The only answer Cindy Lou offered, that gave him any better feeling about the situation, also made him wary and distrustful. Her stone faced, cold-eyed, answer that the marriage had never been consummated seemed far too good to be true and all too hard for him to believe.

When he'd heard all her explanations, he returned to his chair in the study to think, leaving her to fling herself once again on her father's bed. Intending to come up with some resolution to the whole matter of who Cindy Lou really, truly, loved, he sat until the warmth of the room lulled him to sleep.

Late in the afternoon, he woke to the sounds of a dying fire before him and Blasted scratching furiously on the front door. He rushed out to free the dog, noting the stillness of the house, sadly. When Blasted had finished his business and come back inside, he went to the kitchen and heated a small stew at the stove and made fresh coffee. He rekindled the fire in the kitchen fireplace, then went to find Cindy Lou, to wake her and make his apologies for their fight.

When he pushed open the door to her room, though, and saw her sleeping peacefully on the bed, he changed his mind and, instead of waking her, pulled a comforter off a nearby chair and laid it over her. She stirred a little, and opened her eyes for a moment when he kissed her forehead, but continued sleeping when he slipped away from her bedside and lit a fire in the cold fireplace.

When she woke again, over an hour later, Cindy Lou found Jimmy sitting in the chair across the room, pulled close to the fireplace, staring at her. She roused herself when he handed her a cup of coffee and thanked him for the fire, then they fell silent, listening to Blasted snore from his new spot at the foot of her bed. They stared easily at each other, each with their own troubling thoughts.

In the flickering light, all Cindy Lou could think about was how handsome Jimmy was. His jaw, nearly healed now, still appeared strong and smooth. His, now longer, hair nearly covered the indentation in his skull, leaving only his damaged eye staring at nothing, she noticed. His lips, she knew, were chapped and rough, yet they seemed as tempting and sure as they had been the day she'd first seen him. A feeling Cory had never made her feel welled up inside her once more, and almost took her breath away.

To Jimmy, Cindy Lou looked older and more beautiful than she had only a few months before. Her hair didn't seem as yellow as it had in the sunlight, when they'd sat so close to each other on the rock, but her eyes seemed bluer, and wiser, and still sparkled just enough to set his heart racing in his chest.

Though he fought desperately not to think of such things, her kiss replayed itself over and over in his mind and made him wish she'd kissed him longer, and that he'd kissed her back.

When she set her coffee cup aside, he offered to get her more, but she refused. She noticed that he was clenching his teeth and rubbing his jaw, cradling it in his palm when he spoke, and she rushed down to the kitchen, herself, and took up the strips of cloth she'd intended to re-wrap his head with earlier, and took them up, along with two steaming bowls of Jimmy's stew, to her father's room.

After she'd helped him finish his bowl, she told him how much better he looked now that he'd shaved, and held a mirror up for him to see how nicely his scars were healing. He grimaced at the sight of himself and pushed the mirror away without comment, then pulled her into his arms again, kissing her, this time.

Cindy Lou didn't resist, pressing her body into him as he moved her into his lap. There was no awkwardness or surprise this time, and neither let pass the chance to breathe the other in and feel all the warmth the other could give, for a long moment.

Finally, she giggled nervously and pushed him away, reminding him that she'd intended only to wrap his head for him, and they quickly set about figuring out how to secure each strip of cloth, until his jaw was restrained in place again. After admiring their handiwork in the mirror as they sat on the edge of the bed, Jimmy stoked the fire nervously, unsure what he should do next.

Though he wanted very much to kiss her again, he put himself firmly back in the chair at a safe distance, he hoped, and watched her resettle herself against the pillows at the far end of the bed. He didn't think she'd put up any fight, but he resisted a strong impulse to take his place next to her for the night.

Nothing had changed about his girl being married to another man, but there wasn't any doubt left in his mind, at that moment, that she was, and always had been, more his than Cory's. Before he left her to spend the night hours dreaming of her, in the room she'd once shared with Esther, down the hall, he made her promise she'd agree to annul her marriage as soon as possible, and marry him. Cindy Lou agreed, but only after he gave in to her beckoning, outstretched arms and kissed her once more, and held her to him for another short while.

When he'd closed the door between them, Cindy Lou sighed, then cried softly into her pillow for the promise she'd only just made to one man, and now planned to make to another. With no one to guide or council her otherwise, she decided what she was doing was right, more right than she'd been to allow her sister and well-meaning friend, Mrs. Wilcox, to convince her to do.

Cory had been wrong too, she told herself, and he clearly regretted marrying her. He'd left without any concern for her and had never really been her husband at all, but she wondered if Pastor Franklin would agree with her and Jimmy, or would he turn them away to live in scorn?

For an instant, a memory of Esther's words to her, about her not knowing the thrills of a lover's touch, returned to Cindy Lou and she smiled through her tears, certain that the way she felt in Jimmy's arms must be more thrilling than Esther had ever imagined herself to feel laying with her lover in a field. Then a memory of laying with Cory, in that very bed, crashed in on her good feelings and she shuddered at the memory of that night; confusion set in.

With Cory she'd felt wise and safe, but never the sensations that Jimmy brought. Cory's lips hadn't held such excitement as she still felt now, to merely think of Jimmy's. Surely these feelings she'd not shared with Cory signified real and true love, she thought.

The fears that filled her head now, with Jimmy no longer there in the room to force them away, left her feeling miserable. For this night, she finally resolved to herself, she'd think of nothing and no one but the man sleeping just down the hall; the man she loved; and she drifted off to sleep at last, with the beginnings of a faint smile on her lips.

Jimmy could think of nothing but the pride and happiness he felt over the prospect of marrying Cindy Lou, if it was possible. Images of restoring his family home and taking her to live with him there, filled his mind. Though he'd set the fire blazing across the room, he felt warm enough entirely without it.

Unencumbered by worries of recent commitments to break and a reputation to protect, he could think only of how happy he was that Cory had not been at the supply store when he'd gone there to force him to do right by Cindy Lou. Only he, he now felt certain, knew how she needed to be taken care of. It seemed only right that he be able to care for her as her husband; his pride would never allow it to be any other way. He fell asleep confident and trusting that his life had finally given him a good turn, the best any man could hope for.

Chapter 21

Pastor Franklin delighted his wife when he fell into bed that night. She cackled with laughter as he jumped back out of bed, after only a moment, crystals of sugar flying in all directions, throwing sheets, comforters, and pillows in a heap on the floor, shouting and cursing at the top of his lungs. When he turned to berate her, she scurried out of the room and hid in her pantry, not daring to come out until she heard water running in the bathroom. Then she changed out the bed linens quickly and resettled herself against her pillows to greet him cheerfully upon his return.

After boxing Millie with his heavy pillow a time or two, Pastor Franklin left her to giggle herself to sleep at his back, without any blankets to cover herself and keep out the bitter cold. No amount of prying, kicking, or begging, could convince him to release his grip on the covers until he was pretty sure she'd be drowning him in pitiful tears the next instant, then he threw all the covers over top of her and bound her up in them, and tickled her mercilessly.

They quickly tired of their battle and lay breathless with laughter in a completely destroyed bed. Neither righted the sheets, pillows, or blankets, but rather, each chose their own pillow and position, used what cover was available, and went to sleep all askew on the bed. Even as they tried to sleep, one, then the other, would burst out laughing, listening to Pastor Franklin's empty stomach rumble with pleas and protests for food.

The whole day had passed without a morsel crossing his lips, but he was too lazy and weary to, now, get up and do all that would be necessary to feed himself. Millie wouldn't give in and make him anything, he knew, so he'd force her to hear his starving plight all night, he determined.

Millie went to sleep vowing to herself that she'd make up with her husband the next day, starting with a huge breakfast, but the growls from his belly, sounding in the dark room were too entertaining to give up. She tried to block them out, and eventually went to sleep.

In the middle of the night, Pastor Franklin finally gave up and did what he'd refused to do earlier - light a fire in the fireplace. Millie was sleeping soundly, under all the covers she'd stolen when he'd dozed off, leaving him chilled through and unable to stay asleep. When he slipped back into the bed, he ensured that Millie lost a little sleep to the cold too; prying up a corner of her blankets and pressing a cold foot to her leg, then, once she was awake and complaining, he stripped her of all the blankets and went to sleep.

Too tired to retaliate, Millie satisfied her pride by vowing not to give him any food the next day as well. Heaving a big sigh, she got up, put on a warm dressing gown and returned to bed, to sleep, feeling positively abused.

Sarah didn't react to Lee's confession quite the way he'd feared she would for so long. When he'd run out of ways and words to explain what he'd done, she nearly collapsed with laughter.

He chuckled with her, at first, not knowing what about his confession had struck her as funny, but he quickly grew serious and worried again, and escaped to his den, to his safe, to prove his confession was true. She didn't stop laughing, though, even as he counted the many bills out to her, but almost seemed to find his counting more funny still. Confused, he re-stacked the money and returned it to his safe. It was safe to assume, he reasoned, alone in his den, that when his wife finished laughing, he'd have hell to pay.

It seemed the wisest thing to stay hidden from her, and keep his sturdy desk between them when she recovered herself and came after him. He sat, still hearing her laughter from out in the kitchen, to sulk over what was to come and think up some way to make the whole thing up to her, if he survived.

He'd nearly worked himself into a panic, certain she would leave him that very day, by the time Sarah stifled her merriment and knocked on his den door. He called her in and watched her face anxiously as she crossed the long room and sat down across the desk from him. As soon as she took in a breath to speak, a giggle slipped out behind her hand, and he jumped to his feet and began wearing the carpet thin underfoot.

Sarah righted her face and adopted as near a scornful expression as she could muster, then broke into laughter again at the sight of her husband acting and looking as frightened as a child waiting for a spanking. She was shocked by what he'd done to keep all the money given to him for Esther's care and, though surprised at the great lengths he'd gone to deceive her, she was relieved to finally know the reason behind his sudden change of personality since Cindy Lou and her new husband had brought Esther to their home.

She had felt Lee withdrawing from her, lately; nearly always bristling with unhappy tension whenever she was around, to the point she'd feared he was unhappy with her and that their marriage might be slipping away. Her laughter, now, kept her breathing while she tried to fathom the seriousness of what her husband had done, and wrap her mind around the fact that not only was her marriage still secure and safe, but now they had money and lots of it.

All the things they'd done without since their wedding day were now easily within their reach. The land they'd dreamed of buying one day could be theirs - and oh, so much more. She finally set his mind at ease, asking only how long it would take him to get himself over to the land owner who'd promised to sell to them, when they could afford it.

Lee grabbed her up from her chair and hugged her tightly, dancing her around the room. when she'd finished. He promised her, grinning wildly, that he'd go the very next day and buy the land for her.

For the remainder of the day, they talked excitedly about all the other things they could do with the money left over, after they'd bought the land and seeds for the additional corn crop, and speculated about what hell they'd pay from Cindy Lou when she found out.

Cindy Lou woke to the banging of pots and dishes, and Blasted barking, downstairs. She dressed quickly and went down to see what the ruckus was about and was surprised to see Millie,
Pastor Franklin's wife, bustling around in her kitchen.

Millie said a curt "Good morning." her, when she caught sight of her, but didn't stop her work, going into and out of Cindy Lou's pantry with the many items she'd brought from her house.

Flustered by the woman's unexpected,

unannounced, presence and clearly un-engaging attitude toward her, she stood in the doorway observing Millie silently, then she saw the food on the stove top and rescued a pan of bacon just before it turned to char.

Millie appeared at her side in a flash and snatched the skillet away, muttering to herself under her breath, but clearly audible to Cindy Lou. She pushed the girl back from the stove and continued preparing, what appeared to Cindy Lou, a feast for many people.

Too stunned to respond, Cindy Lou toppled into a kitchen chair and continued to stare at the older woman in disbelief. What was this woman doing in her home? How had she gotten in? Where was Jimmy?

Questions flooded her befuddled mind, but she had to take a moment to work up her nerve to try to get answers out of Millie. At length, she got her wits about her and demanded to know what was going on.

Millie slammed a plate of biscuits down on the table in front of her, fully red in the face, and lit into her about coming all the way over to bring her food so she wouldn't starve to death, only to find her shacked up with the likes of Jimmy Fenton.

In a flash, Cindy Lou was equally outraged, and angry words flew between the two until Pastor Franklin heard all the shouting and appeared at his wife's side. Then to Cindy Lou's horror, the normally kind and solicitous man took up his wife's side of the exchange and demanded explanations for Jimmy's presence in her home.

Cindy Lou defended herself aggressively, but only for a moment, before it became clear to her she'd not win this shouting match. Her head began to throb and, without further effort to justify herself to this nosy couple, she jumped from her chair and fled the room in tears. She ran to her father's study and threw herself into a chair in front of the fire, already burning brightly in the fireplace.

Pastor Franklin and his wife followed her, still yelling, so wrapped up in their excitement over their discovery that they didn't see or care that the girl they were chastising was in distress. Millie took up her ranting in front of Cindy Lou's chair, while Pastor Franklin took his fight to Jimmy, on the far side of the room.

Unaware that Jimmy was present, Cindy Lou turned in her chair to see who the pastor was making such vile threats to, behind her. She saw, finally; Jimmy was bristling mad, fists clenched at his sides, standing by the window, unable to get in a word of response to the other man's attack. Headache and tears forgotten, she got to her feet and, giving Millie a harder than necessary shove, crossed the room and grabbed Pastor Franklin's arm.

So angry now she didn't care who this couple was, Cindy Lou raged in Pastor Franklin's face about he and his wife's uninvited visit and ordered them from her home, maneuvering herself as she shouted, to stand between Jimmy and the surprised pastor.

Millie, spitting mad now, flew across the room and tried her level best to get her hands on the insolent young girl, aiming to teach her a lesson about disrespecting her elders, but Cindy Lou slapped her hands away and threatened, quite convincingly, to do a lot more if the woman got near her again. Millie burst into tears at the threat and fled the room, ordering her equally stunned husband to take her home that instant!

Pastor Franklin stood his ground, glaring at

Jimmy over Cindy Lou's head, then, with parting-threats directed at him, and promises to return with men from town to remove him from Cindy Lou's home, he stormed out of the house, his wife leading the way.

Jimmy and Cindy Lou stood staring at each other, shocked, until Blasted's continued barking brought them back to the moment and Cindy Lou went to find the excited dog. She looked around the downstairs until she'd covered every room, then realized he must be outside and sent Jimmy to the back door to check, while she went to the front. The barking stopped before she opened the door and she heard Blasted's toenails on the hardwood floor, running toward her. He met her in the front hall and plowed into her legs, trying to jump up on her, but she held him off and assured the worried dog that she was alright, then he followed her back to the kitchen where Jimmy sat at the table with his head in his hands.

Cindy Lou didn't say anything, instead turning her attention to making herself and him a cup of coffee. Her headache had returned and she suspected Jimmy had one too by the looks of him. For a long while they sat silent at the table, with Blasted between their chairs begging and whining for some of the food he could see on the tabletop.

After a couple of cups of coffee and a little rest, both were awake enough to begin to worry, and wonder if the pastor would really do what he'd threatened to do to Jimmy. Cindy Lou helped Jimmy break up three of the biscuits Millie had made onto a plate with some bacon slices and gave it to the hungry dog, then Jimmy explained, as best he could, how long the other couple had been there and how they'd gotten into her house.

Cindy Lou pressed a clammy hand to her forehead and set about making two plates of food for herself and Jimmy, assuring him she'd not let anyone do anything to him as long as he was an invited guest in her home. She swore angrily about the nerve of the couple trying to take over her home and dictate to her what she could and couldn't do, while Jimmy listened with growing discomfort.

Jimmy had woken to the sound of pounding on the front door and without thinking, had gone downstairs to answer it. On seeing him, Pastor Franklin and his wife had demanded to know what he'd done to Cindy Lou, and had barged past him into the house like they meant to find out.

Millie had searched the house til she'd eyed Cindy Lou, still sleeping in her father's bed, then informed her husband that she wanted Jimmy removed from the house while she unloaded things from their car.

Pastor Franklin had ordered him to explain his presence and, when he had not even tried to answer, threatened to kill him if he didn't get out of Cory's house. He'd tried to push him, to impress him with his intention to see him out, but Jimmy was unmovable. Flustered, the pastor had fled to the yard to help his wife bring things inside from their car.

Jimmy hadn't been sure what he should do about the intrusion. He and Cindy Lou needed the pastor's approval to annul Cindy Lou's marriage to Cory, and then marry them, but it seemed the man felt Jimmy had no right to be anywhere near Cindy Lou. He'd tried to go upstairs to wake her and tell her the pastor had come to call, but decided against forcing a fist fight, when the pastor had blocked his path and informed him that he wasn't going to see Cindy Lou before they did. He'd gone back to the study to wait things out and see what Cindy Lou thought of things before he took up any battle to stay in her house.

The wait had been long, and throughout, he could hear Millie ordering her husband around the kitchen and could smell food cooking, but he stayed put to avoid any further trouble. He felt terribly unsure of himself, and though he didn't want to leave, he tried to tell himself he would if, when she woke up and came downstairs to talk to the pastor, Cindy Lou asked him to.

When he'd heard Cindy Lou yelling in the kitchen, he'd listened closely, trying to hear what she would say about him being there. He decided that if she said she wanted him out of her house, that she didn't love him, he'd leave before she could say it to his face, but before he'd known it, she was in the study with him, and before he could speak to her, so were the other two, only this time, the pastor seemed emboldened by his wife's presence. Unable to speak clearly enough with his firmly bandaged, aching, jaw, he could only stand his ground by the window, and fight the urge to punch the pastor with everything he had in him.

Cindy Lou, though stopping short of telling the pastor or his wife that she and Jimmy wanted to be married that day, made it more than clear that she wanted Jimmy in her home and the two of them out - quickly! Jimmy had been shocked to see her lose her temper that way, but had been relieved to hear what she had to say, right up to the point that she mentioned being a married woman, and therefore allowed to decide for herself who she would or would not have in her own home.

Hearing Cindy Lou call herself a married woman, gave Jimmy a sinking feeling in his stomach.

As much as he would have liked to just run from the house and the whole situation, his feet had felt glued in place, so heavy he could do nothing more than stand mute behind her and let her defend him, willing her to tell the pastor about their newly-found love for each other and their plans to marry, but she did not. The irate couple had left none the wiser, seemingly hell-bent on getting up a lynching party and coming back for him.

    Cindy Lou seemed not to remember anything of the night before, as she raved on about what she'd do if anyone tried to take over her life and home again, seemingly more concerned with the challenge to her independence than her professed love for him. Though Jimmy kept silent for a long while, just listening; she said nothing like she had said to him the night before.

    Finally, he gave up hoping, and when she'd worn herself out and sat down beside him, he ignored her entirely, occupying his hands patting Blasted on the head, and his mind whirling; planning to leave her, the house, and the whole situation. As he stared into Blasted's mournful brown eyes, it occurred to him that he could use the gentle beast as his excuse to get out of there, and in that way avoid any further conflict. He'd take Blasted, who'd protect him from any townsmen he might encounter on the road, and return to Doctor Miles' place. Surely, he thought, the old man must have given his pet up for dead, or might be out on the roads in his car, searching for him and his dog.

    Cindy Lou jumped a little when Jimmy got up and started putting on the coat and gloves and boots he'd worn when he'd arrived. She asked him where he was going, but Jimmy avoided eye contact with her and pointed at Blasted, then jerked his thumb in the general direction of Doctor Miles' house. Thinking he intended only to take the dog into the yard for some exercise, she told him offhandedly to "have fun" and didn't notice the hurt look that crossed his face as he waved goodbye to her, unable to speak he was so upset. Too aggravated over the morning's events, and preoccupied with her own irritated thoughts, Cindy Lou waved back at him in exasperation, and rolled her eyes.

Jimmy took her reaction to his leaving as a brush off, and he grabbed Blasted by the scruff and led him quickly out of the back door, slamming it behind them angrily. He wasted no time crossing the side yard, through the deep, melting, snow, to the road and walked away. When he got to Doctor Miles house, he swore to himself, he'd give back the man's dog and ask for a few food items to take back with him to his own home. He could take care of his own recovery from here, he decided, without any help from anybody.

He and Blasted walked in the tracks of someone's car until they'd nearly reached town, then they turned onto what Jimmy hoped was the footpath cut-through to shorten the walk to Doctor Miles' house. If the car tracks in the snow had been made by Pastor Franklin's car, he reasoned, it would be a very bad idea to follow them all the way to town and find himself trapped by the townsmen who were no doubt gathering there, preparing to come after him, with Cory. He didn't need the hassle. Cindy Lou, he felt, had made it clear that he didn't matter to her, not really. If Cory wanted her, he could have her without a fight from him.

When they neared the doctor's house, Jimmy was surprised that no smoke was coming from the chimneys, and wondered out loud to Blasted, whether the doctor was even home. He could see no car tracks on the road, or in Doctor Miles' side yard, though, so he urged Blasted on ahead of him, and the dog raced away to scratch and bark excitedly at the back door.

A moment later, Jimmy finally reached the back porch and, with a bad feeling starting in his chest, pounded on the door, pushing Blasted back out of his way with his foot. He looked through the glass and saw Doctor Miles sitting with his back to him at the table, apparently sleeping with his head on his arms, so he beat harder on the door and called out to the man, but the doctor didn't move, and the door, he found, was bolted shut.

Blasted began to whine in frustration, waiting for Jimmy to open the door for him and when Jimmy gave up and left the porch to try to get in through the doctor's office window, he returned to his scratching and barking, then stood up on his hind legs to see why his owner was taking so long to let him in. On seeing his owner inside, he began to howl.

Jimmy got inside the house quickly and ran to Doctor Miles in the freezing cold kitchen. Blasted continued howling and scratching at the door, but Jimmy was determined to wake the doctor before letting him in.

He opened the door a moment later, with tears in his eyes, and didn't stop Blasted from rushing to his owner's side. While the great dog took in that his owner wasn't responding to him, Jimmy slumped into a chair and tried to console him. After a moment, Blasted laid down next to Doctor Miles' chair and stared at his unmoving feet.

Jimmy's head was spinning and he couldn't think what he was supposed to do now. He couldn't see any injury on the doctor to explain his death, so he assumed the old man had frozen in the night; his body was cold and stiff, and his head and hands were lifeless and, as reality began to sink in, he cried helplessly into his gloved hands.

The house was cold. Ice had formed from the sink tap until it met the bottom of the sink, and Jimmy could see his own breath as he sat at the table across from his doctor, crying and making terrible noises, praying the man wasn't really dead; that he'd sit up any moment and tell him to make coffee, or pat his dog on the head. There was nothing but stillness all around the room, and sadness, and the bitter cold.

After a good deal of confused thought, Jimmy finally accepted that the man who'd taken him in and cared for him, despite what he'd done to Old Bill, was really gone and that he was desperately alone now. He didn't have a friend in the world and all his family was buried already. Cindy Lou had tricked him again with her fickle charm, and brushed him off again as if he was of no consequence to her. He had nothing and no one, and he was cold.

Blasted got up and pressed his warm body to Jimmy's legs, nudging him back to the moment. He reached over and pet the dog absently, then, in a moment of thoughtfulness, decided to light a fire and make coffee to warm himself. He'd be able to think more clearly if he could feel his fingers again, he decided. There was nothing he could do for the doctor now, but he couldn't just sit and freeze to death at the table, with the man's trusting dog by his side. He lit a fire and went to his hospital room to find some warmer, dryer, clothes. When he returned to the kitchen, Blasted was once again laying at his owner's feet, staring up at him.

After warming himself with coffee and the fire, it occurred to Jimmy that he couldn't leave the good doctor where he was. He needed to take the man outside, where it was cold still, or his body would begin to rot and smell. He imagined already that he could detect an odor in the kitchen near the doctor's body, so once again he put on his coat and gloves, and opened the back door.

He tried to lift the doctor, but couldn't, so he tipped the chair the man was in back as far as he dared and drug him out of the house in it. It was heavy, cold, slow-going, but he finally got the doctor into the shack behind the house and shut the door on it. He gasped for air, once outside again, and leaned against the door for support until he had regained enough strength to get back into the house, shivering harder than he had from the walk over from Cindy Lou's house.

Blasted was waiting for him just inside the door, and he fell to his knees and hugged the dog's neck tightly, crying into his thick fur. They were all each other had in the world now, and Jimmy didn't want to let go of the comforting beast. Only when Blasted pried himself away, did Jimmy force himself back up into a chair at the table.

Chapter 22

Cindy Lou busied herself straightening her house, still muttering to herself miserably over the pastor's visit that morning. She was so busy with her temper tantrum she didn't think, or care to think, of Jimmy. She remade beds and washed dishes, dusted, then set upon the pantry Millie had reorganized for her, taking out all the items the pastor's wife had put in, and returning the pantry to the order she preferred.

Only when the work was done and the silence of the house became severe, did she begin to wonder just how long Jimmy had been gone, and when he'd return with Blasted. Though a gloomy feeling began to settle in around her, it didn't occur to her to worry that Jimmy wouldn't return. She couldn't see them out in the yard or in the surrounding fields, but she assumed they'd only gone for a long walk; a longer one than she'd have considered with so much snow on the ground and the biting, damp, wind.

The sun was nearly setting when the truth began to sink in. She had eaten and taken a long nap, certain her two companions would be back by the time she woke, but when she'd gone downstairs calling for them, neither had appeared. She'd searched the quiet house with a gnawing ache in her chest and had finally burst into tears when she realized Jimmy and Blasted were nowhere to be found. She'd sobbed, sitting on the stairs, suddenly overwhelmed with loneliness and feeling lost.

No one appeared to dry her eyes or comfort her, and the moans of the wind grew steadily as she pulled herself back to her feet wearily and returned to bed to cry into her father's pillow. For the first time since her father's death, she felt hopelessly broken inside, and she cried bitterly for her family, wishing she too could go to sleep and never wake again. She dozed off, hours later, only to dream of her childhood, her father and her sisters, all happy together in this house, and she tossed about miserably each time a creak in the house threatened to wake her and bring her back to reality.

    Pastor Franklin and his wife talked late into the night about their rescue mission gone awry that morning at Cindy Lou's house. The two were very much at odds over what must be done about Jimmy Fenton's presence in the girl's house.

    They'd gone directly to town, after Cindy Lou had kicked them out, to talk to Cory and Tyler about returning with them to remove the murderous young man, but they'd not been able to find either man. Millie had insisted they go home straight away, so she could sit in her room quietly and gather her wits about her, overtalking Pastor Franklin's inclination to drive out to Doctor Miles' place and enlist his help and support against Jimmy. They'd driven home in silence, but Millie had started raving again as soon as they tried to sit at their table and eat a late breakfast.

    They both wanted the Fenton boy out of Cindy Lou's home, but Pastor Franklin reminded his wife, unhappily, that he had tried to get Jimmy out and hadn't succeeded. Cindy Lou was a married woman now, he reminded her; free to do as she pleased in her own home with whomever she liked. Only Cory could insist, against her will, that Jimmy Fenton leave.

    Before Millie would agree to go to bed that

night, she made her husband promise he'd find a way to rid Cindy Lou, and their community, of this last, most troublesome, Fenton and he'd agreed, too weary and frustrated to try again to convince her that his hands were tied, but to himself, he resolved to drive out to Doctor Miles' house the following day to have a strong word with him.

He held the good doctor fully responsible for the Fenton boy's recovery and Cindy Lou's protectiveness of him. If Doctor Miles hadn't taken both young people into his home, Cindy Lou would never have been subjected to encounters with the monstrous young man at such a vulnerable time in her life. The only other man he had a determination to find, after the doctor, was Cory. He'd not be satisfied until he saw to it that the supply store owner get over whatever had taken his mind, and get back to taking care of his own wife and his own business.

Cory had worked all day on Will's broken-down tractor, and had smudges of grease on his forehead and face to prove how challenging the repairs he'd made had truly been. He'd only just fired it up when Will had motioned him in, from the barn door, for dinner.

Now, he stood staring at his own glistening eyes in the bathroom mirror, mesmerized, water running unnoticed from the tap. He couldn't tear his attention away from his reflection.

Darla Mae, hearing water, but no sounds of splashing from the bathroom for a long while, finally sent Will from the table to collect Cory, or at least hurry him along. She'd plated up a fine dinner already, and it was cooling quickly in front of her small family as they waited for Cory to join them at the table.

Cory joined them, making apologies, a moment later, and they all tried not to stare at the peculiar expression on his face. Each of them ate their food quickly, anxious to know what was on their houseguest's mind.

Will asked him what was bothering him, only after Darla Mae and Lisa started clearing dishes from the table. Darla Mae listened, as best she could, over the clattering of dishes and her, still unhappy, teen-aged daughter's snippy comments regarding their guest.

The only thing Cory was able to put his finger on, in explanation for his odd expression, he told Will, was a vague sense of sadness that had grown quite intense, periodically, throughout the day, but for which he could find no reason. Seeing how distraught Cory was becoming as he tried to apologize and explain himself, Will decided he'd better do as he'd intended to do that day, the following morning; he'd leave early and go to Farmersville. He felt certain someone there could tell him what had happened recently to cause Cory such unhappiness.

Jimmy Fenton fell asleep in his familiar hospital room bed, with Blasted snoring beside him through the night. He woke with the sun the following morning, unsure what he should do about Doctor Miles, his house, or his dog.

He talked to Blasted about their situation as they went about their, once rather dull, daily routine, and finally concluded that the faithful old dog must stay with him now; and he planned on leaving for his own long-abandoned home, in short order. Blasted followed Jimmy around the doctor's house, ever watchful, while he collected food, clothes, and other things he'd decided he'd need in order to take up residence, once again, in his family's farm house.

The pain in his jaw sent him to the doctor's office to find pain relievers enough to last him a few more days, then he bundled up all that he'd gathered together, and set out with Blasted for his house. As they walked through the melting snow, in dazzlingly bright sunlight, he could see his new companion was satisfied with the new arrangements, and it made him feel safe to have such a powerful creature by his side, just in case Cory, the pastor, or any other of the townsmen, should find him out on the road.

Surely, he figured, none of them would try to impede his way out of their town, to go back to the home where he and his family had hid their very existence all the years gone by. Seeing him leaving should satisfy them, he thought, even make them happy enough to leave him alone, he hoped, forever.

He'd rather never see or hear from any of them again, anyway. As far as he was concerned, his plans for a life with Cindy Lou were as hopeless as they'd ever been, and the mere thought of her made his heart feel like lead in his chest.

The walk home was long and difficult, and a feeling of depression filled Jimmy when he finally stepped into his own kitchen at last. While Blasted sniffed around, he forced himself to bring in wood and start a fire in the kitchen fireplace. He'd have a lot to do to make the old house livable again, but the idea of having work to do made him feel a little better about things.

While Blasted settled himself in front of the fire, he set about washing down the countertops and made coffee with Doctor Miles' coffee beans. Before he'd finished his first cup, Blasted was snoring loudly, and he had a plan for their new living arrangements.

Deciding it would be warmest in the kitchen, he went up to his childhood room and disassembled his bed. Careful not to strike himself in the head with the cumbersome mattress, he carried it down the staircase and placed it in front of the kitchen fireplace.

After making his bed with the linens he'd brought from the doctor's house, he did his best to seal off the kitchen from the rest of the drafty house. Depression overwhelmed him and he felt like crying, certain he couldn't bear to live in his house, like this, until the weather permitted fixing it up, and opening up the rest of the rooms for living space. Being in his mother's kitchen again evoked unhappy memories, but he tried to push them away and focus on the tasks that lay ahead of him the next day, thankful that he at least still had Blasted to keep him company. He put together a pot of stew and they ate, huddled together for warmth, in front of the crackling fire.

Cindy Lou woke early and, finding herself as alone as she'd been the day and night before, started to cry again. Tears streamed from her tired, swollen, eyes even as she made her coffee and built a fire in her kitchen fireplace. All the near-excitement she'd felt initially, about returning to her own house from Doctor Miles' to live alone, had vanished into the thin cold air around her. When she had no tears left in her, she got herself dressed and sat and stared into the kitchen fireplace til the flames died down and a chill filled the room again.

She was exhausted, but her mind wouldn't rest. Her eyes hurt and her fingers and toes were as stiff as her back, from the cold. Only after a strong gust of wind threatened to lift the roof off the house, did she rouse herself enough to bring the fire back to life. She wrapped a blanket, from her father's room, around her shoulders and slouched in a chair resting her eyes, dozing here and there, until it was early afternoon and her grumbling stomach wouldn't be put off and ignored any longer.

She quickly discovered that eating alone was entirely unsatisfactory and wondered, as she washed her dish, if she should find some way to get word to Sarah that she really must come home right away. Sarah wouldn't come, she knew, since Lee had no employees to watch out for their farm in their absence, but at least, she rationalized, asking might prompt Sarah to invite her to visit them for a few weeks, at least until winter had passed.

She penned out a letter to her sister before it occurred to her that mailing it would have to wait until the snow melted, so the roads were passable. She sighed and put it in an envelope anyway, then resumed her spot in the kitchen, at the table, and stared into the fire.

At the odd moment, throughout that terribly long day, she found herself thinking wistfully of first Cory, then Jimmy, then shaking her head sadly and remembering how perfect and easy her life had been before she'd involved herself with either man. Despite the fleeting thoughts of the one she'd married, she didn't wish Cory would return. The man who brought pangs of hurt and confusion to her heart was Jimmy. It was he who had claimed to love her, then left her without a nod, last.

She dozed off in the night hours, with her blanket wrapped tightly around her still, in her father's bed, alone. In the morning, she promised herself before she fell asleep, she'd figure out what she should do with what was left of her life. She was far too exhausted and miserable to yet contemplate facing any of the townspeople ever again.

Pastor Franklin woke before his wife, anxious to get out to the good doctor's house and give him a piece of his mind, about Cindy Lou. If, he decided while he dressed, Cory was at the supply store where he should be, he'd have a word with him first, about the strange goings on at his and Cindy Lou's house, and demand that he go there at once and take care of things.

Dressed and out of the driveway before his wife woke, he breathed a sigh of relief. He'd be able to do what he knew was best for Cindy Lou a lot faster and a lot easier without his well-meaning, but strong-headed, wife interjecting her ideas and opinions about things, he thought.

He drove through town on the paved road, staring hard at the supply store. He saw the CLOSED sign, still hanging in the window undisturbed, but, noting the busted condition of the door, he stopped anyway, just past the store, to step around behind it and look for Cory's truck. He swore irritably when he saw it wasn't there, and stomped back to his car to make the treacherous drive out to Doctor Miles' place. He'd give the doctor a lecture and a half, as soon as he opened his door, he promised himself.

The drive was slow and slippery from the deep melting snow. Twice, he had to back his way carefully out of the ditch by the roadside, once, only after getting out and pushing with all his strength to unstick the tires. When he finally stopped in front of the doctor's house, he decided to just leave his car in the road and walk the rest of the way to the door in his soggy, cold, boots.

He knocked on the door, stomping his feet free of snow, becoming even more irritated by the moment that Doctor Miles wasn't rushing to let him in out of the cold. He searched the front hallway through the window glass in the door and saw that even Blasted wasn't stirring inside. There was no fire lit in the fireplace and the room looked gloomy.

Frustrated, he decided to check around a bit before he left, just in case the doctor had locked himself up with his dog, upstairs in his bedroom for warmth, and hadn't yet gotten up. He found the back door was unlocked, so he went in calling for Blasted and Doctor Miles, and otherwise making as much racket as he could. Hearing no response, he searched the rooms downstairs, calling and listening, then climbed the stairs and searched each room there as well. Finally, he accepted that the old man wasn't inside to hear him yelling and went back out onto the back porch.

From this vantage point, he could see the tracks Blasted and Jimmy had made earlier, mostly melted into unrecognizable impressions, leading away from the porch. He tried to follow them a short distance with his eyes, but saw no point in pursuing the trail that clearly ended near the woodpile and a small outbuilding. He walked out to the barn where he knew the doctor kept his car and looked inside. The car was clearly visible inside the dimly lit barn, so he called out again for the doctor, then he opened the large door to let in more light and searched around the car for the man and his dog, to no avail.

Not knowing what else to do, and a little worried to find the car, but not the doctor, he stepped back out and shut the barn door securely. There were several outbuildings surrounding the barn, and he decided he must search them all before he gave up and returned home.

He discovered Doctor Miles' body, still sitting

frozen in his table chair, in the next building he searched. He gasped in fright and surprise, backed out the small door as soon as he spotted him. He couldn't believe his eyes and he couldn't move. He gulped down a breath of fresh air and called in to the man, hoping he wasn't really as dead as he appeared to be, but the doctor didn't move.

At length, Pastor Franklin got his thoughts and his nerve back together, and went back into the shed. He made himself touch the doctor's hand, just to make certain there was no life left in him, then he forced himself to call out and search the room thoroughly for Blasted, who he felt sure should be around someplace.

He gave up finding the dog when all the buildings on Doctor Miles' property yielded up only rats, scurrying into dark corners at the opening of each door. He returned to the house, finally, and noticed that someone had rifled through the rooms and closets, wondering if that someone had broken in and robbed the good doctor, then killed him. The thought of such a thing made the hairs on the back of his neck bristle, and he left the house at once, shaken by what he imagined to have happened, and drove back to town as fast as he dared.

The temperature outside was dropping fast as he made his way to the paved road in the center of town, and when he got there, there was no one in it still. Cory's truck was still gone, the supply store door was still askew, and there were no signs of life at Tyler's lumber mill either. But, still upset by his discovery of Doctor Miles, this time he forced his way into, and searched thoroughly, both Tyler's lumber mill and the supply store, praying he wouldn't find their owners in the same condition as he'd found the old doctor.

He was relieved when he didn't find anyone else he knew, dead, but he was greatly disturbed to see that both Cory's and Tyler's businesses and small apartments were completely abandoned. He tried to recall exactly when he'd last seen either of the men, but couldn't. Neither of them, he realized, had attended Esther's funeral service, or burial at Cindy Lou's house, and though it hadn't given him much pause, considering all that had happened since, it now alarmed him greatly.

Before he drove out of town, feeling quite odd and miserably confused, he checked the post office for Ralphie and again found no one. The entire town had been abandoned, he thought unhappily, and the good doctor was dead, and his dog was missing. Something was terribly wrong in Farmersville, and he felt an urgent need to get back to his own home and make sure his wife was still there, and alright.

When Millie let her ashen-faced husband in the back door of their house, a short while later, all the mean things she'd intended to do and say to him for leaving without telling her, earlier, slipped her mind. She felt a stab of panic when he grabbed her up in his arms and hugged her, but couldn't seem to speak.

She pried him off of her, after only the briefest moment, demanding to know what had scared him so badly. She pushed him into a kitchen chair and begged to hear the news, then huffed in frustration when he began to tremble uncontrollably instead, unable to speak. She put a cup of coffee in front of him and sat down, tapping her fingers on the table, trying to guess what was wrong with him, until he gasped out all he had discovered. She was shocked to stillness, then she cried in fright until he took her in his arms again and calmed her, trying to reassure her that they were safe and promising they'd figure out what had happened to everyone.

Though Millie demanded, when she'd recovered sufficiently, that he go out again, immediately, and discover what had happened to everyone in town, he knew he could do no more that day. With no destination in mind, what good would it do for him to drive about the treacherous roads? It was getting late and the temperature was dropping steadily, so the snow that had melted was freezing. It would be far too dangerous until the next day, at least. He talked Millie into making them a hearty, if very late, breakfast, and they ate while he went back over every detail he could remember of his discoveries.

They agreed, before they went to bed that night, that he should return to town, to the post office, and find out what he could from Ralphie, in the morning. Surely, they agreed, he would know why, or at least when, Cory and Tyler had abandoned their businesses and homes.

Chapter 23

Cindy Lou woke to the sun streaming through her bedroom window. Feeling rested and cheered by the brightness, she dressed quickly. She lit a fire in the kitchen fireplace while she made coffee, then sat at the table to warm herself and plan out her day. If she was destined to be alone, she resolved to herself, she'd not waste another day crying for anyone's company.

After eating a small breakfast, she climbed the stairs and searched out Esther's sewing basket. She knew there were several dresses waiting to be mended or altered, so she gathered them all in a heap and took them to the kitchen to work on where it was warm, in front of the fire.

Though her sleep had been plagued with dreams that could only leave sadness, she felt oddly capable and gown-up this morning. She picked through dresses Esther had intended to finish for herself and selected the prettiest of them, then set about altering them to fit her. Things she did not want and items belonging to her father, she set aside to put away, and by early afternoon she was trying on three beautiful new dresses and examining them critically, in the hall mirror, upstairs.

When the dress mending was done, she took a long hot soak in her bathtub, and spent some time pushing her yellow tresses into a new style, then experimented with Esther's many jars of creams and face colors. When she felt she looked most attractive, she made herself a fine dinner and pretended to be entertaining her old school chums on some special occasion, at her kitchen table.

Before she went up to bed that night, tired but feeling quite proud of herself, she filled all the wood boxes in the house and made each fireplace ready to be lit. With new dresses to wear and a house to keep up, she'd decided, she must have an income too. She decided she'd go into town bright and early the following morning and take her rightful place in her father's post office.

Things hadn't been going very well for Ralphie since Esther's funeral. The weather had turned so radically that day, he'd taken ill, forcing him to make his journey home without seeing her buried.

He hadn't kept up with his work at the post office; for two days he'd slept and not eaten anything substantial, and he felt weak and miserable. He was feverish and couldn't rest easy, but he hadn't a thought for trying to climb through the deep snow he could see through his bedroom window, all the way into town to catch up.

On the rare moments he was awake, he kept a blazing fire going, but each time it burnt itself out, he felt all the more sick from the cold. With no one around to notice or help him, he wondered if he was to die this way, as he imagined Esther had so few days before.

The heartache he felt over losing her made him almost entirely without will to live on. His life had no purpose without the promise of their future, and he felt a part of him laid buried with her in her grave.

He'd not let on to anyone how much affected he was that the townspeople who'd attended Esther's funeral hadn't shed a tear for her passing. The women who'd talked so cruelly behind her back had continued to whisper about the dead girl, and her curiously absent lover. They'd come only to fulfill their obligation, and continue to mourn Old Bill's recent death, together, and he was outraged that no one seemed to care for the girl; even her older sister hadn't come to say goodbye, and he was thankful Esther had not been able to see any of it. His anger had kept him boiling hot as he'd walked home, through the beginning of the storm after the funeral service, but it had also made him even more terribly ill.

Despite his tender age, he was quite accustomed to living entirely on his own. Now he was in trouble, though, he'd never been this bad off before.

Jimmy Fenton woke to Blasted's scratching at the door, and it took him a long moment to register where he was. He confirmed to himself that he hadn't dreamed of going back home as he let Blasted out to run around his back yard. When the dog returned, he lit a fire and fed him scraps, from their meal the evening before.

He made coffee, not feeling any happier to be home than he had the day before. As he looked around him, there seemed little that needed doing that could be done before Spring. The big house that had once been so grand, now looked so shabby he could hardly bare it, and though he'd loved his brothers, and missed them, the overwhelming sense of their presence in every room of the house depressed him and made him feel horribly lonely.

As he searched the yard for a project he could start, his thoughts turned to Cindy Lou, but in an entirely unpleasant way. He recalled how his older brother, Len, had taunted him about even thinking she would be interested in him, "a Fenton boy", and his face reddened, though no one was there to see it. Just as he had done before, when the girl had tricked him, then spurned him and made a fool of him, he realized, he'd run here to his family home, seeking a place to hide. This time was no different than the last, save the criticism his brother could no longer speak, now echoing in his head, and realizing that, his temper flared.

    He stormed through his house, shaking his fist at the very walls. He cursed his brothers, in his head, for leaving him this way, for not sticking with him like they'd promised as children, and raged in his parent's room, at their cruelty and the life they'd left him. He ripped the curtains that had long kept secret from the world, the misery of his family's existence, from their hooks and hurled them to the floor, then slumped to the floor at the top of the stairs overlooking the mess he'd made. Blasted ran to his side and nudged him until he reached out and hugged him closer, sobbing into his fur.

    He hated the house, he told Blasted through his tears; he couldn't stay there, he swore, couldn't go back to living the way he and his family had. Blasted licked his hand supportively, until he got back to his feet and made his way back to the kitchen, telling Blasted he had a new plan for their new life together.

    In the kitchen, he gathered up some of the gauze he'd taken from Doctor Miles' office. He carefully removed the strips of fabric Cindy Lou had helped him use to secure his jaw, and replaced them, then he set about putting everything he'd brought home with him, and a few items of clothing from his room, into a bag he could carry over his back. While Blasted watched from the back door, he threw handfuls of dirt on the fire in the kitchen fireplace, then he opened the back door and locked it behind them.

With the duffel over his stronger shoulder, he led Blasted back toward Doctor Miles' house. They'd stay there one night, he told his companion, then they were going back to Cindy Lou's house to tell her about finding the doctor. From there he'd figure out where they should go and what they should do.

Through the night, Cindy Lou dreamed strange dreams of finding Ralphie on the road to town, running to catch up to him, hoping to talk with him about her father's post office, but never being quite able to reach his side, or even get his attention. When she woke in the morning, she couldn't shake the image of the young man, nor the strong feeling that she should go to the post office, without delay.

She drank her coffee quickly, then put on one of the dresses she'd finished tailoring the day before. She put on her heaviest coat and boots, determined not to let time get away from her as it had the day before. Maybe, she thought, Ralphie could use some help sorting and delivering the mail that must surely be piled high at the post office because of the snow storm.

The road was a slushy mess, but she waded to the center of it, and made her way into town. The morning sun warmed her back, as did the exertion of walking so briskly, making her feel a little melancholy for Spring, when she could throw open all the windows of her house and let all the miserable, haunting, memories of the Winter's tragedies float away on the wind.

As she neared town, she felt her heart skip a beat. It was likely as not she'd have to see Cory that day, if she continued on. Her step faltered. How embarrassed she'd be to have to see her new husband in town again, and more humiliating than that, have to deal with the townspeople who would doubtless demand to know why he had run out on her, assuming he'd left her after catching her with her new lover, Jimmy Fenton, thanks to Pastor Franklin and his wife.

She wanted to turn back, but, catching a sob in her throat, she squared her shoulders and forced her feet to march onto the paved road. She'd come too far, and for good reason, to turn tail and run now. She'd done nothing wrong, she consoled herself; if anyone should flee in embarrassment, it should be Cory.

She opened the door to the post office and slipped inside, locking the door behind her, relieved to be out of sight, in her father's old post office, hidden from Tyler, Cory, or anyone else who might already be around. She called out for Ralphie, though he clearly wasn't there, and hadn't been for days.

A pile of mail was indeed waiting just inside the drop door, so she lit a fire in the stove and set to work at the front counter, sorting through it. Halfheartedly, she searched for a letter from Sarah, as she made small stacks of the envelopes, addressed to various people in the community. While she worked, she kept a wary eye on the front window, waiting for Ralphie to show up, and praying Cory wouldn't. All was quiet outside, though.

After several hours of sorting mail and cleaning the two-room post office, she began to feel angry that Ralphie wasn't there. She'd gone, repeatedly, to the door and braved the cold to check up and down the road for him. She cursed him, mildly at first, for being so undependable, but with so little to occupy her in the small rooms, she soon lost her temper.

She put out the fire she'd made and locked up the post office, then marched out of town, toward Ralphie's place, to give him a piece of her mind and order him to town to do his route.

Farmersville felt oddly unpleasant and empty to her as she left it. The supply store's CLOSED sign caught her eye as she'd locked the post office door, but only when she could no longer see the buildings over her shoulder, did she begin to wonder where her husband was.

All the way to Ralphie's place, she pondered the possibilities; that Cory might be sick, or injured, or simply too ashamed of himself to face the townspeople and their gossip. She didn't even think to imagine he'd abandoned not only her, but the community entirely, but she realized, as she sloshed down the road, that she'd really never known Cory that well, and had no idea where he might go, or what he might do. Only her father, if he were still alive, could tell her what had come over his dear friend.

She pounded on Ralphie's front door, chilled to the bone from the long, miserable walk. Part of her didn't blame him for not wanting to make such a trek every day, but he'd promised he would, and the community depended on him to do it.

No one answered her knock.

Noting wisps of smoke coming from the chimney, she felt certain Ralphie was inside somewhere, hiding from the tongue lashing she intended to give him, so she marched around the small house, banging on the window glass and yelling at the top of her lungs for him to let her in out of the cold. When she got to the back door, she found it unlocked, and after a moment's hesitation, she went in, still yelling his name. No one answered.

She peered around corners and into small rooms, and finally found Ralphie in his bed, sleeping. She shook his shoulder and tried to wake him, but he only moaned in protest and slept on. She could see her own breath, and realized, suddenly, how cold the room was and how strange it was that the boy could so steadily sleep through all the racket she'd been making. On closer inspection, it was clear that Ralphie was not well.

Her anger gone in an instant, she quickly stoked the fire back to life near the foot of Ralphie's bed and searched the house for blankets to cover him with. She could find nothing more than Ralphie had already found and wrapped himself up in, so she lit the small stove in his kitchen and fretted to herself over what she should do.

She could see he needed the doctor, but Doctor Miles' place was several, slushy, miles away, and the sun would be setting before she could reach it on foot. Even if she did make it to the doctor's house, she fretted, he'd no doubt refuse to return with her until daybreak, which would mean leaving Ralphie to suffer alone through another night without anyone to keep the place warm for him.

While she considered her options, she found items enough to make a thin broth; she'd feed him, if she could wake him again. With food in hand, she returned to the bedroom and tried to rouse the boy. This time, she got a response.

Ralphie jumped in fright to see Cindy Lou at his side, in his bedroom, then thinking he must be delirious, he fell back on his pillow again, almost at once. When she roused him again, with a sharp tone in her voice, he almost wept with relief.

His hands shook violently, but he grabbed the

hot bowl of broth and drank it down as fast as he could make himself swallow the scalding liquid. When he'd emptied the bowl, he felt warmer, but his head throbbed with pain and he fell limp against his pillows once more.

Cindy Lou could see he had exhausted himself with the effort, and wondered how long he'd been this way. He was asleep again before she could ply him with questions, though, so she sat quietly by his bedside and watched him closely as he slept. She'd have to stay with him, at least til morning, she decided, then she'd give him more food and go get Doctor Miles.

Pastor Franklin and his wife woke, feeling defeated and uncertain. Though they prepared everything for Sunday services as usual, none of the townspeople came to the church. Millie made lunch for the two of them, when they were certain the hour was too late for anyone to show up, and they ate in stained silence.

The snow had prevented the pastor from speaking to the townspeople about the one remaining Fenton in their community, the sad news that another of their own, Doctor Miles, had died, or demand explanations for the mysterious disappearance of both Tyler and Cory. Frustrated, Pastor Franklin finished his dinner, and while Millie cleared their dishes, he sat staring into the fireplace in his den, still trying to figure a way to get rid of Jimmy Fenton before Millie put up notices around town to announce Doctor Miles' funeral service.

Unable to think of anything to try, he finally went out to his shed to build a suitable casket, the third he'd made in as many months, for the good doctor. He'd put it off, with distracting thoughts about gathering the townsmen to go to Cindy Lou's house and make the Fenton boy leave, but he knew it had to be done. He wore out his temper and his miserable sadness, cutting and shaping the fine wood he'd chosen for the doctor's casket.

As he worked, he could picture the reaction of the emotionally exhausted townspeople; there would be such gloom as they met together in the small cemetery to lay Doctor Miles to rest, he could hardly bear to imagine it.

"Life goes on." Millie had warned him many weeks before. He could hear her words ringing in his ears, and the sadness in them, still. If what she claimed was true, he thought, why didn't the future seem any less dismal?

Jimmy and Blasted spent one night, as he'd planned, in Doctor Miles' house, and left it locked and secure, on their way to Cindy Lou's house, the next morning. They took the short-cut path to avoid town, and in doing so, didn't see that Cindy Lou was at the post office, not at her home waiting for their return.

When they arrived on her doorstep some time later, Jimmy had finally broken down and forced the door open, so he and Blasted could get out of the cold. Blasted made himself comfortable while Jimmy lit a fire, worrying that Cindy Lou had gone out after him a full two days before, searching for them, and fallen in harm's way.

The kitchen was warming quickly, but Jimmy's fears kept him cold inside, and he paced the kitchen, growing more distraught by the moment, hoping Cindy Lou would walk in soon, even if she became angry to find him there and kicked him out. Hours ticked by uneventfully, and Jimmy, growing weary from the long walk over, and all his frantic pacing, found himself sitting pensively on the edge of a table chair.

The idea that she might have gone out into the snow after him made him feel sick with regret. He'd been angry with her, had wanted to know that she'd miss him, and had meant all the wonderful things she'd said to him, but he hadn't meant for any harm to come to her because of his leaving. All he could think to do, as daylight began to slip away, was pray that she was alright, that she'd only gone to stay with a friend somewhere nearby, and wait for her to return right where he was. As darkness settled in, he fell asleep in his chair, feeling hopeless.

Mrs. Wilcox had weathered the blizzard in her cozy home, well outside of Farmersville, but cabin fever had set in, late the following day. She'd gone to bed promising herself that she'd get out and do some shopping in the nearby town the next day, despite the melting snow. She knew Calvin, the General Store owner, would be happy to have her company for a bit, and she needed some human interaction after so much upset.

She made the treacherous walk to town and spent several hours spilling her heart out to the shop owner, there, filling his sympathetic ear with all that had happened of late, in Farmersville. He in turn left her speechless with his tale of recent dealings with the Farmersville supply store owner, Cory.

All that he told her affirmed her worst fears for Cindy Lou. The girl had married a lunatic, and now she had proof. She wasn't the only one, now, who'd seen Cory's much changed disposition. Empowered with this new information, she promised Calvin she'd make it her business to rid Cindy Lou of her new husband if it was the last thing she'd do.

Throughout the walk home that day, she lamented leaving Cindy Lou with such a wild man, cursed herself for being so spineless when the Farmersville gossip had come to her home and threatened her to stay clear of "her town". She'd be damned if she'd deprive herself any further, in cowardice, of the company of the girl she'd considered her own. No one would stop her, this time, from being the mother Cindy Lou needed so much.

After a good night's sleep, she vowed to herself, she'd close up her house for a while and take herself to live with Cindy Lou again; and if all went well, she'd stay on and protect the girl's interest until she could get Cory out of their home. Feeling the strength of her new-found will, and eager to get to the morrow, she went to bed early and fell asleep envisioning a blissful future in Farmersville.

The following morning, she roused herself early, and busied herself at once, drinking her tea while she put her house in order and packed a small bag. As she collected her things, she put larger bags, filled with more of her personal affects, in the hallway near the front door, for Cory to gather easily, without any excuse to violate the privacy of her home, when she dispatched him to collect her things.

She rehearsed exactly what she'd say to Cory when she got to Cindy Lou's house, as she started out, with bag in hand, for Farmersville. By the time she reached the paved road in town, she was prepared for any encounter she might have with one of the hateful people who might be there. She marched, with her chin in the air, looking neither left nor right, to show anyone who might think to harass or question her, that she meant business and would not be deterred, or detained, from her destination. The

CLOSED signs in Tyler's and Cory's respective storefront windows escaped her, she was so distracted with her righteous indignation, and nerves; she was nearly out of breath when she reached the far end of the paved road.

Though she felt quite weary from her walking, and the small traveling bag felt surprisingly heavy in her hands, she continued on through the slush, with the wind in her face, toward Cindy Lou's house. She rehearsed her speech once more as she approached the front door, sucked in a deep breath, and knocked loudly, setting her mind and her lips firmly in preparation to do battle to get in.

Chapter 24

Jimmy, having spent nearly half the day wandering aimlessly around Cindy Lou's quiet house with Blasted, was startled by the sharp rapping on the front door. In an instant he was convinced that Pastor Franklin must be returned as he'd promised. Louder, more insistent, banging jolted him with anger and he threw the door open, prepared to attack.

Seeing Jimmy Fenton suddenly filling Cindy Lou's doorway at her insistence, completely undid Mrs. Wilcox. Her scream pierced Jimmy's ears as she turned to flee, dropping her bag, and slipping uncontrollably, nearly to the point of falling on the porch.

Jimmy was surprised, then outraged at the older woman's reaction to seeing him. He yelled after the confused, sobbing woman, ordering her inside so he could shut the door, through clenched teeth.

Unable to process a single thought, she followed Jimmy's order, scrambling to right herself, collect her bag and her composure, and hazard the trip past him, to enter the house. She stood speechless and shaking where Jimmy had pointed her, just inside the door. Nowhere in all her vivid imaginings had she planned to run into him again. She cowered under his glare and struggled to comprehend his muffled questions and demands.

Seeing the older woman was hysterical, Jimmy finally gave up asking what she wanted, and stormed back to the kitchen. Blasted, roused by all the noise, rushed to the hallway, then shied away a bit to see her in such a state.

After Jimmy had returned to the back of the house, she stood clutching the front of her coat at the throat, swaying and feeling terribly ill. When she became aware of the massive dog by her side, she wept with relief, telling the animal how happy she was that his master was close at hand and would, no doubt, protect her from the monstrous Fenton boy, if he would only lead her to him.

Blasted licked her hand, seemingly willing to take her to Doctor Miles, and she followed him trustingly into the kitchen, but when she saw only Jimmy at the table, she demanded to know where the doctor was.

Jimmy stared at her for a long moment, trying to decide how to answer her question. Finally, he pushed out a chair with his foot and waved her into it, and when she'd stripped off her coat and sat holding it in her lap, looking desperately uncomfortable, he told her the sad news.

Mrs. Wilcox's fainted to the floor. Jimmy and Blasted rushed to her, and between them they woke her and Jimmy put her back upright in her chair. While the news of Doctor Miles' death sank in, he made coffee, then tried to busy himself at the sink. He handed her a dish towel for her many tears, and pet Blasted's wide head absently, unnerved by the emotional display.

When she felt herself strong enough to speak again, Mrs. Wilcox asked about Cindy Lou, but Jimmy only stared at her, unwilling to tell the already overwrought woman that he didn't know where Cindy Lou was.

She stared back at him expectantly, then burst, again, into loud, gasping sobs, thinking his silence meant to tell her Cindy Lou was dead too. Blasted crowded up to her legs and pushed his head in her lap, but she ignored him, struggling to quiet herself when she could see Jimmy was protesting, and then she heard him saying Cindy Lou was nowhere to be found and dissolved in another fit of wailing.

Unable to endure any more of the woman's emotions, Jimmy swiftly made for the relative quiet coldness of Old Bill's study, and paced the floor, wringing his hands, hearing the woman's wails continue. Finally, he remembered the liquor bottles and poured two glasses out. He drank one and refilled it, then made himself return to the kitchen with them, thinking it would surely calm the old woman to have a stiff drink.

Mrs. Wilcox stared at the glass Jimmy set on the table in front of her, and quickly quieted herself. She brushed away her tears, and without comment, gulped the dark liquid down. Then she questioned him thoroughly as to the details of Doctor Miles' death, and accepted his answers solemnly. What little he could tell her only added to the alarm she felt that Cindy Lou had left, and Jimmy and Blasted had arrived, without any search for the girl since. She excused herself to powder her face, and returned a few minutes later with an idea.

Jimmy agreed that they must find Cindy Lou, but he was weary and it was already after noon, so they agreed they'd go out first thing in the morning and search everywhere until they found her, if she didn't return in the meantime. While they waited, Jimmy made dinner for them and explained, as best he could, how he'd come to be in Cindy Lou's house.

All the information was too much for Mrs. Wilcox, though, on the heels of such devastating news, and she retired just as the sun was setting, in the room she'd once occupied, upstairs. Jimmy built a fire in Old Bill's study and drowsed in a chair in front of it, still hoping Cindy Lou would walk in at any moment.

    Ralphie woke early the following morning, and was startled again to find Cindy Lou at his bedside. She reminded him of her arrival the day before, as she left his room to get him a cup of coffee.
    He didn't feel as sickly this morning as he had for so many days on end, and he was thankful that Cindy Lou, as much as she'd always irritated him, had come looking for him. When he'd finished drinking his coffee, he thanked her over and over again, until she confessed that she'd come to his house only to give him a piece of her mind for neglecting his duties at the post office. The revelation made him more embarrassed and he apologized profusely. She told him of her intention to go get Doctor Miles, but he refused to have her go to the trouble, pointing out that she too might end up terribly sick if she went out on such a mission in such cold, damp weather.
    He had a stash of old books he'd collected from others in the community, he told her, so if she would only stay a bit longer, she could occupy herself reading, while he slept a while. She assured him she had no intention of leaving him, in his condition, and went to search out a book she liked, then while he dozed, she read aloud to him to create a little noise in the otherwise quiet little house.
    Cindy Lou was secretly well-pleased with herself for discovering that Ralphie was so terribly sick, and so quickly getting him to feeling better. She smiled at the thought of word spreading around the community that she was as good as any doctor, if a doctor wasn't handy, though she suspected that the

news wouldn't please Doctor Miles even a tiny bit.

Jimmy was already drinking his coffee when Mrs. Wilcox came down to the kitchen looking tired and swollen in the face the next morning. She muttered greetings to him, then got herself a cup of coffee and sat down at the table across from him. With all the tormenting news she'd heard from him the day before, she'd refused to bring up Cory in any of her many questions, but in the light of day, she realized she must deal with whatever had become of him sometime, so she forced herself to ask.

Jimmy's jaw felt remarkably good despite all the talking he'd done the day before. He felt certain that it was nearly completely healed now, and the thought that his painful ordeal might finally be over had made him greatly optimistic, until Mrs. Wilcox brought up Cindy Lou's absent husband. He wasn't sure what the woman thought of Cory, or him, and he didn't want to start her weeping and wailing all over again by telling her too much, so he told her only that Cory had left, and did so in a tone that discouraged further discussion.

Hearing Jimmy's evasive answer for what it was, she pressed on, still unable to quite understand why this Fenton boy felt so comfortable in another man's house, keeping his wife company while he was away. She was determined, now, to convince this distrustful Fenton to open up to her, but he refused to be enticed into any conversation regarding Cindy Lou's husband.

She concluded that he was in denial about Cindy Lou's marriage to Cory, entirely, and possibly very much in love with the girl, himself. Realizing this, she was anxious to see whether Cindy Lou knew the young man felt this way about her, and if felt the same for him. Though nothing would make her happier, she felt sure, than hearing that Cory might be so easily replaced, but the idea of Cindy Lou with a Fenton boy was certainly one she would not have considered.

When they'd eaten a small breakfast, they fell into a heated discussion about which of them was to go into town and which should remain unseen as much as possible, searching the countryside, for Cindy Lou. Both had engendered such hostility, and been the target of such violent threats, it seemed wisest and safest for both to stay well clear of town. Finally, grudgingly considering the more recent, more obvious, injuries Jimmy had suffered at the hands of townspeople, Mrs. Wilcox agreed to be the one who faced the unforgiving lot of them. She'd go to the post office first, she decided, then if she had to, she'd confront Cory again at his supply store. One of them would surely know where Cindy Lou had gone off to, she felt sure.

Jimmy knew Cindy Lou wasn't at Doctor Miles' place, having been there himself, on two occasions since he'd left Cindy Lou's house, so he took to the dirt road and wandered out into the countryside. Mrs. Wilcox had told him where Cindy Lou's oldest sister lived, but he didn't have any intention of going that far.

His search was short lived, and aimless, barely keeping him away from the house a full three hours. Searching for Cindy Lou, to him, seemed pointless and a dangerous waste of time for both he and Mrs. Wilcox. He'd made an effort, to shut the old woman up, but he firmly believed the best course of action was to wait for Cindy Lou to come to them - to her own home. To his guilty mind, to search for her on the road and in fields meant he might find her dead, fallen victim to some wild animal attack because he'd walked out and left her, and he couldn't accept that possibility.

When he stepped back into the kitchen, Mrs. Wilcox was already at the table waiting for him with a hopeful expression on her face. She'd been into town, but not one business had been open. No one had answered her knocks at Tyler's or Cory's, she said, and the post office was locked up too. Jimmy reminded her that he'd found the town just as she had, on his last trip through, but she didn't take issue with his retort. She could plainly see that he hadn't found Cindy Lou either.

Frustrated that her idea had not gotten them any closer to finding the girl, she took out her anxiety on the stove, making all the food she could think of, filling the large old house with aromas that made Jimmy's mouth water.

Though he tried to stay out of the woman's way, Jimmy found himself wandering through the kitchen repeatedly, each time being rewarded with this morsel or that, meeting each gift with enthusiastic approval. He continued his wandering and snacking, stopping every few minutes to ask for assurances Mrs. Wilcox couldn't give him, that Cindy Lou was alright.

By the second morning after Cindy Lou's arrival, Ralphie was well enough, and on his feet once more. With her cooking, and surprisingly un-irritating company, he was nearly ready to resume his work at the post office.

Cindy Lou was happy enough to see the boy doing better and anxious to tackle the mail that had stacked up at the post office, but she knew he shouldn't jump right back into his deliveries. After battling the issue over between them, Ralphie finally agreed to wait til the following morning to return to work.

Cindy Lou was tired, and still wearing the dress she'd been wearing when she'd arrived, only now it wasn't as clean and crisp and new looking. She was restless to go home and it showed. Ralphie assured her he'd take it easy for the rest of the day, sleep well that night, and be back at the post office the next morning, and suggested she go home and get some rest, herself. Within the hour, he'd closed the door behind her.

Coat wrapped tightly around her, Cindy Lou stumbled, with the wind hard on her back, toward home. What remained from the heavy snowfall was pure ice underfoot that, at times, allowed her to plant her feet side by side and slide a bit. In only half the time it had taken her to reach Ralphie's house, she was near enough her own home to see smoke coming from the chimneys.

Her heart skipped a few beats as she pictured her father and Esther waiting at home for her, then she felt a sharp pang, realizing that they were really gone, and that it was more likely that Cory had returned. The thought of having to face him now, now that he'd made a mockery of her, and their marriage, filled her with anxiety and she rushed to cover the remaining distance to her door, ready for a fight. She wouldn't have the man, now, she swore to herself, she'd send her new husband packing as soon as she laid eyes on him.

Blasted, only just let out to roam the yard a bit, caught sight of Cindy Lou, and bounded out to meet her on the road. She was so relieved to see him she nearly cried, but only for an instant. She'd been prepared to deal with Cory, but she wasn't as sure how she felt about the young man she knew must have returned with the doctor's dog.

She walked in the back door, fully expecting to see Jimmy, and squealed with surprise when instead she found Mrs. Wilcox in her kitchen. Mrs. Wilcox ran to hug her and they cried happily in each other's embrace.

When she'd pried the woman off her, at last, she asked where Jimmy was, and confirmed to Mrs. Wilcox, in doing so, that she indeed knew Jimmy Fenton, and knew he cared for her deeply, and seemed very pleased that he was there, like she'd expected him to be waiting for her when she returned from wherever she'd been. She pointed Cindy Lou toward the study and watched her rush off through the house.

When Cindy Lou opened the door to the study and spotted Jimmy on the far side of the room, staring back at her, she ran to hug him, no longer unsure about anything. Jimmy lifted her in his arms and she buried her face in his neck, crying. He chastised her for making him worry about her for so many days, then he kissed her and set her back on her feet again to quiz her about where she'd been.

Mrs. Wilcox left the young couple undisturbed, smiling to herself while she finished preparing a feast for the three of them, and the hungry dog that sat staring at her from his spot in front of the fireplace. Then her face fell as she realized that Jimmy would most certainly have to be telling Cindy Lou about Doctor Miles' death.

When hot food filled all the counter space in the kitchen, a short while later, she sat down at the table to rest a moment. Then, hearing nothing from the study, she grew worried and called Jimmy and

Cindy Lou out to sit with her and eat the fine dinner she'd made.

She gave Jimmy a questioning look as the two sat down at the table, but it was clear that he'd not told the girl the sad news. Unwilling to spoil the dinner she'd worked so hard to prepare, she refused to broach the subject herself. After dinner would be a better time, she felt sure, to have Jimmy tell her.

When they'd finished eating, on her suggestion, they retired to the study where Jimmy poured them each a glass of liquor, then sat next to Cindy Lou. Mrs. Wilcox hovered close by her on the other side, and Jimmy told her he'd found Doctor Miles' frozen to death, the day before and had come back with Blasted to tell her the sad news.

Cindy Lou's face crumbled, and she was inconsolable, despite their combined efforts to calm her. Finally, Jimmy pulled her over, into his lap and held her, letting her sob against his chest.

Mrs. Wilcox left them and took Blasted out to the kitchen with her, hiding her tears as she went. She cried softly as she cleared away all the dishes she'd dirtied making dinner, and those that remained on the table, and filled a bowl with scraps for Blasted. When she heard Jimmy taking Cindy Lou upstairs, she slipped back into the study to sit for a while and finish her glass of liquor.

When Jimmy returned a few minutes later, she invited him to sit with her a while, and told him about her many-years-long affair with Doctor Miles. He listened without comment, staring into the fire, consumed with his own thoughts for a time.

When, a long while later, she stifled a yawn behind her hand, he helped her upstairs to the bedroom she'd slept in the night before, cautioning her, as they went, that he'd put Cindy Lou in there already. She said good-night and closed the door, thankful that he'd thought of this sleeping arrangement. Her sleeping with the girl would surely prevent any rude gossip that might spread through the community, about Cindy Lou sharing her house with the Fenton boy inappropriately.

Chapter 25

By sunup the next morning, Ralphie was already half way to the post office. He was anxious to get back to work, and knew there'd be plenty of deliveries to make that day. He'd agreed to stop by Cindy Lou's house for dinner when his route was finished, so he mentally adjusted the order he'd deliver the mail in, as he walked.

    Will roused himself, and he and Cory went to the kitchen to talk and make coffee. Over their coffee, Will confessed that he'd planned on taking his truck that morning and paying the folks in Farmersville a visit to see what might have happened to disturb him so. Cory didn't seem upset to hear his plan, but he protested that he'd already told him all about Old Bill's death, and how the grief he felt over losing his dear friend had tainted his desire to live in Farmersville any longer.
    They sat talking quietly in the kitchen about how much the people in Farmersville had changed since the death of their beloved post master. Cory related the several times the miserably affected men of the community had paid him visits at the supply store, and how they seemed determined to hold him responsible for Old Bill's death, and subsequently, what remained of Old Bill's family, namely Cindy Lou.
    Will was sympathetic, and not a little relieved to hear Cory talk so much about what his life had been, of late. He didn't blame him for not wanting to

live on, and try to do business, with people so irrational that they blamed an equally injured, innocent, man for their suffering.

Pastor Franklin woke several hours after the sun came up, dreading the day and still weary from his labors on Doctor Miles' casket, the evening before. The roads were clear enough, now, to go in his car to pick up the good doctor's body and prepare it for the service. Millie would ride with him, and put up the notice of the funeral date, two days from then, en-route.

After breakfast he began urging Millie to get herself ready to go, irritably. She ignored him, as best she could, as she put on her clothes and brushed her hair. She didn't see any need to rush.

She dreaded the trip into town to put up the funeral notice almost more than going out to Doctor Miles' home to pick up his body. It seemed to her like her every trip into town lately had been to officially announce more terrible news. Her visits to town were never fun, and always meant that the community would be getting together very soon, to sit in tears, in her beautiful little church. She was tired of burying her friends. She wished she'd been able to convince her husband to post the notice, himself, this time, since he had to go through town anyway.

An hour later, despite all her stalling, they pulled out onto the road, still slushy with melting snow, and drove without speaking, into town. She slammed her car door extra hard when she got out at the post office, and did her duty putting up the notice, and slammed it again when she got back in, but her husband refused to comment. The drive out to Doctor Miles' place was treacherous still, slick and muddy, and it only added to the bristling tension between them.

Millie refused to get out when they pulled into the doctor's side yard, planting her feet on the floorboard, with her fists clenched in her lap and an evil scowl on her face. In retaliation, Pastor Franklin slammed his car door as hard as he could when he got out, rocking the heavy car, impressively. He swore at her under his breath as he opened the door to the shed where Doctor Miles' body lay, and hefted it over his shoulder.

Though very angry with her, he did his best to prevent her from seeing the man he carried as he passed by Millie's car window to the back door of the car, then he realized the door was still locked. He kicked the door to get her attention, but Millie sat still, rigidly facing forward in her seat, so he kicked her door, angrily. Finally, she twisted over the seatback and opened the door for him and he placed Doctor Miles' body on the seat, and covered it quickly.

There was no silence to enjoy on the return trip, for Millie, nor any due respect shown for the dead man lying on the seat behind her.
Pastor Franklin seethed threats at his wife until she retaliated, announcing her refusal to help him, in the future, deal with anyone dead - no more writing up notices, posting notices, nothing, she swore. At that, he became more angry and ordered her out of the car, to walk the remainder of the way home.

Millie opened her car door and moved like she might just do that, forcing him to slam on the breaks and reach over her to pull the door shut and lock it, before carrying on. Enraged, Millie bit his hand, then threatened never to cook or clean house, or church, for him again, and he met her challenge with a promise to lock her out of every building on their land, making her homeless on the spot.

When they got home, at last, Millie jumped out of the car before her husband could, and ran to lock herself in the house. He yelled after her, and cursed her roundly, then busied himself tending to the doctor's body. He filled out the death certificate and set it aside, then put finishing touches on the casket he'd made and placed the doctor's body in it. When Millie had gotten over her tantrum, he decided, he'd ask her sign the certificate too, to make it legal, but until then, he had no intention of speaking to her.

An hour later, he roused himself and beat on the back door of his house until, for fear he'd break it in, Millie unlocked it and scurried off to lock herself in their bedroom. Unwilling to carry on their fight any longer, he let her go unchased and instead cooked himself a small dinner, too small to be shared, since he was certain Millie had already fed herself for the evening. He took his food into his den and locked himself in to work on his funeral sermon for Doctor Miles, undisturbed.

Cindy Lou woke up alone in the big bed, feeling dismal that a new day had already begun. She could hear voices in the kitchen, but it took a moment for her to register who they belonged to. She put on a robe and padded down to see if there was any coffee left, hoping no one would talk to her.

Mrs. Wilcox and Jimmy stopped talking when Cindy Lou came into the kitchen looking disheveled and unfriendly. Both told her "Good-morning", but otherwise left her alone to get her own cup of coffee, and a sweet roll Mrs. Wilcox had just finished making. They resumed their conversation, haltingly, only after Cindy Lou had settled herself in front of the fireplace with her back to them, but they soon discovered how late it was getting and separated; Mrs. Wilcox to clean the kitchen, and Jimmy to make the long walk to Pastor Franklin's home to tell him of Doctor Miles' death.

When she'd finished her sweet roll, Cindy Lou mumbled a thank-you, then disappeared back up the stairs. She made herself a hot bath and soaked in it til the water turned cool, then went to the room she'd shared with Esther to find a dress for the day, her mood entirely unimproved.

Mrs. Wilcox finished her cleaning, then closed herself up in the study to sit by the fire Jimmy had made earlier, reading a well-worn book until she was sufficiently tired to nap.

Only a few minutes after he'd settled himself behind his desk, with a tablet and pen under one hand, and a plate of hot food under the other, Pastor Franklin heard loud knocking on his front door. Certain that Millie would not take care of this unexpected visitor if she could make him do it, he huffed and went to answer it. His temper flared the instant he saw Jimmy Fenton on his front porch, but he kept his voice level, and the meanness out of it, and invited the young man in.

He could see, from Jimmy's demeanor, that whatever was on his mind was gravely serious, so he led him into his den and closed the door behind him, then resumed his place behind his desk, shoving his food aside so it wouldn't distract him.

Jimmy stared at the steaming plate while he told the pastor what he'd come to say, explaining how he'd found Doctor Miles, frozen to death at his kitchen table, with tears streaming down his face.

The pastor was stunned. He offered Jimmy his handkerchief and gave him a moment to collect himself, then told him, with kindness that surprised even him, that he had already discovered and recovered the good doctor's body. He offered his sympathy to the young man who was so obviously grieving the loss of his doctor; seeing Jimmy Fenton this way challenged his perception of the young man he'd so recently threatened to rid the community of, forever. Suddenly he saw what Doctor Miles had seen in Jimmy the day he'd decided to take him in. Overcome with new-found respect for the young man, he stood and put out his hand, and Jimmy shook it, still crying.

His duty done, Jimmy made to leave, but Pastor Franklin stopped him, asking him, more calmly than he had before, just how he'd come to be in Cindy Lou's house, and what his intentions were with the girl considering her recent marriage to Cory.

Jimmy, unsure of himself and unprepared to talk to the surprisingly calm pastor about his feelings for Cindy Lou, hesitantly confided that he loved the girl and swore on his honor that she loved him too. He told the him that Cindy Lou had agreed to marry him, but that they needed him to first annul her marriage to Cory, then marry them.

Pastor Franklin could hardly believe what he was hearing. He shook his head, taking in the idea of such a thing, then his face softened and he patted the nervous young man on the back and assured him he'd give what he'd said some thought. Jimmy thanked him and started to leave again, but as he did, it occurred to the pastor that the hour was getting late for walking, wherever Jimmy intended to go next, so he offered to drive him.

Jimmy jumped at the offer, telling him to take him back to Cindy Lou's house, but the pastor was immediately hesitant. Then Jimmy told him Mrs. Wilcox's was also staying with the girl and would stay on with them to keep appearances, for Cindy Lou's sake, above reproach, and he relented. Jimmy helped him put the last of his meager gas supply into the car and they took off for Cindy Lou's in silence.

As they neared their destination, he assured Jimmy that he'd ask Cindy Lou about everything he had told him, when they arrived, and if she agreed that what he'd said was true, he'd be willing to marry them and destroy her marriage certificate to Cory when he got back home, that very evening. Who was he to stand in love's way, he thought to himself; Cory could take it up with Jimmy and Cindy Lou if he took issue with her annulment of their unusual marriage. Why should she be made to suffer for Cory's leaving her the way he had? If Jimmy was telling him the truth, she didn't love the man her father had wanted her to marry, anyway. And if Jimmy was lying, he'd find out that very evening and he'd make sure the young man was well away from Cindy Lou before he left her house again.

Jimmy was floored by his good fortune. He had no doubt Cindy Lou would agree to keep her promise to him, now, and he couldn't keep the smile off his lips all the way home to her.

Chapter 26

Mrs. Wilcox opened the door as soon as Pastor Franklin's car pulled into Cindy Lou's side yard, anxious that something terrible had happened to Jimmy. When he jumped out and gave her a thumbs-up sign, she demanded to know why he'd brought the pastor; Doctor Miles' body was at his home, from what he had told her. She let the two men pass by her and closed the door, still waiting for an explanation, but there was none forthcoming.

Jimmy led Pastor Franklin through the house calling for Cindy Lou; they found her upstairs, in her childhood room. Jimmy explained to her why the pastor was there and the three closed themselves up in the room for a very serious, very private, talk.

While the three upstairs were busy with their secrets, Mrs. Wilcox let Ralphie in the front door and put him in the study to wait with her. She was happier for the boy's company than he was of hers, though. She shushed all of his questions and they sat together quietly, waiting to find out what was going on.

Cindy Lou called down the stairwell for the bewildered woman, nearly a half hour later, and shocked her when she reached the top of the stairs and found Cindy Lou breathless with excitement and blushing brightly. Before questions could fly from her lips, she found herself whisked down the hall into the bedroom she'd shared with the girl the night before, following orders to help tidy Cindy Lou up for her wedding. Not too dull of wit, she caught on to Cindy Lou's meaning quickly, even while she was helping the girl struggle out of her day dress and into the most beautiful gown she'd ever laid her hands on.

A few minutes later, they emerged from the bedroom; Cindy Lou, radiating happiness in a satin and lace dress Esther had made, one that she had modified to flatter her more generous figure, and Mrs. Wilcox beaming and fully red in the face from all the sudden excitement. Cindy Lou tapped on the bedroom door where the pastor and Jimmy sat waiting and went in, leaving Mrs. Wilcox to call Ralphie up to join them, and explain what he was going to witness, for Cindy Lou.

A few moments later, with their backs to the window that overlooked the places where her mother, her father, and her sister, had been laid to rest, and with a proud Mrs. Wilcox, again serving as witness, alongside a flustered and confused Ralphie, Cindy Lou and Jimmy stood holding hands, unable to take their eyes off each other, as Pastor Franklin pronounced them man and wife. Then Jimmy kissed his beautiful new bride.

Two days later, as Millie played solemn hymns, the townspeople gathered for Doctor Miles' funeral service. Many tears flowed, even from cold, staring eyes, over the loss of their community's well-loved doctor, but when the service was over, tongues began to wag.

Pastor Franklin, anticipating an uproar, gathered the crowd together tightly and introduced the newest couple to be married in Farmersville. Before anyone could speak another word, he explained to them all that Cory, the supply store owner, had left their community, abandoning Cindy Lou, a few days before and had not told anyone where he was going, or why. He told them that since he could not be found, Cindy Lou had asked to have her marriage to him annulled, and that he had done so.

He held up a hand to silence them again, then explained to all everything that had happened recently in their small town, that had resulted in Old Bill's death, and Cindy Lou's subsequent marriage to Cory, her father's dearest friend. He explained the change of heart the good doctor had had when he'd seen Jimmy's condition, and buried the last of his family. Then he told his neighbors and friends that he too had seen good in Jimmy Fenton, something he had felt made him worth a second chance in their community. He told them what Doctor Miles had done, with Cindy Lou's help, to give the young man back his life, and challenged them to accept Cindy Lou's decision to marry him.

The townspeople were horrified. They stared at him, angrily, as did his wife, but after a disconcertingly long moment, Mrs. Sylvester stepped forward and took Cindy Lou's hand, pushing Mrs. Wilcox away from the girl as she did. She congratulated the girl loudly enough for everyone to hear her, then turned to eye her husband until he too stepped forward and acknowledged the unnerved couple. When he extended his hand to Jimmy, the men around him grumbled, and moved to take their wives and children a safe distance from Old Bill's murderer, and, to their minds, his foolish daughter.

Finally, under an intimidating glare from her husband, Millie moved forward and half-hugged Cindy Lou, but Cindy Lou shrunk away from her and leaned more heavily into Jimmy's side. She knew Millie's support was feigned and after the way she'd treated her, she couldn't make herself accept the older woman's attempt to sway the townspeople.

Jimmy put his arm around Cindy Lou and pulled her away from the others, his eyes scanning the crowd for any indication that they might move against him. He had come to the funeral service unaware that the pastor intended to make a spectacle of them. He'd thought himself lucky to have made it through the brief funeral service without having to fend off any blows from the townspeople.

Mrs. Wilcox pressed into Jimmy's other side, also seeking protection from the townspeople. Mrs. Sylvester, and several other women close to her, eyed her reproachfully, but no one made any move to molest her. She'd promised herself she'd stand tall, and attend Doctor Miles' funeral service with Jimmy and Cindy Lou, but with all the unexpected focus on the three of them, she felt like fleeing for her far away cottage.

Seeing the townspeople's reaction to the news, and feeling the growing tension around him, Pastor Franklin quickly turned to the men behind him and gave the nod to begin the procession to the graveyard where Doctor Miles would be buried. He followed closely behind them, with Millie trailing him, unhappily, hissing at him for putting her on the spot the way he had, not caring who overheard her.

Some of the townspeople formed a small group and headed the other way, back toward their homes, leaving those who remained confused and uncertain who to follow. Mr. and Mrs. Sylvester flanked Jimmy and Cindy Lou, again pushing Mrs. Wilcox back from the couple, and steered them along behind the pastor, wordlessly, while more of their neighbors turned away to begin their walk home. The remaining few straggled along behind at a distance, determined to see their beloved doctor through til the end even if it meant suffering criticism, later, from those who'd turned away.

By the time Doctor Miles' casket was lowered into the grave, the townspeople's had divided themselves, the ambivalent and those who supported the new couple, and those whose hatred of the Fenton family had so hardened their hearts that they would not make themselves even acknowledge this last remaining of them, married to the daughter of the man he had killed.

A new couple had been born in Farmersville, but the road ahead of them would not be easy. The townspeople had suffered such shock and so much loss that even Ralphie, for all the appreciation he felt toward Cindy Lou for her recent care of him, could not bring himself to fully believe that Cory had left their community, and his new wife, so suddenly, without any explanation.

Though he'd witnessed the ceremony that bound the supply store owner's wife to the murderous Fenton boy, he felt certain that when the truth came out, when Cory returned, there would be nothing but more trouble for Jimmy Fenton. And when that day came, he promised himself, he'd be as far away from the new couple as humanly possible.

Other Books by Amy K. Jones

Her Place In Time, Part 1

Old Bill, Farmersville's postmaster, losses his wife in a terrible fire everyone knows the Fenton's started. Left to raise his daughters alone, he struggles to keep them on the straight and narrow as they come of age. Cindy Lou, the youngest, finds herself torn between two men: Cory, a very successful, much older, friend of her father's and Jimmy Fenton, the son of her mother's killers - the town outcast. While her father's eyes and attention are focused on Cindy Lou, Esther, her older sister, takes comfort in the arms of another young man whose commitment to her is fickle and fleeting.

What's a girl to do with the best catch in town is ready and willing to marry her? How can she resist the advances of the town outcast when the very sight of him makes her and her father tremble - for very different reasons? Will Cory, the owner of the general store, win her love or will she risk everything to be with a boy whose reputation could destroy her own?

Coming of age in Farmersville proves more challenging than Cindy Lou could ever have dreamed, when an innocent crush turns her tight-knit community upside down. Nothing is simple and everything has its price.

More Books by Amy K. Jones

MISREAD
A Murder Mystery

Nearly losing his life when his best friend's house explodes, Peter Shaw is tormented by his need to find out who is behind not just his near-death experience, but a series of violent crimes that threatens those closest to him: his wife, his best friend, and his best friend's only child.

Despite his best efforts, the one person who can help him most side-steps his every attempt to solve the crimes she seems to know too much about.

As those around him fall victim, 'Pete' and his former partner, and best friend, retired Detective Jim Swartz, drive unswervingly toward the discovery of the menace that threatens their city and everything they hold dear.

More Books by Amy K. Jones

Strange Association

Private Investigator, Mike Tine, finds himself empty-handed, beaten and unable to return to his home, a small apartment above his most trusted friend's restaurant, Mitchy's. As he searches for the girl a mysterious client has hired him to find, and then the client himself, he finds his friends turning into dangerous enemies he cannot avoid. Someone is watching his every move and that someone today is you.

Made in the USA
Lexington, KY
02 July 2013